THE CIRCLE EIGHT

BRODY

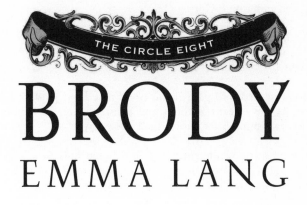

THE CIRCLE EIGHT

BRODY

EMMA LANG

𝓑
BRAVA

KENSINGTON PUBLISHING CORP.

www.kensingtonbooks.com

BRAVA BOOKS are published by

Kensington Publishing Corp.
119 West 40th Street
New York, NY 10018

All Kensington titles, imprints, and distributed lines are available at special quantity discounts for bulk purchases for sales promotions, premiums, fund-raising, educational, or institutional use.

Special book excerpts or customized printings can also be created to fit specific needs. For details, write or phone the office of the Kensington special sales manager: Kensington Publishing Corp., 119 West 40th Street, New York, NY 10018, attn: Special Sales Department; phone 1-800-221-2647.

Brava and the B logo are Reg. U.S. Pat. & TM Off.

ISBN-13: 978-0-7582-6905-8
ISBN-10: 0-7582-6905-6

First Kensington Trade Paperback Printing: July 2012

10 9 8 7 6 5 4 3 2 1

Printed in the United States of America

CHAPTER ONE

September 1836

Olivia Graham was about to melt into a puddle in the late summer heat. Bees droned incessantly over the wildflowers nearby, while katydids buzzed from the trees. It was a lazy Tuesday afternoon, which she might have enjoyed if she wasn't yanking up weeds from the garden. Her hands pulsed with blisters, irritated by dirt and stickiness the weeds left behind on her skin.

The garden was small, built beside the ashes of what had been her mother's garden. No matter how uncomfortable she was, Liv would nurture those plants until every last vegetable was harvested. It would help feed the clan for the winter, and with twelve of them living on the ranch, there were many to be kept fed. Her mission didn't make the work any easier though.

If there was any justice in the world, it would rain. She would give up just about anything for relief from the heat. The summer had sunk its claws in deep and refused to let loose. Even now when fall should be in the air, shimmers of heat hung all around her.

She used her sleeve to wipe the sweat from her forehead, dislodging her hat. It fell to the dirt below, allowing the scorching sun to hit her square in the face. She mumbled a curse beneath her breath and snatched it up, succeeding in spraying the loamy earth into her mouth.

Olivia wiped at the dirt, her teeth coated in grit. She reached for the mason jar of water nearby only to discover someone had knocked it over, spilling the precious liquid into the parched ground.

"Dammit."

"That's no way for a lady to speak."

The slow drawl instantly put her back up.

"Ranger Brody Armstrong." He was the last person she wanted to see.

She spit as much of the dirt out as she could. Right on his boot. "Oh, I'm sorry about that." Inside she grinned.

The Texas Ranger was supposed to be helping them with their parents' murder investigation, but he'd done nothing as near as she could tell. Nothing except for get their hopes up. Now three months after his big promises, Liv didn't believe a word the man said.

She glanced up at him, dressed in his standard black trousers and a black coat, white shirt with a silver string tie. Did the man own any other clothing?

A flat-brimmed black hat shaded his face, but she didn't need to see his cold blue eyes or the jagged scar on his jaw. She knew exactly what he looked like, even with her eyes closed. To her chagrin, Liv had nurtured an infatuation for the man for at least a month before she'd realized he had lied to her. And in her opinion, he was a poor excuse for a man of the law.

"I think your apology has à few holes in it." He wiped his boot on the tall grass nearby. "But I won't call you on it."

"If you're looking for Matt, he's not here. He and Hannah went to Houston for a couple days." She spat out another mouthful of gritty dirt after explaining the whereabouts of her brother and sister-in-law. "I'm in charge while he's gone. What do you want?"

She could've been nicer about it, but she was feeling gleeful to know she could tell the ranger to get off the Graham ranch. She had no use for him or any man for that matter. Not since her fiancé had talked her into giving up her virtue, then backed out of the wedding after she lost her parents and little brother. Men were fickle and faithless. And occasionally as annoying as Brody Armstrong.

The ranger frowned, as she knew he would. "When will he be back?"

"Thursday, maybe Friday. They left early this morning." She rocked back on her heels, a grin on her face.

"Damn. I needed to talk to him." To her consternation, the ranger turned and walked away.

"Where are you going?"

Without even slowing down, he threw his answer over his shoulder. "Inside out of this heat."

She wanted to be mean to him, but she wanted to know what he had to tell Matt even more. "Wait." He slowed down but didn't stop.

"Please." The word was ripped from her throat. It was the last one she wanted to use in the ranger's company.

This time he swung his head to look at her over his shoulder. "I'll wait for you inside with Eva and Mrs. Dolan." He pointed at her mouth. "You might want to wash the dirt off your teeth before you join us."

Olivia's cheeks heated at his observation. She would have used her sleeve to scrub her teeth but that would have made it worse. She left her garden implements lying on the ground and went over to the well pump. After using the pump handle to get the water flowing, she leaned down and opened her mouth. The water was warm, a testament to the summer heat. However, it was clean and she rinsed her mouth four times before the grit was gone. She cupped her hands and rinsed her face, then finger combed her hair.

Pronouncing herself presentable, Olivia stepped into the shade of the house. The cooler air inside hit her wet skin and she sighed in relief. Goose bumps danced down her skin and she closed her eyes at the welcome sensation.

"Ahem." Eva's amused tone told her she had done something she would be embarrassed about.

Olivia opened one eye and saw the housekeeper, Granny Dolan and the ranger sitting at the large table in the kitchen. The man's gaze was glued to her chest. Mortified, she realized goose bumps were not her only reaction to the cool air.

Olivia crossed her arms and looked for a hole in the floor to fall into. "It feels good in here."

"Apparently." The ranger's drawl made her want to hit him. Brody watched her, his hat lying on the bench beside him. She'd never seen him without it. His hair was straighter than a pin; so thick and black, it probably shone in the sun like a blackbird's wing.

"You've been working hard this afternoon. Why don't you sit down and I'll get you a drink?" Eva shepherded her to the table, pushing her into her sister-in-law Hannah's chair, which was right beside where the ranger sat. What in the world was the housekeeper doing?

"You are a passionate girl, Olivia." Granny Dolan's observations usually brought a smile or a chuckle, but today, her comment just made Olivia's discomfort worse. "No need to be embarrassed by what your body does."

Oh, where, oh, where was that hole in the floor when she needed it?

"Martha, would you go check on the girls? They're supposed to be practicing their reading." Eva came to the rescue, shooing her old friend, and Hannah's unorthodox grandmother, out of the kitchen.

"You have an interesting family." Armstrong's tanned fingers fiddled with the tin cup in front of him. They were slender but strong, with blunt and surprisingly clean nails.

"You've no idea." Olivia put her face in her hands, again wondering how she could still be obsessing about the ranger. He was an obnoxious ass.

"I have some idea, but I'm sure you know better." He tapped the table. "I have news I wanted to tell Matt, but I have to be someplace on Friday so I can't be here when he comes back."

She waited, oh, so impatiently, while Eva set down a cup of buttermilk in front of her.

"Drink, *hija,* you need to refill your body." The housekeeper retreated to the stove again.

Olivia took a big swallow of the buttermilk, its sweet rich flavor coating her tongue. She swallowed half the glass before she realized she had groaned. Out loud.

His blue eyes didn't look cold anymore. They were warm as his gaze moved over her face. What was it about this man that set her off kilter so easily?

"Good milk, hmm?"

"Uh, yeah, it is good." Olivia licked the milk off her top lip and witnessed his gaze drop straight to the movement. A jolt of something hot flashed through her. She managed to take in enough breath to gather her wits. "What news did you need to tell him?"

"Huh? Tell who?" Brody squinted at her.

"Matt. What news did you need to tell him?" She gripped the cup, its smooth curves keeping her grounded in reality while her traitorous body kept bouncing off into strange, dark pockets of sensation.

He looked down at the cup and took a swig of the coffee before he spoke. She didn't prompt him again, holding onto her patience by a thread.

The next time he looked at her, the ranger's cold gaze had returned. "I found out some information about your brother."

"Something about Matt?" She didn't understand what Brody possibly could have found out about her older brother that would warrant a visit to the ranch.

"No, not about Matt. About Benjamin."

Olivia could hardly suck in a breath. *Benjamin.* The youngest of the eight Graham children. The precocious five-year-old who had been missing for more than six months. His absence had left a hole in their family, a break in the circle of eight.

"What about Benjamin?" She could hardly take in a breath, her heart beat so hard.

"I need to talk to your brother. I'll wait until he comes back." The taciturn ranger sipped at his drink, making her want to upend the cup right in his lap.

"When Matt isn't here, I am in charge. I'm only a few years younger than he and I take care of the books for the ranch." She gritted her teeth to keep from cussing the man out. "Whatever you can tell him, you can tell me."

"Nope, won't do that. We had a deal, him and me, and it doesn't involve you." He glanced at Eva. "Your coffee is good, as always. Do you have any bread to go with it?"

"Don't you dare give him any bread." Olivia knew she was more likely to catch flies with honey than vinegar, but the man's refusal to talk with her was infuriating.

"He needs to tell me what he knows before he gets anything else from the Grahams."

She folded her arms across her chest and gave him her best "you will do what I say" look. He only shrugged and kept sipping his coffee.

Eva frowned at her. "*Hija,* you must be nice to Ranger Armstrong. He is a good man."

Olivia snorted. "I'll believe that when he treats me like a person instead of a pain in the ass."

"You are a pain in the ass."

At first she could hardly believe he'd said it, but then when it sank in, a chuckle burst out of her mouth. She didn't want to be amused by his smart mouth, but she was.

"So are you. Now tell me what you know. I won't tell anyone. I just need to know." She fiddled with the cup in front of her, embarrassed to be reduced to begging. "He's my brother too."

The ranger stared at her with his unblinking gaze long enough to make her squirm. Olivia didn't look away though. She refused to let him intimidate her. Too many men had tried that, unsuccessfully.

"Please." That she'd said please to the man twice—twice!—in one day stuck in her craw.

He finally looked away, out the window. "I found a man who worked for Jeb Stinson."

That was a piece of news. Jeb was their neighbor, a friend who had betrayed the whole community by sending a gang to kill ranchers, then buying their land for pennies on the dollar. He had hanged for his crimes but had refused to name his accomplices.

The Circle Eight was one of the ranches that had been attacked, and Olivia had lost both her parents and her little brother that day. She still had nightmares about seeing her mother and father's bodies. She also had a hard time trusting anyone, even her neighbors, because of Jeb and what he'd done.

"Did you arrest the man?"

"Only for being drunk, but he wouldn't give me anything until I told him his neck would stretch if he didn't tell me what he knew." Armstrong looked back at Olivia. "He said Jeb had a place south of here where all the stolen goods were hidden."

"What about the missing people from the ranches?"

She wasn't sure she wanted to know the answer, but with Benjy still missing, there were hard choices everyone had to make.

"Mexico."

Olivia's stomach quivered at the word "Mexico."

The war was still so fresh in everyone's mind, the idea Jeb would have easily betrayed his country and the veterans who had fought, was unfathomable.

"My God." She glanced at Eva, who looked as horrified as she felt. "He's so small. What do you suppose has happened to him?"

The ranger shook his head. "I've said too much."

"If you think for one minute you are not telling me everything, you're mistaken." She got to her feet and leaned toward him. "Tell me now."

He regarded her for a few moments before the corner of his mouth kicked up. "Anyone ever tell you that you have brass balls?"

"No, and I don't know what that means. Just tell me, for God's sake." She gripped the table to keep from shaking him.

"It means you are standing there yelling at a Texas Ranger, telling him what to do, without a bit of fear."

He got to his feet and Olivia remembered just how tall Armstrong was. She had to crane her neck to look at him. "That takes brass balls."

"Fine, then I've got brass balls. Now tell me what I want to know."

His lashes were absurdly long and thick. They looked like a woman's lashes, but she wasn't about to tell him that. It was an awkward time to be noticing his features. She was too distracted to think straight.

"I'm headed out in the morning to follow my lead. You can tell Matt I'll be back in a couple of weeks." With that, the ranger stood up and nodded to Eva. "Much obliged for the coffee, *señora*. *Es delicioso*." Pretty as he pleased, the ranger left the house.

"*De nada*." The housekeeper gave Olivia a look that told her to pursue the man.

She already planned on it.

Brody Armstrong walked out of the Graham house and sucked in a breath of the humid air. No matter how sticky it was outside, it was better than staying in the house. Olivia Graham was as annoying as a tick burrowing into his skin. Even though she was pretty enough to make his eyes hurt, her mouth made his head hurt. She never shut up and the woman was bossier than any military general.

He really wanted to talk to Matt, but he couldn't wait around for him. The shack he'd found out about was just a few miles outside of town. Brody planned to investigate the shack before his source woke up from his drunken stupor and was released from jail.

"Where do you think you're going?"

Armstrong didn't answer her but his hands fisted at the sound of her schoolmarm tone. He kept walking toward his paint. The pinto was his best friend, confidante and the only companion he ever wanted to travel with.

"I asked you a question."

"I don't have to answer." He untied the horse's reins and had just put his foot in the stirrup when she clamped onto his arm like a hundred-twenty-pound cocklebur. There was no way he was going to notice just how soft her breasts were, or how she was tall enough that he didn't hurt his neck looking down at her.

"You will not leave this ranch without telling me everything." There was a frantic note beneath the annoyance in her voice. "I have to know."

He had never been pressed up against her before. Her sweet breath spread across his face. Damned if her eyes weren't almost the color of turquoise, the bluish-green color unique to the Graham family. Her skin was honey colored, perfect except for a mole right at the corner of her mouth.

He wanted to kiss that mole.

Holy hell. Where had that thought come from? Brody wanted nothing to do with Olivia. Nothing. *Nada.* She was trouble and more work than any man ought to put up with. He had no time for a woman, least of all one like her.

"There are things I don't think you should know. And there are things I don't know yet. I ain't about to tell you partial truths or the drunken stories of a half-Indian I found in a tavern twenty miles from here." He leaned in even closer until their noses almost touched. "I am a man of the law. Let me do my job or I will put your pretty ass in jail."

She stared at him, her eyes getting a sheen that looked suspiciously like tears. Impossible. Not the unflappable, tough as nails Olivia Graham. She glanced away and cleared her throat.

"Where are you going? Can you at least tell me that?"

"I told you. Mexico. I'll be back in a couple of weeks." He didn't realize he was holding his breath until she moved back and he sucked in a much needed gulp of air.

"Isn't it dangerous? I mean, it's been such a short time since the war." She frowned, the hint of tears gone.

"Of course it's dangerous. Being a Texas Ranger is about danger, but it's also about doing what's right for Texas and its citizens." He patted her shoulder awkwardly. "I'll be fine. I've done it before." He didn't have the suave tongue that others did. His skills were in fighting, tracking and shooting. None of which helped him now.

Brody got up on his horse before she could grab him again. He tried not to look into her eyes, at the anger and confusion he would see there. She had to realize there were things a man did and things a woman did. He wasn't about to involve her in his investigation. It was much bigger than the kidnapping of Benjamin Graham. The child's disappearance was a piece in a larger puzzle, but Brody would do his best to find the boy, even though his discovery might bring the family as much heartache as his disappearance.

As he rode away, he thought about all the things that could happen to a young white child in the wild. He could have been sold to an Indian tribe, to a Mexican family, or even another Texas family. No matter what the case, Benjy was not going to be the same little boy who'd disappeared six months earlier.

It was a piece of truth he couldn't bring himself to tell

Olivia. If he did, she might not believe him, or worse, might try to find him herself. That was all kinds of wrong, more trouble than Brody cared to contemplate.

It was best for all that Olivia Graham stayed put.

He rode for two hours toward the deserted cabin that had held the stolen goods from Jeb's gang. He thought hard as he rode, trying to puzzle out just what Jeb could have done with the people he'd taken. The women were easier to figure out than the children. Jeb had given the law no information after his arrest, and now that he'd hanged for his crimes, there would be none forthcoming.

Then there was the disappearance of Jeb's own sister, Margaret, who'd been missing for three months. Supposedly she'd been having tea with Olivia when she'd vanished without a trace. Their father, Frederick, was now a broken man who rarely left his house, and had sold most of his land and cattle.

Jeb had decimated his own family for profit. That left a rotten taste in Brody's mouth. No matter what he believed, family was blood and blood was thicker than anything. He and his brothers had been through hell and back, and he was the only one who'd survived. He sympathized with the Grahams and the pain of losing Benjamin.

The loss of their parents had been bad enough, but at least death brought with it a kind of closure. Benjy's disappearance kept their pain and grief alive, without any end in sight. The Grahams assured him they had moved on, but he knew they hadn't really. Every time he came to the ranch, they asked him about the boy. It killed him not to be able to give them news, any kind of news. The boy had vanished just as Margaret Stinson had. Into thin air.

He slowed his horse to a slow walk as he got closer to where he thought the cabin was. He was always on guard, even if he didn't see a speck of dust move or hear a peep. Being a Texas Ranger was a dangerous job, but after his brothers' deaths, it seemed a good choice for him. He didn't regret signing up, and when his year was over, he would continue on. He saw the good that could come of keeping law and order.

He pulled the horse to a stop near a copse of trees. The cabin was tucked behind them, a tiny shack with only one window and a broken hitching post out front. He dismounted and left the horse ground-tied. Domingo was trained to stay put, untied, to allow Brody to leave in a hurry. The horse's training had worked to his advantage many times.

He stood there for several minutes listening to the sounds around him. There were birds rustling in the leaves above, but no human sounds, and no horse sounds either. If anyone was around, nature would tell him, and he always paid attention.

After taking the rifle from its scabbard, he approached the shack. He needed to look for clues, but only had a couple of hours before he had to find the Mexican he'd been told about, one of Jeb's hired thugs. The half-Indian, Bluehound, would be out of jail as soon as he sobered up, and Brody was sure he'd warn the Mexican first off. That left Brody just enough time to snoop around the shack.

The soft grass swayed around his legs as he walked toward the building. He scanned the woods as he moved toward the door. The wood was warped with age, its cheap hinges hanging off the frame. The window only had half its glass, the jagged edges gaping like sharp teeth. He peered in, seeing nothing but shadows and dust.

Brody glanced behind him before he pulled the door open. A gust of stale air hit him and he waved away the rancid stench. Something, or someone, had died in there.

Brody hesitated for only a few seconds before he went inside. He pulled his neckerchief up over his mouth and nose to block the stench. His eyes were watering already and he hadn't even found the rotting corpse yet.

Broken crates littered one corner with what appeared to be canned vegetables. Beside the broken crates were piles of clothing, nothing high quality, just everyday folks' clothes. Some of them had rust-colored spots he suspected were blood. He tried not to look at the tiny dress crumpled at the corner of the pile, its yellow fabric stained. A burlap sack was near the back wall, a three-legged stool lying in the dirt nearby. The sack had dark blotches that told him whatever smelled lay beneath it.

He used the end of his rifle to pull up the burlap. Before he could even get a good look at whatever it was, he spun around after hearing a shuffle near the door, his rifle cocked and ready.

"Good Lord!" Olivia Graham dropped to her knees, her arms over her head. "Don't shoot me, Brody."

His finger twitched on the trigger; the rifle was customized to his touch, and the only reason she wasn't dead. "What the hell are you doing here?"

More important, how had she sneaked up behind him without a whisper of noise? He was a trained tracker and a Texas Ranger. Rancher's daughters did not sneak up on him. Ever.

Until now.

"Following you. I couldn't let you leave without knowing what happened to Benjamin. I figured the best way to do that was travel with you."

"Not a chance." He gestured to the door. "Go home."

"Not a chance." She threw his words back at him, then grimaced. "What is that smell?"

He had a moment's consideration for the fact that she was a woman, then decided maybe a rotting corpse was the perfect way to shake her off his tail. "A dead body."

Her gaze widened but she got to her feet. "Who is it?"

"I don't know yet. I was going to find out when you decided to try to kill yourself by coming up behind me." He sounded annoyed and maybe a tiny bit petulant. What was she turning him into?

"I didn't want to kill myself. I just wanted to show you I was serious about finding my brother."

To his surprise, she stepped toward the burlap. He almost stopped her but decided to see exactly what Miss Graham would do.

"Whoever it is, it's small, either a woman"—she paused to swallow—"or a child." She glanced at him. "Did you check the pile of clothes too?"

She was smart and observant. He scowled at her. "Not yet. You interrupted me."

"Of course I did." Olivia leaned down and pulled at the corner of the sack. He watched her face, waiting for the horrified screech, for the quick exit from the shack, but she did neither. "Oh, Margaret."

It appeared they had found the missing Stinson daughter. The rich beautiful girl who had had everything to live for and a brother who must've wanted it all for himself. What was left of her was nearly unrecognizable except for her bright red hair. The decomposing body had stained the bright blue dress she'd been wearing. Olivia had been her friend and now had found her dead body. Any other woman would have been a blubbering mess.

But not Olivia Graham.

"Frederick will be heartbroken again." She glanced up at him, her eyes wide but dry. "I think they must have strangled her because there don't seem to be any bullet or knife marks on her dress."

Damned if the woman wasn't right. If she'd been a man, she would've made a good Texas Ranger.

He banished that thought before it went any further.

Brody knelt beside her and examined the body. The remnants of a rope were still tied around her wrists, attesting to the fact she'd been taken forcibly, likely by her own brother. Olivia was right about the strangling though. There were no other marks on the body that he could see. And if she'd just been tied up, she would have left the shack and crawled for help.

"She must have been here the whole time we were looking for her." Olivia shook her head. "I hope she didn't suffer too long."

Brody didn't tell her he thought perhaps the young Miss Stinson had suffered plenty before she passed. The men who worked for Jeb were not human—they were animals.

Olivia pulled back the burlap completely and sighed when she spotted the other woman's underthings bunched around her ankles. Oh, yes, she had suffered plenty.

"Can we bring her back to her father?" She replaced the burlap and got to her feet.

"I can't. I've got a man to chase, remember? You can stay here and do what you want." He didn't think she would be willing to transport the rotting corpse alone.

"I would but I don't want to lose sight of you." She walked over to the pile of clothing. "Now let's finish searching in here so we can find your man's trail."

"He's not my man and you are not coming with me." To his annoyance, she ignored him and focused on sorting through the clothes.

He watched her as she picked each piece up and held it at arm's length, turning it this way and that, before folding it neatly beside the pile. What in the hell was she doing?

"I recognize at least three of these as belonging to folks I've seen in town. I've got an eye for detail, and for clothes, so I usually pay attention to what people wear." She kept on examining the clothes while he stood back, plumb amazed by the way she approached such a gruesome task. "Oh, Brody, this is Benjy's."

Olivia held up a small brown coat. She carried it to the door and held it up in the sunlight. "I don't see any bloodstains. Thank God."

He expected her to fall down and start sobbing. Yet the woman proved him wrong at every turn.

She set her jaw and narrowed her gaze. "We're on the right trail."

"You are not coming with me."

"Yes, I am." She set the coat down by the door and returned to the pile of clothes. "If you had a lick of sense, you'd realize having a partner will only help your investigation."

"Partner?" He chuckled hoarsely. "You're nothing but a pain in the ass spoiled little girl. You wouldn't be worth spit on the trail."

She was silent for a few minutes, and he thought perhaps she was done with her crazy talk. After all, who ever heard of a woman partner? Nobody. Texas Rangers worked alone, only pairing up when they needed to. And he sure as hell didn't need her.

He took the opportunity to finish searching the shack, but found nothing but raccoon shit, rabbit shit and some spent casings.

When he turned around, he found Olivia had finished sorting the clothing and was going through the broken crates. She pulled out all the broken pieces and set them aside. There were seven unbroken jars that she put next to the coat by the door. He had to admit the woman was meticulous; no doubt the books at the Graham ranch were just the same.

She peered at the crates, looking at each broken piece. Brody wanted to get on his horse and get the hell out of there, but his curiosity over what she was doing kept him rooted in place. The woman was a natural investigator.

"These are a mixture of homemade crates and ones from mercantiles." She pointed at the pieces she'd laid out on the floor. "This is marked Brown's, this one Barnaby's, this one O'Hara's and this one." Her finger traced the lettering. "This one is from La Tienda." Her gaze met his. "It's Mexican."

Brody had seen Brown's and O'Hara's in his travels, both within fifty miles of there. Barnaby's was unfamiliar, as was La Tienda, but she was right. The crates had come from various mercantiles, all gathered together in this small shitty shack in the middle of nowhere Texas. What had Stinson been up to? Why was he stealing supplies and clothes, only to stash them here? Olivia had found a lot of information but no answers; her observations brought more questions to an already cloudy investigation.

He should have been the one to look at the evidence, but instead she had. Brody could not say whether he would have examined everything so carefully, or recognized what he had found. He wasn't about to admit it to her but he was impressed.

"Did you find anything?" She got to her feet and wiped her hands on her riding skirt.

"I found shit." He left the building and walked straight into the barrel of a shotgun sticking into his gut.

CHAPTER TWO

Olivia stood in the shadows, her heart thumping like mad. She heard the other man's voice and Brody's deep response. He was in trouble.

She had not come unarmed out into the wild; even now the pistol pressed against the small of her back. She'd shot it a few times, at coyotes and such, but never at a human being. However, she would protect the ranger, even if he was an ass; the man didn't deserve to be murdered like poor Margaret.

She was glad she'd worn her cowhide riding boots with the soft soles. One of the hands had made them for her as a birthday surprise; Lorenzo had nursed a crush on her for years unfortunately. But lucky for her, he was a wizard with cowhide and a needle. The boots were sturdy and quiet as a mouse when she walked. She crept toward the door, keeping to the gloom, and pulled the pistol out. The weight of the weapon was unfamiliar, but she gripped it firmly. Her father had taught every one of his children how to shoot every weapon they had. Texas was no place to live without knowing how to take care of yourself.

She reached the edge of the door and peered through the crack. The ranger was on his knees in the tall grass, his hands on his head. Two men stood in front of him;

one had a rifle, the other a shotgun, both pointed at Brody's head. She could squeeze off one shot before they reacted, but which one should she aim for?

"You're snooping around where you don't belong, Armstrong. Some people don't like that and they send people like me to stop you." The greasy-haired one was skinny, with dirty brown trousers and a gray shirt. His hat was even dirtier than his hair, which seemed impossible.

The other stranger was bigger, a barrel-chested man who would be harder to take down with one shot.

She stuck the barrel through the crack in the door and closed one eye. They were at least fifteen feet away, but if she aimed carefully, she could hit the skinny one holding the shotgun. She sucked in a shaky breath and cocked the pistol.

"I'll stick you in there with her and you can rot in hell together." The man raised the shotgun.

Olivia fired.

She fell back, right onto the broken crates. The boom was so loud she couldn't hear anything but the ringing in her ears. She scrambled to her feet and looked outside in time to see Brody fighting with the bigger man. The skinny one was on the ground and she knew her shot had been true.

She loaded another bullet in the gun as quickly as she could, then stepped out of the shack. Without being closer, she couldn't hit the other man without risk of hitting the ranger. The skinny man screeched when he saw her, blood covering his chest. He spat a bloody gob at her, but she jumped back, her eyes wide and her heart in her throat. She had done that, shot the man in the chest and now he would die because of her. But there was no turning back.

No matter what, she could not go back to who she had been two minutes before.

Olivia walked closer to the two men wrestling on the ground. The big man had Brody beneath him and was beating his face with meaty fists. She picked up Brody's gun and pressed it to the back of his head.

"Let him up or he'll be picking pieces of your brain out of his hair for a week." She hardly recognized her own voice. It was full of grit and rage.

"You best back up missy or I'll fuck your eye sockets after I kill him." The man's voice was colder than anything she'd heard before. He kept right on punching Brody, whose face was a bloody mess.

"One more chance, mister. Let him go or I'll kill you." Her palm was wet with fear, but she kept her hand steady, the trigger cocked.

"Fuck you." The man swung around to grab her leg, but she jumped back and fired.

The man's head exploded in front of her. Blood, brains and bone sprayed in a gruesome cloud all over the grass, and Brody.

"Oh, you kilt us both, you bitch." The skinny one had crawled to his shotgun. As he fumbled to aim it at her, Olivia crouched down and fired off another round, stopping him cold.

She dropped to her knees, then to her elbows until she pressed her forehead to the ground. The smell of dirt and grass filled her nose, temporarily blocking out the iron stench of blood and gunpowder. Brody put his hand on her back.

"Hell, Liv, you just saved my ass. I never thought you would be armed or could kill two men." He sounded impressed, which at any other time might have pleased her. For now she just kept her eyes closed and focused on not vomiting.

"Let me have that." He pried the gun from her hand and disappeared for a few moments. The sound of water hitting the ground reached her and she realized he was wiping the gore off his face. In another minute, he pressed a wet cloth to her face. "Here, just try to relax."

Relax? She'd just killed two men. *Killed them.* Olivia had never thought she would have to kill one person in her life, much less two men in two minutes. The wet cloth felt good against her face and thank God, it didn't smell like blood.

When she finally got control of herself, and was sure she wouldn't cry in front of him, she sat up. He crouched beside her, his cold blue eyes assessing her.

"I guess I've got a partner now."

She stared at him, wondering exactly what she had gotten herself into. Eva knew Olivia had left to follow Armstrong, but no one else knew where she was or what she was doing. The impulse to follow the ranger had now turned into something else altogether. She had killed for him and their lives had become inexorably linked. There would not be a time in either of their futures when they would not have this moment embedded in their memories.

Olivia shivered in the slight breeze that brushed against her damp cheeks. "I'm sorry."

Brody's grin would have knocked her to her knees if she hadn't already been there. The man was stunning without smiling, but with it, he was lethal to her equilibrium.

Perhaps it was due to her brush with death, or her growing infatuation with him, but she impulsively grabbed him and pressed her mouth to his. His lips were softer than she expected and they stayed that way as she put her heart into convincing him to kiss her back. Her tongue lapped against the seam of his mouth, needing, wanting more. He groaned low and deep in his throat before he pulled her flush against him and his tongue plundered her mouth.

Sweet heat spread through her body, making her nipples pop and her pussy throb.

To her consternation he pulled back, breathing hard, his lips wet from the kisses. "Shit, woman, do you want me to take you in a field full of blood?"

Olivia put her hand over her mouth, horrified by her actions. What had she been thinking? Death had turned her into an idiot, making her do things that made absolutely no sense to a normal person.

"I-I'm sorry. I just . . . I don't know." Her mouth felt strange, adrift without his.

He ran his hand through his hair. "Killing makes a man think of living. I guess the same is true of a woman. Sometimes folks just need to feel alive."

Oh, she felt alive all right. More than alive; she was pulsing with the need to join with him. Embarrassed by her desires, she simply nodded and got to her feet before he realized just how close she'd come to losing all her inhibitions.

The words he'd spoken just before their kiss finally sank in and she realized what he'd said.

"Partner?"

"That was before you made all the blood leave my head." He took another minute before he rose. She realized he was fighting to tame an erection, one she'd been responsible for.

"Oh, well, I'm sorry about that." She shrugged unrepentantly.

"I did say you'd be my partner." He peered at her, the cold stare of the ranger firmly back on his face. "But you've got to keep it to business only. We can't be jumping into each other's britches. That kind of distraction could get us killed."

Olivia understood his logic, but that didn't make it easier to accept. How was she going to control her wild attraction to him?

"Agreed." She walked back to the shack to retrieve Benjy's coat and the rest of the canned food. They could use it on the trail. "Where are we going?"

"We need to find a man named Sanchez. He is our lead to Stinson's outfit." Brody kept his gaze moving, constantly scanning the horizon for movement. "Where is your horse?" He picked up his hat from the ground where it had fallen, then wiped it on the grass. She didn't want to watch, knowing he was getting rid of the last vestiges of the gore from the stranger's head.

"Right near yours." She'd ridden her mare, the quarter horse that had been her eighteenth birthday gift from her father.

"Is it fast?" He started searching the men's bodies, taking their weapons and whatever else he found.

Olivia had no right to be shocked; after all, the men would have done the same thing to them. They might have even raped her before killing her. Yet taking from the dead left a bad taste in her mouth.

Of course, the men wouldn't have been dead if it wasn't for her. She had no call to cast stones.

"Yes, she's a good horse." Olivia wrapped the canned goods in the small brown coat, keeping her calm by remembering the jacket had no blood on it. Benjy was alive when he'd lost it.

"A mare?"

"Don't go judging Mariposa until you see her fly." She followed him as he walked toward the woods where the horses were. The man had a swagger that distracted her, again. She focused on the woods instead, anything to keep her mind off her attraction to Brody.

"Mariposa, huh?" He snorted. "Figures I pick a woman for a partner and she has a horse named 'butterfly.' Somewhere God is having a laugh at my expense."

Olivia ignored his jibe and kept walking. He didn't know her horse and therefore couldn't possibly judge her. Mariposa had heart.

When they arrived at the horses, he eyed the mare but didn't say anything else. Olivia was so glad to see Mariposa, her silly eyes pricked with tears. She swallowed the huge lump in her throat as she carefully put the coat and cans into her saddlebags.

By the time she was done, the ranger was on his horse looking down at her.

"We're going to have to have rules if we're going to travel together." His gaze was unblinking. "First rule: Don't make me wait for you."

He kneed his horse into motion, leaving her standing there, mouth open, and temper rising. Olivia threw herself into the saddle and went after him. There was no way he was going to leave her behind.

Brody rode in silence for the next hour. He wasn't ready to talk to his new partner, to face the reality of what had just happened. He'd let his guard down because of her, yet she'd saved him by killing two men. If he hadn't lived through it, he wouldn't have believed it.

He'd thought Olivia was a spoiled rancher's daughter with a sharp tongue and a stubborn streak a mile wide.

Now he realized that beneath the exterior she showed the world, Olivia had a spine of steel and more guts than most men. She should have been hiding in the shack while he dealt with the men. Yet she hadn't and without her courage, it might have been his brains decorating that field back there.

She was also perceptive, smart and observant. Her skills put her far above many men who might want to be a Texas Ranger.

She must have been thinking about what had happened as well because she didn't say anything. It was a blessing to have quiet. Their partnership might not be too bad after all.

They came upon a stream and he pulled his horse to a stop. She, however, kept riding. Brody realized he could either call her back or wait until she realized he wasn't beside her. He decided to let her keep going.

The paint eagerly lapped at the water as he watched her riding away. She had an amazing seat on a horse, which showed him she had lived on a ranch all her life. Her ass was nicely shaped too. He should not be noticing her at all, much less staring at her hind end.

"Olivia." He was surprised to find himself calling her.

She pulled the horse to a stop and looked back at him. "What are you doing?"

He didn't answer, waiting for her to ride back to him. Brody wasn't one to talk much and he wasn't going to change for her.

After apparently wrestling with herself for a few moments, she rode back toward the stream. Her jaw was set tight enough that he thought he heard her teeth grinding together.

"It would have been nice if you had told me you were stopping." She dismounted with grace, even though she was clearly annoyed. Another positive feature he wouldn't tell her about.

"Stop leading and you would have noticed." He refilled his canteen and splashed water onto his hair. There were still bits of gore stuck there. He hadn't put his hat on yet because he didn't want it to smell for the next five years. The water was clear and he felt better just having rinsed his hair. If Olivia hadn't been there, he might have stripped down and jumped in.

"I wasn't leading. I was riding beside you." She came up beside him. "I thought you said I was your partner. Is this how you treat a partner?"

He wiped his hands on his pants. "Don't know. I never had one before."

She waited exactly one minute before she opened her mouth again. He wanted to groan. Did the woman never shut up?

"You've never had a partner before? Don't most rangers have a partner?" She wiped her hands clean in the stream as she chattered. "I guess you fought in the war. Wasn't there anyone you had at your side?"

The memory of his brothers was sharp and bittersweet. He didn't know her well enough to tell her about his life or his loss. It wasn't her business.

"You talk too much."

She put her hands on her hips. "You talk too little. How can we be partners if I don't know anything about you?"

"You know enough. I'm a ranger and I uphold the law. That's it." He hung the canteen on his saddle and did a quick check of his horse's hooves.

Olivia stuck her face right in his. "No, that's not

enough but it'll do for now because you've agreed to be my partner."

He snorted at her. "Your partner? No, Miss Graham, I've allowed *you* to be *my* partner. Don't forget that."

Olivia didn't speak after that but he could almost hear her yelling at him in her head. The woman had too much passion for her own good. He liked his women meek and quiet. She was neither—quite the opposite actually. If he'd had to pick a partner, she wouldn't have been it. Rangers never let anyone get under their skin, but she could probably accomplish that task.

The idea that he was stuck with her until they finished the investigation hadn't really sunk in yet. It could take weeks, possibly even a month.

And he was stuck with Olivia Graham until then.

Brody let his decision wash over him as they rode. She was going to be helpful, but at what cost? His sanity more than likely. Then there was the attraction he'd been fighting since the moment he'd seen her three months earlier. Those apple-sized breasts, that beautiful skin and eyes, and her hair. He'd had dreams about her soft, brown hair, about how it would look spread out on a pillow.

It was stupid to spend his time fantasizing over a woman he could never have. When he'd signed up to be a ranger, he'd never expected to have a permanent woman in his life. It had been he and his brothers for so long, he didn't remember how soft women were or how good they smelled, until Olivia. She'd showed him what he'd been missing and he resented her for that, whether or not it was her fault.

A sharp snap in the woods beside him surprised him. How long had he been woolgathering? Foolish man. He dragged his attention back to the task at hand. Blue-hound had told him about a man named Sanchez, the one remaining member of Jeb's gang who was still in the area. From what the half-Indian had said, Sanchez was heading to Mexico real soon. Finding the man and interrogating him was important.

"Are we close?"

At first, Brody didn't answer. He almost asked if she wanted to be close to him, but caught himself before he said something so stupid. Then it dawned on him she was referring to their quarry, not their relationship. If he'd had less control, he might have even blushed.

"Yep. A couple more miles, just over that rise." He pointed to a small hill ahead. "There is no way to sneak up on him, so we need to wait until he leaves and follow him."

"Why wait?" She turned and grinned at him. "I'll ride up and pretend I need help. Does he know your face?"

"Well, no—"

"Good, then you can be my dumb husband." She pointed at the rifle. "Keep that on the other side so he doesn't see it. I'll have my pistol in my pocket. We can convince him to tell us whatever we need to know. If he doesn't tell us, we make him." The feral gleam in her eye made him pause to consider her plan.

It was better than waiting until the man left. After all, the information could be wrong. It could be hours before Sanchez left, maybe even days. Was he prepared to wait that long? Not if her plan could actually work.

"I've been told he has a mean streak. The one thing he loves more than a good lay is a bottle of whiskey." He wanted to shock her, to make her consider what she was doing before it was too late.

"What if I act the wanton, maybe a traveling whore, and you my houseboy?" She frowned at the horizon.

"Convince him that I would trade time in his bed for traveling money."

Brody pulled his horse to a stop and stared at her. "You're going to turn yourself into a whore to get information?"

She glanced back at him. "No, of course not. Once he's distracted by my, ah, offer, we can tie him up and make him tell us what he knows. Won't that work?"

Damn, it just might.

"You'll need to look a little looser." He glanced at her chest, trying to avoid focusing on those perfect tits. "Unbutton until you're showing skin. Put your hair down too. Do you have any face paint?"

She shook her head. "No, but if we find some berries I can make my lips red, maybe even rub some on my cheeks."

"That would work." He looked around. "Do you know what the bushes look like?"

"Do you mean we're going to do this?" Her eyes sparkled in the mid-afternoon sun.

Brody thought about all the reasons he should say no, but there weren't any. "Yep, let's do it."

Olivia looked triumphant. "If Matt saw me now, he would try to paddle my behind."

CHAPTER THREE

Caleb Graham rode into the yard of the Circle Eight, with his brother Nicholas behind him. Lorenzo was waiting by the barn, his expression concerned. There wasn't panic, so Caleb wasn't too worried but he knew the vaquero was hard to ruffle.

He stopped and dismounted, then yanked off his gloves. "What's wrong?"

Nick jumped down with a jingle of spurs. "What do you mean what's wrong?"

"Shut up a minute and let Lorenzo talk." Caleb stepped toward the ranch hand, his worry growing.

"Mariposa is gone."

"What do you mean, she's gone? Did someone take Liv's mare?" The theft of one of their best broodmares would put a dent in their plans to raise their own horses.

"*Sí*, Olivia did." Lorenzo shook his head. "She's been gone since before dinner."

Caleb closed his eyes and counted to ten. "Do you know where she went?" His older sister wasn't the type of female to take off on flights of fancy. She ran the ranch like a military camp and was more disciplined than anyone he knew. When Matt and Hannah were gone, Olivia took great pleasure in ordering everyone around. She just didn't ride away for eight hours for no reason.

"No, but Mama does." Lorenzo frowned. "The ranger was here this morning."

Ranger Armstrong was a good man. There was no reason to be worried if he'd visited. Liv must have told him Matt wasn't there. But where had she gone?

A terrible thought occurred to him and he turned and ran to the house. He burst through the door, startling Eva and Mrs. Dolan, who sat at the table drinking coffee. Wide-eyed, they both opened their mouths to likely admonish him but he spoke first.

"Where is she?"

Eva didn't pretend to misunderstand. "She's gone. When she is done with what she has to do, she will return."

Caleb heard but didn't quite believe the housekeeper. "Gone where?"

"With the ranger, of course. Olivia has gone to find Benjamin."

Oh, shit. Matt was going to kill him.

Olivia shouldn't be excited to be dressing up as a whore and throwing herself at a murderer and robber, but a kernel of thrill had blossomed inside her. Growing up on the Circle Eight had been relatively normal for the Graham children, with the dangers anyone expected in Texas. But the day her parents died had changed that life forever.

Now she would protect her family no matter how hard it was, or how far she had to go. The excitement originated from her heart, from finally doing something to help find Benjamin, and to bring to justice the men who had murdered her parents. Perhaps it was a little bloodthirsty but she was going to accept her feelings, good or bad.

She searched the brush for berries and found some in only a few minutes. These weren't the kind to eat, so she had to be careful not to lick her lips. They would cause vomiting and diarrhea—she and Rebecca found that out a long time ago—but nothing more serious than that. If she had to kiss Sanchez, he would get a bad case of the runs from it. A fitting side effect for a bastard who might have had a hand in murdering her parents.

Olivia took a handful of berries and used a small rock to smash them on a larger rock. She rubbed the juice between her fingers, then carefully applied it to her lips, and rubbed it into her cheeks. Brody held out a canteen to wash her hands off.

He watched as she unbuttoned her shirtwaist, then glanced up at him. His gaze locked on her breasts and the air between them nearly crackled with awareness.

"Is that enough?" Her voice came out a little hoarse.

"No, you need to keep going. More buttons." His tone was flat calm, damn it.

She wasn't sure if he wanted to see her bare herself entirely, which Olivia knew wasn't outside the realm of possibility, or if he was telling her the truth about showing more.

Three more buttons and she spread out the shirt so the entire top half of her chest was showing. Her breasts poked out, almost to the nipple. He licked his lips and her stomach jumped. She wanted to feel his tongue on her skin, on her lips, on her body. With a mental slap for her continued foolishness, Olivia pushed aside her attraction to the man. She had to keep her focus on the man she had to fool into thinking she was a whore.

"Your hair too." His voice had finally become deeper, huskier than it had been. She was immensely satisfied to see that he was as affected as she was. It gave her a certain amount of satisfaction to know she wasn't the only one struggling with desire.

Olivia pulled the pins from her hair and unraveled the braid.

"Here, let me." He stepped behind her and finger combed her hair, rubbing her scalp until she closed her eyes against the pleasure. No one had ever told her a head rub could be so pleasurable. She would have to remember how much she enjoyed it, because she sure as heck wanted to repeat this experience.

Brody stepped away and walked around her. His gaze raked her up and down, then back again. His normally cool blue eyes were blazing hot when they finally met hers.

"Well, hell, woman."

She preened inside at the expression on his face, the heat in his gaze. She felt a pure feminine pleasure at bringing a man to want her by simply looking at her.

"You, ah, make a good ah . . . you clean up good anyway." He cleared his throat and walked back toward the horses.

Olivia told herself she wasn't disappointed. He hadn't called her a good whore, but he hadn't actually complimented her either. If she was respectable, there was no way she would have followed him, or killed two men, or dressed up like a fallen woman. If she was respectable, she would have been swooning about the whole day.

Did that mean she wasn't respectable? Perhaps, but she was feeling good about everything, including the way she'd protected herself and Brody. There was no way she would trade this experience for respectability.

She fluffed her hair a little more and glanced down at her nearly exposed breasts. It was time to put on a show, and she hoped to God it was a good one.

After tucking the pistol in her skirt pocket, Olivia arranged herself on the saddle and pronounced herself ready. Brody moved his coat so it partially covered the rifle. Sanchez would have to walk around to see the weapon if they played their parts right.

"You will be my, ah, manager? Husband?" She wasn't sure which role he would feel comfortable with.

"I'll be your brother."

That was unexpected. A brother wouldn't be ogling her chest or looking at her as if he wanted to throw her on the ground and lose himself inside her.

"I have four brothers. I don't need another one." She made a face at him, but he kept his eyes facing forward. "I think you should be my manager. You make business deals for me and I do the work on my back." It sounded just as raw as it was. She knew there were women reduced to this kind of situation, women who had no one to help them. Olivia wouldn't judge them for what they did because she was about to do almost the same thing. She would do anything for her family, no matter the cost.

Brody didn't answer her so she decided her idea was the best. They came up on the rise and she made sure to sit up straight, thrusting her chest as far forward as she could.

A man appeared out of the woods to her left, rifle at the ready and it was pointing straight at her head. Her mouth went cotton dry and she knew the smile she gave the man was as shaky as her hands. This had to be Sanchez.

"Why, good afternoon, sir." She leaned forward enough to give him an eyeful of her cleavage. "I hope you don't mind us stopping by unannounced."

"Who the hell are you?" His voice was oily and rusty

at the same time, a combination that made her skin crawl.

"My name is Belinda and this here is my manager, Ferdinand." She smiled widely. "I'm meeting such nice folks on my journey, making some money so we can continue on our way."

The man's grip loosened slightly. "Making money?"

"Why, sugar, you know what I mean." She winked at him, grateful he couldn't see how much she trembled.

"How much?"

"Dollar for half an hour. Two for a whole hour." She hoped that was a reasonable amount because she had no idea how much to charge.

"And him?"

"Oh, he likes to watch, but for you, he can wait outside with the horses." She noted the sheer size of the man, his dark black eyes and bronze skin. "I surely do like a big man."

Brody made some kind of noise beside her but she didn't react, hoping the man didn't hear it.

"Ride on to the house. I meet you there." He disappeared back into the woods, leaving Olivia and Brody alone.

She let the air out of her lungs slowly, although she really wanted to let a gust loose. The man was likely watching them and they had to keep up the pretense of being a whore and her manager.

"He seemed like a good customer. Let's get on then before he changes his mind. We need to eat tonight." She spurred her mare forward, aware that every move she made was monitored.

"Don't overdo it, Belinda." Brody's whisper was more like a hiss, almost too low for her to hear.

"Be quiet, Ferdinand."

They walked the horses at a leisurely pace, while her heart thundered instead of the horse's hooves. She was about to cross a line. There would be no turning back now. She didn't know whether to be terrified or excited.

The house turned out to be even less than the shack they'd left behind hours before. It was smaller, dirtier and leaned to the right. More than likely it was an old line shack a rancher had built twenty years ago and then left to the elements. This man had made it his own. Olivia hoped she didn't have to smell the inside.

The trees had grown around the house, sheltering it like a mother's arms would hold an ugly child. The foliage kept it hidden from those that might seek it. Brody had the right of it—sneaking up would not have worked.

Olivia swallowed the dry spit in her mouth at the size of Sanchez as compared to the house. The trees had dwarfed him and now he did the same to the shack. He held a rifle on his shoulder, but his finger was still on the trigger. The man was much bigger than she'd thought he was. She resisted the urge to glance over at the ranger. Instead, she pasted on a smile.

"You have a nice house, sugar." She was proud of just how calm her voice sounded.

"Climb on down and I'll show it to you up close and personal."

Olivia took her time dismounting. "You didn't tell me your name."

"I didn't plan on it." He kept his gaze on Brody, who had stopped ten feet away. "What's your manager doing?"

"Oh, he is giving us privacy." When her feet hit the ground, her mare shied away a little, probably sensing Olivia's discomfort. "He'll go back in the woods if you want."

"I want him close so I can keep my eye on him." Sanchez's dark gaze was sharp and suspicious.

"Ferdinand, please come closer so our host doesn't think you're up to no good." She held onto the horse's reins as she waited for Brody to move closer. The pistol pressed against the outside of her thigh, a comfortable weight. She hoped she wouldn't have to use it again today but was prepared to. There wasn't anything she wouldn't do to find Benjy.

Brody rode up slowly, keeping the side of the horse with the rifle out of the man's view. He dismounted clumsily, and snorted at his own mistake.

"Get on with it then. I gotta date with a bottle and a pair of tits over in Eagle Creek." He leaned against his horse and pulled out a cheroot. As he lit the match on his boot, he met Olivia's gaze. "I'm gonna start charging you for standing there instead of servicing your customer."

She managed to keep her mouth closed at the change in his demeanor. The man would have never been mistaken for a ranger the way he looked right about then. He had thespian skills she wasn't even aware of, and although she might not admit it, she was impressed with them.

Olivia turned to the stranger. "You heard the man. How long do you want me?" She ran her finger along the edge of her blouse. The man's gaze snapped to the digit, following its path. He licked his lips and she held in a shudder with great effort.

"Half hour. Don't have no more than a dollar, but I need a good fuck." He pushed the door open with his boot. "Inside."

"Oh, you know I have to see the money first." She wagged her finger at him. "It is business after all."

He reached into his pocket and pulled out a crumpled bill. "You don't get it until I get my dick sucked."

Olivia's stomach rolled and she tasted bile in the back of her throat. "Your dollar, sugar." She walked up toward him and his gaze locked on her cleavage.

Before she even realized Brody had moved, he had his arm around the man's throat and his rifle planted in Sanchez's armpit. She stopped in mid-stride and stared.

"Fucking bitch. I knowed you was just after my money." Spittle flew from the man's mouth and landed on her cheek.

"Oh, she didn't want money from you." Brody's cold tone was so far removed from his clownlike act a few minutes earlier, she had trouble reconciling the two.

"What the hell do you want?" The man tried to break the ranger's hold, but it appeared to be impossible.

"Jeb Stinson." The name rippled through the air, leaving a bad taste in her mouth. The stranger stopped struggling.

"I don't know that name."

Brody tightened his grip, twisting the man's arm until he groaned. "Don't lie to me, Sanchez."

There was a pause when the man appeared to be weighing his words. "You got the wrong man."

"I don't think so." He leaned in so he spoke into the man's hairy ear. "You tell me or I show you what pain really is."

"Who are you?" Sanchez didn't look afraid, but he didn't look as confident as he had before.

"Nobody you want to fuck with. Someone who needs information." Brody glanced at Olivia. "There's rope in my saddlebags."

She turned to follow his directions, glad she wouldn't have to see whatever he planned to do to Sanchez.

There were many things she had already done that no one would approve of. She shouldn't start judging the ranger's methods.

By the time she returned with the rope, Brody had the man on the ground and his knee firmly planted in his back.

"Tie his hands, then his feet."

She leaned over with the rope, giving the ranger a clear view of her breasts. His eyes widened just a fraction before his gaze snapped to hers.

"And button your shirt."

Olivia's temper reared and when she finished tying Sanchez's hands, she stood up and let loose another button. She very much enjoyed how Brody's mouth tightened at her gesture. Too bad. There was no way he was going to order her around. A partner was an equal, not a dog to be told what to do.

After she tied his feet, she needed to wash her hands. Just touching the stranger made her feel unclean. Thank God, Brody had stepped in before Sanchez had touched her. She wouldn't have the memory of that to contend with for the rest of her life.

The ranger flipped the big man over like a ragdoll. Brody might be lean, but he was strong as an ox. She'd do well to remember that.

"Now Sanchez, you're going to tell me about Jeb's operation. Where he stashed the goods, where he sold the people and where he parked his carcass after a robbery." Brody's voice was cold enough to give her goose flesh up her arms.

"I don't know nothing." The other man wasn't struggling anymore and she saw worry in his dark gaze.

"Oh, I think you do." The ranger pulled a huge knife out of a hidden sheath on his back. It had to be as big as her forearm. The sharp blade winked in the sunlight, lethal and intimidating. "And I think I can change your mind about telling me."

Olivia watched the blade as Brody slid it toward the man's ear. She wondered what he would do to get the information he needed. He was bound by the law, wasn't he?

"You know I can do about anything I want and tell people you died in a gunfight and I buried your body." The knife's edge left a thin trail of blood along Sanchez's dirty neck. "Nobody will care. Nobody will miss you."

Olivia was startled to realize he had not told Sanchez he was a ranger. For the first time since she'd met Armstrong, a frisson of fear slid down her spine.

Matt always told her she acted like a bull, pushing her way through life, no matter who she knocked down. She may have knocked herself down by choosing to be with Armstrong, no matter how much she was drawn to him.

The ranger slid the knife around the front of Sanchez's throat as Olivia stared, her heart thumping hard enough to make her ears hurt.

"You want to tell me what you know before I start cutting off parts?" Another knife appeared in Brody's other hand. He pressed it against Sanchez's crotch.

Apparently, the man valued his balls. "I tell you. I tell you. Don't cut my *cojones, cabron.*" The tough man had been reduced to begging.

Olivia let out a sigh of relief, but a niggling doubt about Armstrong's tactics stayed. Would she have gone that far to get information about Benjy? She didn't want to find the answer to that question.

"Start talking." Brody straightened up but kept the knives in position. His cold eyes locked on Sanchez.

"There is a shack a couple hours north where we

meet. Each time Stinson tells us the ranch to hit. He didn't care about what we took." Beads of sweat rolled down the man's face.

"What about the people and goods you took? Did you bring them into Mexico?"

"*Sí*. Higher price."

Olivia knew the answer to the question before Sanchez answered. It was her worst fear. A sweet, blue-eyed white boy would be sold to the highest bidder for God only knew what. Her stomach heaved. She turned and ran for the bushes, her hand pressed to her mouth to hold back the vomit.

At the edge of the woods, she dropped to her knees and retched time and again. If she let her mind drift to what her little brother was enduring, it made her vomit again. Olivia crawled to a sunny spot a few feet away. She shook as she rocked back and forth, hugging herself.

"You kill two men without blinking an eye, but the sight of an ounce of blood makes you puke." Armstrong stood beside her, holding out a canteen.

She took it without answering and rinsed her mouth. If there was one time to be strong for her family, this was it. She wouldn't let the knowledge that Benjy was in Mexico make her fall apart. Olivia had suspected he was there, but now that she knew the truth, she would follow. Little boys didn't deserve to be sold like cattle. She would find him.

Armstrong handed her a folded handkerchief. She was surprised by his solicitousness but took the cloth, wet it with water from the canteen and wiped her face.

"Thank you." She waved the wet handkerchief. "I'll wash this and return it to you."

"Much obliged." He shifted his feet. "Sanchez says he isn't the one who took your brother, but he was there."

"Did you let him go?" She wasn't ready to talk about Benjy with him yet.

"Hell, no. He's tied up inside that hovel. First town we get to, I'll send a message to Austin to have him picked up." Armstrong held out his hand. "Are you ready to ride?"

This was the moment she decided whether she would go farther than she'd expected to. Whether she had the courage to take his hand and ride into the very country her father and brothers had fought. Whether she would risk her life to find the smallest Graham and make the circle complete again.

Olivia took his hand and got to her feet. "I'm ready."

CHAPTER FOUR

Brody kept glancing at Olivia. He couldn't seem to stop himself. She had done nothing but surprise the hell out of him all day. The sun was sinking into the horizon when he spotted an ideal spot to stop for the night. He wondered if his traveling companion was regretting her decision to accompany him.

He wouldn't blame her if she did. She'd already killed two men for him, not to mention turned herself into a whore, albeit temporarily, and seen things a rancher's daughter ought not to. Yet she'd held on to her control until he had been interrogating Sanchez. She'd been tough as nails all day, and he sure didn't expect to find her puking in the bushes.

Olivia Graham confused him, but he wasn't going to admit that to her. She was one of the toughest women he'd ever met, but still soft. It was a conundrum he didn't know how to handle. Not that he'd admit that either.

"There's a spot up ahead where we can make camp." He turned his horse toward the clearing, expecting her to follow.

She didn't.

"We're going to stop now? You can't mean that. There's at least an hour or more of light left." Ah, that glimpse at the softer side of her was gone.

"It's a good spot with a few rocks to keep the wind off us, trees to protect against any rain, and the sun is almost down." He kept riding. "Your choice, Liv, but I'm stopping."

Her gaze nearly burned a hole in his back. She was annoyed with him, but he didn't care. It wasn't as though she had the experience to be out in the open prairie alone. Armstrong knew more than she did and there wasn't a damn thing she could do to change that.

"Did you just call me Liv?"

That made him pause. He glanced back at her, not knowing her well enough to understand the tone of her voice.

"Isn't that what your family calls you?"

Her gaze narrowed. "You are not my family, Ranger."

This was the woman Armstrong was familiar with. He kneed his horse into motion and didn't bother responding to her. Common sense would kick in, even if she didn't want it to.

By the time he had his horse unsaddled and taken care of, Olivia rode up to the clearing. He still didn't speak to her—there was no need to. She had done what he'd expected and chosen safety over her pride. That didn't mean she would keep her mouth shut. This was Olivia Graham, the biggest mouth in Texas.

She didn't disappoint him.

"I don't appreciate your treating me like that. We are partners after all."

He unsaddled his horse and rubbed him down briskly before he looked at her. She was still mounted on her mare, glaring at him in the late afternoon light.

"You fixing to stay up there all night?" He tethered his horse to a sturdy tree branch, making sure the animal had ample access to the sweet grass nearby.

She scowled so hard, a line appeared between her brows. If her shirt had been buttoned up, he would've been amused by her annoyance. However, her damn breasts were distracting as hell. Brody turned back to setting up the campsite.

"Get off the horse, Liv. Get a small fire going while I find water." He snatched the canteen off her saddle and stomped off toward the sound of water in the distance. No matter if she listened or not, he had to have a few minutes to stuff his dick back in his britches before she realized it was howling to bust out.

Olivia considered her options before getting off Mariposa. She knew she couldn't go into Mexico alone, but Armstrong was bossy and condescending—two of her least favorite flaws in a man. He damn sure wasn't treating her like a partner either.

She couldn't push him around like she did her brothers. Apparently, he didn't budge an inch, ever. That meant she needed to find another way to get him to do what she needed.

After gathering some kindling, she made quick work of starting a fire with the matches she had in her saddlebags. Olivia was nothing if not prepared. There was a time folks would've made fun of her for her habits, but today wasn't that day.

She had a nice blaze burning in minutes. The temperature had cooled and the warmth of the fire drifted past her cheeks to disappear into the fading sunlight. She took out the coffeepot from her bag and set it aside to use when Brody returned with water.

Olivia pulled out the supplies she'd packed, feeling comfortable for the first time since she'd left home. Making a meal was something she could do well. Olivia could do most everything in a kitchen, but it had been at least five years since she'd attempted to cook over an open fire. Her mother had supervised her then.

A shaft of pain squeezed her heart before she pushed it away. Her mother wouldn't want her to wallow in self-pity. Olivia had to do what she had to do.

After a moment to compose herself, she took out the pan she'd brought, and put it on the fire to warm up.

"What the hell are you doing?" The ranger's growl startled her badly. She nearly fell face-first into the fire but, lucky for her, he grabbed her hair and yanked her back in time.

Her pride and her scalp smarting, she gulped down the lump of fear lodged in her throat. Before she even caught her breath, he was kicking dirt onto the fire.

"What the hell are *you* doing?" She threw his own words right back at him. "You told me to start a fire, Ranger."

"I didn't tell you to build a bonfire you could see from twenty miles away." He kicked enough dirt onto the flames to shrink the merry fire into a weak pile of embers.

"How was I to know that?" She scrambled to her feet, righteous fury coursing through her veins. "You bark orders at me and walk away."

He scowled down at her, his expression as dark as thunderclouds. "You'd do well to listen to those orders. I said get a small fire started. The important word there was 'small.'"

"You are a bully and a jackass." Olivia poked him in his chest, which was so hard her finger smarted. Was the man made from an oak tree?

"You are a know-it-all and a loudmouth." His hot breath gusted over her face as he yanked her close.

Their lips met in an apocalyptic clash. Her breath stopped in her throat, trapped by the rush of utter astonishment.

His arms tightened around her waist, bringing her even closer to his incredibly firm body. Each nerve ending sang a different song, some in pleasure, some in horror, others in hunger. Her arms crept around his wide shoulders as the kiss deepened. She knocked his hat off, not caring where it landed.

His tongue slid into her mouth like a conquerer's, guiding her tongue along with the rest of her. She was swept along by a wave of uncontrollable passion. Her nipples budded against her chemise, rubbing deliciously against the cotton fabric and his chest.

Thank God she wasn't a virgin or the reality of being in Brody's arms would turn her into a mess. As it was, she was hanging onto her control by a slim thread. She hadn't experienced such intensity in a kiss before. Ever.

He growled low in his throat as she broke the kiss to suck in a breath of air. He took the opportunity to feather kisses along her jaw until he reached her ear. The hot wet assault on her continued, stealing her thoughts and her objections.

There was nothing but the two of them and the heat between their bodies. She let loose a feminine growl when his hand landed on her aching breast.

"Oh, yes." Her voice was breathy and husky, needful too.

"If you don't stop me now, I'm going to take you." His deep voice sent a shiver from her nipples to her core. "Do you understand, Liv?" He cupped her face with his big hands, staring down at her as they both shook with the power of what was happening.

As they locked gazes, their hot breaths mingled, just as

their bodies had. Olivia needed that mingling and more. She *needed* for him to take her.

"Yes."

His thumbs brushed her cheeks, trembling, oh, so slightly. "Have you been with a man before?"

"Yes."

"Thank God." He picked her up and set her on a flat rock, which was conveniently at the right height for her to spread her legs.

He stepped between them, his cock harder than the rock beneath her behind. She pulled him closer until he pressed up hard against her clit; she closed her eyes at the pulse of pleasure that shook her.

His mouth found hers again, clashing teeth, tongue and lips. In a ballet of desperation, her skirt was ruched up, the slit in her drawers breached and his staff nudged her entrance. Olivia pulled at his shoulders, then his back until he slid forward, entering her in one powerful thrust.

She shook from the ecstasy coursing through her, at the sensation of having him fully sheathed inside her. It was more than pleasure, more than anything she'd ever experienced. The sex she'd had before was child's play, literally.

Brody was all man.

Olivia hung onto the rock beneath her as he slid in again, filling her. She could barely put two thoughts together, her mind scrambled by the force of her own reaction.

She'd had so many dreams about him, but the reality was far better than she'd expected. His scent surrounded her, all man, all heat. Olivia was whirling in a powerful force named Brody and she could only hang on as her body took control.

"Open your shirt." His gruff command didn't annoy her this time. No, Olivia knew what he wanted and she wanted it even more.

With trembling hands, she unbuttoned her shirt, then pulled her chemise down her arms until her breasts were exposed. The corset beneath them served up a banquet for his questing mouth. Both of them groaned when his mouth closed around one dark pink nipple.

Her body contracted around him with each tug of his teeth on her breast. The dirt and pebbles scraped her hands as she clenched the rock, her orgasm building. He lapped at her breast, the cool evening air making it pucker more as he switched to the other nipple.

"Oh, God, Brody, I'm so close," she gasped against his dark hair. "Please."

Hearing herself beg was embarrassing, but she had no time to think about it. She needed a release, needed to feel the ultimate bliss with his cock inside her.

He reached between them and found her clit, flicking it once. Twice. The orgasm ripped through her like a tornado, and she was certain she shouted his name as waves of ecstasy washed over her.

She pushed her breast into his mouth, his teeth grazing her, yanking another groan from deep inside her. Before the shivers of raw pleasure subsided, he withdrew from her core. Olivia watched as he gripped his cock, pumping it three times before he exploded, wetting the rock below her.

He put his hand on her thigh and met her gaze.

"What did you just get me into, woman?"

It was a good thing the coffeepot was metal or it would have been busted to bits the way Olivia slammed it around. Brody hadn't expected to have sex with the prickly Olivia Graham, and he sure as hell hadn't expected her to be angry at him because of it. She was purely furious at him and her reaction confused the hell out of him.

What right did she have to be angry?

He watched her make coffee with a vengeance, never once glancing in his direction. She mumbled under her breath a lot though and he swore she used "son of a bitch" and "bastard" more than once. He'd often wondered what had made Olivia so damn ornery, much more so than anyone else in her family, and now he might have figured out why.

She'd been hurt by a man, likely the same one who had taken her virginity.

Whoever he was, he was obviously a complete idiot. Brody had bedded plenty of women, many of them working gals, but not a one of them had the passion Olivia had shown. She was a hellcat, scratching and writhing more wildly than he'd expected. It surprised him, pleased him and scared him. He could get addicted to a woman with that kind of fire burning inside her. Of course, he could get scorched if he wasn't careful.

It would be better to keep his hands off her, no matter how ferocious she was in bed. Or on a rock.

"You fixing on throwing that pot away after you're done denting it?" The words popped out of his mouth before he could snatch them back. It was the wrong thing to say.

Her anger, which had been bubbling to a boil, cooled to a dangerous low. He liked her better yelling at him. Now she was glaring a hole through him. He wondered if he should be careful when he went to sleep that night.

"I'd like to dent your head with it." She poured herself a cup of coffee, then pretty as you please, poured the rest of it on the ground.

"That was a waste." He'd been looking forward to that coffee, dammit.

"You can make your own, Ranger. I wouldn't serve you if you were a king and I was a serf. I'd rather be whipped." She pulled out what appeared to be biscuit, canned peaches and dried meat, then proceeded to eat the impromptu meal in front of him.

His stomach yowled and she smirked at him.

"I've got my own vittles, you know." He did but they weren't nearly as appetizing as what she had. His jerky was older than dirt, just as tasty too. He also had a bunch of broken crackers and a can of beans. He had planned to stock up after he'd stopped at the Grahams', but things had gone haywire.

Hell, they were still going haywire as far as he was concerned.

"Good, because you may not share my food."

"You sound like a little girl, you know. Not wanting to share her toys with anyone. Selfish." He got up and she held onto her biscuit as though he meant to grab it from her. "I ain't gonna take your food, Liv. Jesus, is that what you think of me?"

Her cheeks colored. "No, what I think of you does not include your taking my food."

Brody snorted and headed to his saddlebags, purely done fighting with Olivia. He had to plan his route into Mexico and what he would do afterward, and that did not involve Olivia Graham. No, he was going to bring her to the next town and pay someone to take her home. There was no way he was going to bring her into Mexico, for two reasons. First, her brother Matt would kill him. Second, she might be killed there because she was white. With Brody's dark hair, and some help making his skin a little darker, he could sneak into Mexico unnoticed. He'd done it before; he'd do it again.

Olivia had light brown hair and skin like cream with cinnamon sprinkles. She would stand out too much to risk it. He did not look forward to her reaction when he told her, which he would do at the last possible moment, of course. He didn't want to wake up tied to a tree with his horse gone—no doubt she would do it too.

He sat back down with his meager meal and tried to ignore the fact she'd dumped out perfectly good coffee. The water in his canteen would wash the dry food down his throat just fine.

"My brothers accuse me of being bossy."

"I find that hard to believe," Brody responded dryly.

"Shut up while I get this said." She clenched one fist. "Please."

He held up his hands in surrender, wondering just what she had to say that was so important. The woman talked enough for two people as it was.

"I didn't used to be so hard but with so many young'uns in the house, I had to be bossy or get run over. Mama was a wonderful person, a wonderful mother. I helped as much as I could." She fiddled with the remains of her biscuit. "I fell in love when I was eighteen, but with Pa and Caleb and Matt away at war, I couldn't leave Mama with all the responsibility. I asked him to wait a bit before we got married."

Brody frowned at that piece of news. She'd been engaged? Couples anticipated their weddings every day, but she wasn't married. He wasn't sure he wanted to know what had happened.

"A month before we were to be married, my parents

were killed and Benjy taken." He heard her swallow. "My intended broke our engagement a week before the wedding." She met his gaze, her blue-green eyes shining in the firelight. "Said he couldn't be married to a woman who wailed and carried on so much."

So many things made sense to him now. She'd lost her parents, her brother and her future husband in a short period of time. He'd left her because she grieved too much? Because she wanted to find her parents' murderer and her missing brother? Whoever he was, the bastard deserved to be castrated.

Now Olivia didn't cry at all, and she wasn't a puddle of grief. She was a tornado of anger and vengeance. Brody wondered whether they'd have gotten along better if he'd met her a year ago, whether he would've noticed her at all. She was not the same woman; he would bet every cent he had on that.

"He's a foolish man," was all Brody could say. "Who was he?"

She narrowed her gaze. "No one. Just a foolish man as you said. The reason I told you the story was so that you'll understand whatever happens between us does not mean marriage."

Olivia could have hit him with a rock and it would have had less impact than her words. Marriage? The dry crackers in his mouth turned to dust and he had to take a huge swig of water to dislodge them before he choked.

"What the hell are you talking about?"

"I am just being clear, Ranger. I didn't get us into anything. I simply scratched an itch." She got to her feet. "Now if you point me to the water, I'm going to wash up for the night."

Brody was speechless. It was the first time in his life he remembered not even knowing what to say. The woman had *cojones* bigger than his. Scratched an itch? The world had just turned upside down in seconds.

"Never mind. I know which direction you came from. I'll find it." She walked off, leaving him sitting there holding his balls as though she wanted to rip them off his body. Olivia Graham was more dangerous than he ever expected. She acted like a wildcat, screwed him until he was cross-eyed, then threw her anger and a sob story at him. He wanted to follow her and give her a good spanking.

And possibly get into her drawers again, judging by the way his body was aroused just by talking to her.

What had he gotten himself involved in? And why did he think it would be impossible to get out of?

CHAPTER FIVE

They slept apart that night, yet still beside each other. Olivia had rolled herself into a cocoon of blanket and gave him her back. She woke slowly, which wasn't normal for her, confused by the body beside her. Sometime in the night she'd snuggled up beside him, her hair loose from the braid she'd put it in the night before. She sat up suddenly, yanking all the covers off them.

Brody's gun was in his hand before she could even catch her breath.

Although, she did notice his cock was as hard as stone beneath his trousers. When she licked her lips, it jerked beneath the fabric.

He cocked the pistol. "You trying to get yourself killed?"

"What are you talking about?"

He gestured to her with the gun. "You look like you were just tussling under the sheets with a man, your hair wild and mussed. Your lips are red and wet like you've been kissed and damned if that blouse is still open. You, woman, are aiming to drive me loco. That's what I'm talking about."

She was driving him loco with her hair, breasts and lips? Who would have thought a tough ranger like

Brody could be distracted by her less-than-spectacular feminine wiles? This was a piece of knowledge she would tuck away and use to her advantage soon. It was purely satisfying to see she affected him as much as he affected her.

"I didn't mean to do anything. I woke up and was startled because I didn't remember where I was." She got to her knees. "I don't need to get shot for it, though."

He blew out a breath and uncocked the pistol. "Jesus, woman, you are gonna kill me."

"I hope before you kill me." She rose on shaky legs, her body betraying her with one look at his hard, and utterly virile form. Loathe to admit it, Olivia had dreamed of his cock inside her again, of his mouth on her breasts and his hands between her thighs. It had been a night filled with salacious dreams starring Ranger Brody Armstrong.

"I won't kill you, for God's sake. I was just startled." He ran his hands through his jet-black hair, making it stick every which way. "You'd best get up so we can get going."

Olivia turned toward her saddlebags. "I'm not the one still in bed."

He cursed under his breath but she heard it anyway. With a smile, she headed toward the small creek to get ready for the day. After morning ablutions with water that could've come from a glacier, she came back to the camp, shivering. To her surprise, Brody had made coffee and had cleaned and packed the bedrolls.

"You have skills as a housekeeper, Ranger." She didn't know why she kept baiting the man, but, oh, how fun it was to see his nostrils flare at her jibe.

"Just efficient as any man who lives on the trail is." He poured himself coffee, then to her annoyance, poured the rest of it onto the ground. "You've got two minutes to be on your horse or get left behind."

"You are a bastard." She stepped up and tried to take the coffee away from him. With longer arms, he easily kept it out of her reach.

"Nope, my parents were married." He glared down at her. "You wanted to be partners but you treat me like a naughty schoolboy. I'm a man, Liv, and I deserve better than that."

"You deserve nothing." She stepped up until she was nose to chin with him. "You earn my respect. I don't give it easily."

He dropped the cup with a clang and yanked her against him. Their lips slammed together and heat flooded through her so fast, she could've used that ice cold water again. His tongue invaded her mouth, even as his cock pressed against her throbbing pussy. Just like that, she was ready and willing to be with him again.

Utter madness.

He tore his mouth away and stepped back. "Holy hell, woman. What was that?"

"You kissed me."

"Like hell I did. You pushed up against me and I reacted."

"By kissing me?"

"No, by pushing you away. You kissed me."

"Then why did you drop your precious coffee?" She picked up the cup, shaken to her core, her heart pounding so hard it was about to bust out of her chest.

"You knocked it out of my hand."

Olivia's laugh was devoid of humor. "You are fooling only yourself, Ranger. I think we've got less than a minute to get moving, right?" She tucked the cup and coffeepot away, nearly burning her hands in the process.

The ranger didn't say a word, but he turned to his horse and mounted.

With no breakfast and no coffee, Olivia saddled Mariposa with little grace and was ready in minutes.

"You're late," he groused as he kneed his horse into motion.

"You're a jackass." She had the satisfaction of seeing his shoulders tense. Ha! Olivia Graham was not going to lie down and take his rejection. Oh, no, she would be the victor in this war, no matter what.

The buildings of Reidsville rose in the distance before Brody spoke again. He was angry, at himself mostly, for being stupid enough to kiss her. Again. Not only that, he woke up wanting to plunge into her. Again. Then he fought with her. Again.

Leaving her in Reidsville would be the best thing for both of them. He could track the rest of Jeb's gang into Mexico and be done with the Grahams for good. There was a slim chance he would find Benjamin Graham. The odds were not good he was alive, much less untouched.

The warmth of the morning had given way to afternoon heat. Sweat trickled down the center of his back. Olivia rode in front of him, and to his satisfaction, she had a few sweaty spots on her blouse. He certainly shouldn't be glad she perspired just like everyone else, but he was glad she wasn't unaffected by their situation. There was no reason to believe she was as hardnosed as she appeared to be.

In the half a day since they'd been riding in silence he had had half a dozen conversations with her. All of them ended in him yelling at her for twisting him into knots. He needed to get her back home before he truly did lose control.

"What are we doing here?" She finally glanced back at him.

"Stopping to get supplies. I can't make it for much longer on cracker crumbs and dried beef." He spurred his horse faster, eager to get away from her as soon as possible. A trained soldier and Texas Ranger did not lose control over a rancher's daughter with a big mouth.

"You should have packed more." She flipped the braid over her shoulder. "Then we wouldn't have to waste time here."

He counted to ten before he spoke again. "I had planned on packing more, but you came along for the ride before I could."

"Poor planning on your part."

"Jesus Christ, Liv, can you let loose your grip on my balls for just five minutes?" He couldn't believe she'd driven him to this.

She stopped and stared, her mouth open. "What?"

"You have pushed, bullied and manipulated me into this. I don't think I've ever met a woman who twisted people into knots like you do." A cork popped out and he couldn't stop his words if he tried. "I didn't want a partner. I don't want a partner. I sure as hell didn't want you."

Her eyes widened. "What are you fixing to do about it?"

"You are going back home. I will find a wagon, a buggy, or even a goddamn turtle for you to ride back to the Graham ranch." He pointed at her. "I won't take you into Mexico with me."

"It's a little late for that. You won't get rid of me that easy, Ranger." She narrowed her eyes. "I am your partner until we find Benjy. I will follow you into the bowels of hell if I have to."

He kneed his horse into a run, leaving her behind. Cowardly perhaps, but it was either that or get into a fistfight with her. He wouldn't degrade himself into losing what was left of his honor over her.

Reidsville was a little stop along the trail, with typical wooden buildings, a mercantile, a restaurant, a hotel, a couple of taverns and blessedly, a whorehouse. He didn't care what Olivia said or did—he wouldn't lose his control over her again. She would stay at the hotel tonight and in the morning he would send her on her way.

Brody headed directly for the tavern closest to him. There wasn't enough whiskey in the world to make him forget Olivia Graham, but he could numb the pain for a little while at least. As he dismounted, he spotted her riding in behind him. No doubt she'd follow him into the tavern too and spoil his drink.

He walked in, blocking out his annoyance for a few minutes. The man behind the bar was burly and hairy, with a scar down his cheek. Obviously noting the scar on Brody's face, the man nodded at him.

Brody sat down on the tired-looking stool. "Whiskey."

With no conversation to weigh things down, he sipped at the rotgut. It burned its way down his throat, leaving a path of blessed fire. Yep, that was exactly what he needed.

"Woman troubles?"

"I'd like a whiskey too." Olivia's husky voice came from beside him.

The barkeep raised his bushy brows, but poured her a shot and slid it to her.

To Brody's utter surpise, she slung it back as though she regularly spent time in taverns.

"Will you never do anything normal?"

She snorted. "I am normal to me. Who says what's normal?"

He threw back the rest of his whiskey and let his tongue and throat burn for a moment before he gestured to the barkeep to pour two more shots.

"You want to get drunk, Miss Graham?"

She turned to him, her eyes full of shadows and a myriad of emotions he didn't want to know about. "Yes, I do." When she threw back the second shot of whiskey, even he was impressed.

"I didn't know you had a taste for whiskey."

"There is a lot you don't know about me, Ranger." Her grin was almost feral, and it sent a shiver up his spine.

"This one's a keeper, fella." The barkeep eyed her with more than selling whiskey in his expression. "If'n you don't want her, just say the word."

Although it was the last thing he would admit to her, his protective instincts roared to life. No matter how much she annoyed him, she was his responsibility. As a man of the law, he would not be derelict in his duty. Even if he'd been intimate with her not twelve hours earlier.

"She's not available." Brody couldn't disguise the growl in his voice.

"Hey now. I am the one who gets to decide that." She pointed at the barkeep. "You keep filling my glass and we'll see what happens."

"The hell with that." Brody grabbed the bottle off the bar. "I'll pay for the whole bottle, but you don't get the girl. Ever."

The barkeep shrugged. "I like a woman who can hold her liquor."

Olivia raised one brow and smiled. "You see, I'm not a bitch all the time, Brody."

His name on her tongue was like a caress on his bare skin. His cock twitched against his buttons.

"No, but you choose to be."

"Ouch, fella. I can't let you talk to the lady like that." The barkeep was a big son of a bitch, but he didn't scare Brody even a smidge.

"Easy. I'm a Texas Ranger." He flashed the badge he kept tucked in his belt. "She's helping with an investigation and I'm her keeper."

Olivia took a long tug right from the bottle of whiskey. "Let's get drunk, Brody. I wanna get drunk and get messy with you." She leaned forward and pressed her breasts into his arm, then kissed the ever-loving smarts out of him.

Brody forgot his name.

"I want you. Now." Her breath gusted across his face, the scent of whiskey strong.

He shouldn't be touching her again. Or ever for that matter. Yet he was in a hotel room with her, alone. What the hell was he thinking? Well, that was it. He wasn't thinking at all.

"I said now." She grabbed at his shirt, popping a few buttons before he could stop her.

His cock nearly tore open his britches wanting to get out. His self-control, already dulled by too much whiskey, jumped out the window when she licked his neck and grabbed his staff through the material.

"Please come out and play. I need you. Now. Now. Now."

He couldn't very well refuse a woman in need, now

could he? What was left of his conscience spoke up. "You're drunk."

"So are you. It doesn't matter. I wanted you from the second I saw you." She stripped off her clothes with amazing speed, given the amount of liquor she'd inhaled. "I had dreams about you, did you know that?"

Why no, he didn't know that. And he didn't need to know it, but now that he did, there was no way he'd forget it.

"Olivia, we agreed not to do this again."

"Ha! I didn't agree to anything. You accused me of tricking you into having sex with you." She waggled her finger and to his dismay, her breasts jiggled right along with it.

His mouth watered to taste them, lick them, bite them.

"I didn't accuse you."

"Yes, you did." She pushed him back into the chair in the corner, the seat hitting the back of his knees. He dropped onto the cushion and suddenly had a lap full of naked woman on top of him.

He almost came in his britches.

She leaned in and pushed her breasts against his lips. "I want you, Brody," she repeated. "I want to come again."

His control shredded the moment his hands cupped her beautiful breasts. They were softer than anything he'd ever felt. He pulled one taut nipple into his mouth and sucked while he reached for the other.

"Oh, God, yesssss. More." Olivia reached down and unbuttoned his trousers. He groaned when she took his cock in hand, running her slender fingers up and down its pulsing length. "You're so big. Did any girl ever tell you that?"

Apparently liquor turned her into a wanton. He

couldn't have resisted her then. If ever. Brody didn't like simpering, whimpering, whining girls who fluttered and flittered about. Olivia drank like a man, had sex when she wanted, and did what she knew was right. If she'd been a man, they would've been friends.

Instead, she had his cock in her hand and he had her breast in his mouth and his hand inside the moist folds of her pussy.

"I need you inside me." She shifted until she was poised above his cock, her moist heat already coating him.

"Then put me in there." His voice was nearly unrecognizable, rough and gravelly with the intense arousal coursing through him.

She slid down his shaft with aching slowness, until they were both shaking with the need to move. Brody sucked at her nipple while his other hand flicked her clit. Each time his finger moved, her body tightened around him. He wouldn't last long that way. He tried to take his hand away, but she bit his shoulder.

"Don't you dare stop. I want to come, Brody. Now." She pushed her other breast at his mouth. "Make me come."

He couldn't resist the lure of her words or the way they seemed to fit together like a hand in a glove. With just three more flicks on her clit, she came, shuddering and squeezing him so hard his eyes rolled back in his head. His balls tightened as he lost his mind completely and came inside her, buried deep within her heat.

It was the most exciting, exhilarating, frightening moment of his life. Also quite possibly the stupidest. He might have just put a babe in Olivia's belly.

What had he done?

★   ★   ★

Olivia's mouth had turned into a ball of old cotton. She tried to find enough spit to swallow, but there was none. Not even a drop. She cracked one eye open and glanced around. Where was she? The moon shone through the window, illuminating a hotel room she didn't remember entering. And she was stark naked.

A soft snore beside her scared her enough that she sat up, stifling a scream as her head nearly exploded from the sudden move.

Oh, what had she done?

She peered at the man beside her and recognized Brody. The last thing she remembered was stopping in town for supplies. He'd ridden ahead, hightailing it to the tavern without a backward glance at her. She'd been annoyed at his high-handedness and the way he'd dismissed her.

Olivia had made some mistakes in her life, but having sex with Brody wasn't one of them. It felt good and she wasn't ashamed of that. He took precautions and didn't spend his seed in her so there would be no child. They were adults. No matter how people might judge her, she wouldn't regret being with him.

And apparently she liked it enough to get drunk in the middle of the afternoon and do it again. There had been whiskey and a hairy barkeep, then the rest was a blur of sensations and pleasures. Her body was well sated, that she could feel even over the pounding in her head.

Her skin fairly throbbed with the aftereffects of whatever they had been doing in the hotel room. She only wished she could remember the details.

Wait, hadn't there been a chair involved?

She peered through the shadows but could only see vague shapes. It was no use, she wasn't going to recall all of it. The bald truth was she had consumed too much liquor and tumbled into bed with Brody Armstrong.

Olivia eased her legs out of bed and got to her feet as slowly as she could. Her head swam a little, but it was her stomach that heaved. She wasn't able to swallow, since her mouth was a pit of dryness, so she had to make her way to the washstand and pray some competent person had left water in the pitcher.

Her body was sticky and sore. She almost sobbed to find lukewarm water in the pitcher and poured some into the basin. She cupped her hand and took a small drink of the water, enough to wet her mouth but not too much lest her stomach decide to heave.

With hands that trembled for more than one reason, she used the water to rinse herself. Feeling marginally better, she felt around the room until she found clothing, recognizing the plain cotton chemise her sister-in-law Hannah had made for her. She slipped it on like a suit of armor, no longer naked and vulnerable.

Olivia sat on the floor with her back to the wall. She wasn't the same person who had left home two days earlier. There was no doubt in her mind that she would change because of her decision. However, waking up in a hotel room naked with the ranger who drove her mad in every which way, was not what she expected.

"Liv?" His husky voice made her heart hiccup. Now wasn't the time to develop feelings for the cold man of the law.

"I'm here." If he was as naked as she'd been, she didn't want him to jump out of bed.

"What are you doing?" The bed creaked as she saw him rise in the gloom to a sitting position.

"Just sitting and thinking." How could she explain to him that she was contemplating just how much she'd lost control of herself. She was not this person, not at all. Brody had turned her into a loose, foolish woman with no regard for consequences.

"Oh." There was a short pause. "Do you want me to sit with you?"

Would she invite him to her spot on the floor? Did she have a choice?

"Yes." She answered before she had time to think about why she wanted him there.

The bedclothes rustled and she heard him walk toward her, curse when he stubbed his toe and pull on what she thought were his britches. When he sat down beside her, he pulled a blanket up over both of them.

To her dismay, tears pricked her eyes at the gesture. She didn't want to think Brody Armstrong was a gentleman. He was a temporary presence in her life, not the man she wanted to love.

"It's chilly down here."

She couldn't answer yet so she just nodded, not caring if he could see her in the darkness.

He slid his arm around her and she snuggled against his bare chest. It surprised her that she felt safe and comfortable with him. Just hours earlier they had been fighting and snapping like two dogs sizing each other up. Their time together had been nothing but one impossible situation after another. She had done things she had never done before, including killing two men.

She shivered at the memory and pressed closer, needing to feel his life, his heat. Brody was many things, but he was an honorable man, that much she would admit to herself. She needed him to find Benjy and she needed him for herself. That was a hard truth to accept, particularly considering just how shameless she'd behaved that day.

"I didn't mean to get drunk," she whispered.

"Yes, you did, but so did I." He chuckled, its rumble making his chest vibrate against her ear. "We drank nearly half a bottle."

"Oh, Lord. If my family knew." She stopped that thought before it went any further. Right now was about her and Brody, no one else.

"They never will unless you decide to tell them." He sounded as exhausted as she felt.

"Brody?"

"Hmm?"

"I will find Benjy, no matter what." She hadn't come this far only to be pushed aside by her own stupidity or his sideways gallantry.

"I know you will." He sighed heavily. "It will be dangerous. We have to disguise ourselves."

She hadn't thought that far ahead but he was right. There wasn't a chance she would be mistaken for a Mexican with her light complexion and freckles.

"You won't leave me behind, will you?" She ran her fingers through the crisp hairs on his chest, loving the warmth of his body and the way it felt comfortable to be there at his side. He was quiet for too long. "Brody?"

"No, but I should. Your brother is going to kill me."

She smiled against his chest. "No, he won't. I'll protect you."

He chuckled again. "Somehow I believe you will."

The craziness of the day before slid away and she closed her eyes, this time giving herself over to sleep, knowing whose embrace she was in.

The next time Olivia opened her eyes, the sun was streaming through the same window the moon had graced the night before. It was past sunrise already and she slept on the floor cuddled up with Brody Armstrong.

She couldn't have thought of a stranger situation.

"My arm's asleep." His sleep-tinged voice surprised her. "Can you move off it?"

Oh, yes, that was the ranger for sure.

Olivia shifted away from him and got to her knees. Her body felt as though she'd been beaten with sticks, sore and bruised. After riding for so long, then engaging in other activities twice in two days, well, she deserved to be sore. Then sleeping on the floor just made it all worse.

Why was she on the floor anyway? There was a perfectly good bed, yet she had chosen the floor, away from the man she couldn't stop being with. And he'd followed her, held her while she slept.

"God, I hate those pins and needles you get." He got to his feet, still wearing only trousers, half-buttoned trousers. As he shook the sleep out of his arm, she watched him, fascinated by the man fully revealed in the light.

He was more slender than her brothers but had muscles on top of muscles, scars on top of scars. He had a warrior's body, silly as that sounded, and wore his battle wounds as a true man would. The big scar on his jaw just lent him an air of suave danger. His shoulders were wide, his chest covered with dark black hair, leading down his belly to—

"Do you plan on getting off the floor?" He peered down into the basin. "You could've gotten rid of the dirty water."

Olivia started chuckling, which turned into a full-fledged laugh. She laughed until her stomach hurt and tears leaked from her eyes. Brody just went about the business of dumping the water out the window and pouring some fresh into the basin. He didn't even look at her, giggling like a lunatic on the floor.

A sudden thought had set her off. Here she was, sitting in front of a man in only her chemise on the floor of an unknown hotel room somewhere in Texas, and yet she was not frightened. Brody was the only man she could picture in this scene.

The only man.

Something about the two of them fit together, black to white, a key to a lock. She couldn't explain it to anyone but she recognized it as the truth. God surely did have a strange sense of humor to leave her with a man she wanted to kiss and kick at the same time.

Olivia was falling in love.

Brody sipped at the hot coffee and stared across the table at Olivia. Her jaw was set, her chin up and her eyes flashing. Miss Graham was not going to go down easily on this fight.

"It's not just dangerous like getting lost in the dark out on the prairie. You can and might be killed." The coffee was nice and strong, which he desperately needed after last night.

"I understand that. I heard what you said and I know Mexico is dangerous." Her brows slammed together. "I'm twenty-one years old and capable of making my own decision on whether I will risk my life."

"You're twenty-one?" She acted so independent, Brody had thought she was older.

"Not a word out of you about my advanced spinster age." She speared her egg with a vengeance.

He was glad he hadn't sprouted from a chicken's ass.

"I wouldn't think of it." Brody considered how he

could convince Olivia to stay behind. He didn't want her to think too much about what her younger brother might be going through, but he wasn't above punching low. Sometimes he had to push people away to keep them safe.

She would not thank him for it though.

"Why are you doing this?" He watched her carefully, looking for anything he could use.

"Because it's been more than half a year since Benjy disappeared. Our circle is not complete without him." She didn't flinch, blink or blush. That told him she completely believed every word she said.

Damn.

"You would risk your life to go on a hard ride into hostile territory on the slim chance we'll find him." He knew he would have done the same for either of his brothers, had they survived the war. But men were different; there was honor at stake.

"Without a second thought." She pushed a forkful of eggs in her mouth and there it was. He saw it. Her hand trembled. Now was his chance to scare her back home.

"You will probably not make it back home. If you do, you won't be the same." He leaned toward her and lowered his voice. "There will be men who will kill you for looking at them, or rape you for not. There are men who will steal every stitch of clothing from your body, then rape you and leave you to die. There are others who will steal from you, rape you, torture you, and only then kill you."

She blinked rapidly. "Only if they catch me."

Brody frowned at her. "I ain't funnin' with you, Liv. I'm not trying to scare you."

"Yes, you are but I expected that." She took another forkful of eggs. "I won't change my mind though."

He sipped his coffee and watched for a minute before he spoke again. "He might be dead."

Her fork froze in mid-air. "I know." This time her voice was softer.

"Or worse."

Her gaze snapped to his and those blue-green orbs were fairly shooting fire at him. "I know."

"No, you don't. You think this is going to be like riding in to town to fetch him from a schoolhouse." He leaned even farther forward until he was six inches from her face. "There are men and women who would pay top dollar for a little white boy. They don't want him to shine their shoes, Liv. They want young boys so they can play with them in their beds and sometimes in their parlor during a party."

Her face blanched, making her freckles stand out. "You don't have to say that."

"Yes, I do. I need you to understand what we might find so you don't get the vapors if we do find it." Before he knew it, he had taken her hands in his. They were cold, clammy and shaking. "He won't be the same boy you loved and lost. He is no longer Benjy Graham. Even if we find him, you won't get Benjy back."

Tears hovered behind her lashes, but she didn't let them fall. "I don't care. I can't just abandon him because bad things happened to him. He's a little boy and he needs his family. Right now that's me. *Me.* If there was a fire in the house, I would go after him, no matter if I got burned. If he fell into a ravine and would die within an hour, I would go after him, no matter if I died too." She pulled her hands away. "I will not give up looking for him, no matter what."

Brody sat back, strangely satisfied by her response. He expected most women would have turned tail and gone back home where they belonged. Olivia Graham was not that kind of woman. She was the strongest woman he'd ever met, not that he'd tell her that.

"I wanted to make sure you were riding into this with your eyes open."

"Oh, they're open, Ranger. And I can see you trying to scare me back home. It isn't going to work. I will never give up looking until I find him or—" She swallowed hard. "Or his body."

He was satisfied she at least understood what might or probably would happen to her, and what, on the slim chance they found Benjamin Graham, they would find. There couldn't be any misunderstandings now.

"Fine then. Finish up your breakfast so we can get going."

He'd just accepted the fact he was riding into Mexico with Olivia Graham.

Ah, hell.

They finished their breakfast in silence. His mind was whirling with ideas of how to get into Mexico with a woman at his side, one who stood out for more than one reason. They needed to hide her whiteness.

As they rose from their seats, she stopped his musings in their tracks. "If we use some red clay, we can mix it up with water, make my skin and hair darker."

"What?" He frowned at her. "What did you say?"

She rolled her eyes. "If you expect me not to think, it's never going to happen." She took his face in her hands. "Now listen to my words so I don't have to say this a third time. I'm going to use red clay to darken my skin and hair. It stains everything else, why not me?"

Brody wanted to shake her for talking to him like that. Damned if she didn't sound just like him too. That annoyed him more than anything.

"Fine. Let's go get you some mud."

"Clay."

"Shut up, Liv."

They found a vein of rich red clay on the bank of a creek just outside the small town. Olivia didn't want to be smug until she made sure it was going to work. She dismounted and looked down at herself. If she was right, the clay would stain everything. There was no help for it, she'd have to take off at least the first layer of clothes. She had two buttons undone before he made a noise.

"What the hell are you doing?"

"Trying not to stain my clothes while I stain me." She was halfway down her blouse when his hand landed on hers.

"That's foolish."

She shook off his hands. "I don't have money to spend for new clothes. I want these to last."

He stared at her as though she had grown a second head. "I don't understand females."

"That's probably a blessing." She took off her shirt and his mouth tightened. "I'm wearing a chemise, Brody. It's not as though I'm naked."

"Might as well be." He glanced around as though someone was about to come upon them and attack.

She took off her riding skirt and he slapped his forehead.

"Jesus Christ, Liv."

Olivia chose to ignore him and laid her clothes on the saddle. She put her hair back in a leather strip and stepped toward the creek. After finding a level spot, she knelt down in the grass and took a handful of red clay and a scoopful of water. Mashing them together between her fingers felt good. More than good, it reminded her of playing in the mud with Matt when she was a little girl. She almost enjoyed the cool squish of the clay on her skin.

"You appear to like that mud a bit too much."

"It's clay, Brody."

"I don't care what the hell it is. Don't play with it." He stood beside her, arms crossed, exuding annoyance through every pore.

She rolled her eyes and started rubbing the clay into her skin in a circular motion until she reached her elbows; then she moved to her face.

"You might want to try this yourself." She closed her eyes and made sure to get her eyelids and forehead covered. "You don't look Mexican."

"A little dust and different clothes are all I need." She heard his boots shift in the dirt behind her. "You plan on keeping that mud on you long?"

"I still have to do my hair." She sat down cross-legged on the grass and lifted her face toward the sun. "Give me ten minutes to let the clay soak in and then I'll do my hair."

More shuffling and cursing behind her; then a gust of air went past her ear.

"Just sit still and I'll do your damn hair."

Olivia couldn't do anything but sit still, mostly from shock. He was helping her?

Sure enough, he tugged on the strip in her hair, then ran his hands through it. Memories of the last time he'd done that rippled through her. He had wonderful hands, even if he had a bossy streak a mile wide. With a surprising amount of speed, he worked the clay into her hair.

"Damn disgusting is what it is," he grumbled, followed by a lot of splashing. She presumed he was getting the clay off his hands.

Her head felt heavy, weighed down by the thickness coating her skin and hair. The first batch she'd smeared on her arms was already starting to dry and it itched. She should have expected that, but that didn't make it any easier not to scratch.

She cracked her eye open and peered at him. He sat back on his haunches watching her, the strangest expression on his face. It was the first time she'd seen an emotion other than annoyance or cold anger on his face. If she wasn't mistaken, she saw concern, a first for the cool-eyed ranger.

They sat in silence for ten minutes while the mud dried on her skin and she tried in vain to ignore the itchiness.

"You look like a mud doll."

"It's clay, not mud." She waited for him to snap back at her but he didn't.

"You still look like a mud doll."

Her lips twitched and the clay cracked on her cheeks. "If it works, you're going to have to apologize."

"Like hell I will."

This time she smiled and a chunk of clay fell onto her arm. "I think it's time I wash it off." She opened her eyes and glanced down at the dried remnants.

"Do you plan on jumping in the creek?"

It wasn't a bad idea actually. He might not approve, but her underthings would dry quickly. It would be easier to rinse off her hair if she could dunk her head.

Before she could change her mind, she got to her feet and took off her boots.

"I wasn't serious, Liv. We don't have time for you to frolic in the water."

"I don't plan on frolicking. I'm just getting clean." She waded into the water and sucked in a breath as cold water hit her feet. It was definitely no deeper than two feet, but that was enough for what she needed to do.

"Now you look like an abandoned mud doll someone threw in the creek." He stood on the bank and put his hands on his hips. "Your chemise just turned into a peekaboo."

Olivia tried to ignore him and his jibes. It wasn't as though he hadn't seen her breasts before, and giving her underclothes a quick rinse wouldn't hurt.

The clay came away from her skin easily, turning back into a mushy mess that she sloughed off into the gentle current. However, it stuck to her hair and she had to scrub at it for a good five minutes before her hair squeaked between her fingers.

When she emerged from the water, she shivered in the breeze that ran across her wet skin. Goosebumps raced up and down her body. Brody stared hard, his gaze as cold as the water she'd just left.

"Why are you looking at me like that?" She resisted the urge to cover her breasts, knowing her nipples were standing at attention.

"Damn, woman, you almost look Mexican."

It was the closest thing she was probably going to get to his admitting she was right. She nodded, unwilling to dance triumphantly around him, but she kept the knowledge she was right close to her heart.

As she dressed in her dry clothes, he watched, still as stone. Olivia wasn't one to hurry for a man, especially one who was so doggone bossy, but she found herself moving quickly. Perhaps this was the beginning of a dangerous adventure, or better yet, the promise of doing something to find Benjy.

"Keep your hair tucked under your hat for now. Maybe later we'll find some more of that mud to darken it again." He rubbed some dry dirt into his cheeks and neck. "You might want to dirty yourself up too."

"I just got clean." She finished buttoning her blouse and began twisting her hair into a tight bun.

"You want to look like a Mexican woman? Your skin isn't bronze yet, Liv. You need to darken it more." He rubbed his dirty hands on her cheeks, then dipped down toward her chest.

Darned if her nipples didn't pop again after just having relaxed. She moved back a step, out of his reach.

"I can dirty myself up, thank you."

"I don't doubt that," he mumbled as he turned toward his horse. "Let's get going then. Daylight's burning."

Olivia's heart slammed into her throat and the reality of what she was about to do hit her hard. All of the horrible possibilities Brody had outlined ran through her head. She might never see her family again but it would be worth it if she found Benjy. It didn't matter what happened to her. He was more important than anything. Without the eighth link in their circle, they'd never be whole again.

CHAPTER SIX

B rody didn't need a map to find the place on the Rio
Grande where he wanted to cross into Mexico.
During the war, he and his brothers had crossed at that
particular spot numerous times, mostly because it was
hidden from view and out of the way of prying eyes.

They rode through the morning, stopping only briefly
to eat before pushing on. By sunset, he saw the big river
sparkling in the orange rays shining from the west. His
gut clenched at the sight.

This was the last chance to turn back, to send Olivia
packing to her ranch. He had tried to scare her and bully
her, neither of which worked. His only other option was
to force her, but that would have an even worse out-
come.

There was no chance she was going to change her
mind, so he had to accept the fact he was stuck with her.
He'd been the one to start their partnership, such as it
was. Though he'd never intended to take her so far.

His intention was to scare her enough she would stay
at home. Unfortunately it had the opposite effect. She
was even more determined to put herself in harm's way.
He couldn't be blamed for what happened to her from
now on.

He pulled his horse to a stop a hundred yards away

from an oft-used campsite. "We need to stay put until dark, then cross over."

"Why?"

"The fewer people see you in daylight, the better."

She made a face at him. Although her skin was colored by the clay, she didn't look Mexican close up. From a distance, and in dim light, she'd be fine.

"If there's more clay nearby I can put some more on my skin."

He leveled a stare at her to shut her up. "You look fine. We just need to be as quiet as we can when we cross. That's all."

"Fine. I was just trying to help." She stopped at the edge of the campsite and dismounted. "I'll get a fire going."

"We don't need a fire. Just sit still and stop talking." He stayed in the saddle, scrutinizing the river for signs they were being watched.

She huffed and puffed but, otherwise, she was quiet. He heard her fussing with her mare, which gave him a chance to think. Sanchez had told him the pueblo where they met their buyer was twenty miles south into Mexico. It was far enough to make a quick run to the border improbable but not impossible. He wanted to think through what to do once they got there without Olivia nearby to confuse his thoughts.

He was worried about what she would do when they spoke to someone. Hell, he didn't even know if she spoke Spanish. He could tell them she was mute, but then he'd probably have to gag her to keep her quiet. There was no help for it, he had to ask.

"*¿Hablas español?*"

She glanced at him. "*Sí, hombre. Vivo con una mujer que me enseñó. Hablamos español todo el tiempo.*"

"*Bueno.*" He kept his face impassive, but damn, damn,

damn. Not only was her Spanish perfect, but her accent was even better than his. If he closed his eyes, he could believe he was in a tavern in a pueblo deep in Mexico. He had no excuse to leave her behind. Or to gag her.

"Are you going to tell me what we're doing next? Besides sit here and stare at the river?" She perched on a rock with her chin in her hands, scowling at him.

"I'm still thinking on that. My original plan didn't include you." He scowled right back at her.

"My plan didn't include leaving the ranch but here I am." One brow went up. "You need to think quick out here."

For that, he ought to throw her over his knee and spank the sass out of her. His hands itched to do just that, but a tiny part of him knew it was more than just a spanking he wanted from her. Olivia had gotten under his skin.

If he was smart, he'd tie her up and leave her here, or better yet, put her on a wagon headed home. A tiny little voice somewhere deep inside stopped him. It wasn't very loud, but it was enough. She had been a good partner, albeit a frustrating one. She was smart, observant and strong. Hell, the woman had killed two men to save him. He had no call to doubt her courage or abilities.

It was his own self-control he doubted.

Admitting that to himself was hard, real hard. Brody had been the youngest of the Armstrong boys, the one who took the teasing, punching and all-around misery from his older brothers. He didn't flinch, couldn't flinch. Now he found himself wondering how one woman could make him doubt that iron-clad wall he'd erected for protection.

She wasn't anything special to look at. Oh, she was pretty and had really great breasts, but she wasn't classically pretty and her ass was a little big. It wasn't her looks that gave him pause; it was what she did to him.

Brody had to stop thinking about her and start thinking about what they were doing and what they needed to do in Mexico. If he could find out who Jeb Stinson had been using to move his stolen items and people, he could stop the operation. If the men were Texan, he could bring them to justice. If they were Mexican, he could make sure they didn't cross back over the border.

His main concern was stopping the gang, which was still raiding ranches even after Jeb's death. Olivia's focus on her brother was not Brody's. He couldn't forget that there were more folks affected by the gang's activities than just the Grahams.

"We're going to cross the river after dark, quietlike. We don't want anyone knowing we're even breathing Mexican air." He stared at the river and the light sparkling on its surface until his eyes hurt. "I need you to act as a woman should, with your head down and your mouth shut. We also need to take off some of that finery you're wearing. I hope you don't mind if we dirty up your clothes."

"What finery?" She glanced down at her plain cotton shirtwaist and riding skirt.

"What you have on underneath, Liv. If we get caught, someone might see you're wearing lacey things and wonder why a poor woman who lives on the trail with her no-account husband had such things on." Brody had to think of every detail of their disguise. Their lives depended on his thoroughness.

"I have to take off my underthings?" She cupped her breasts. "And my chemise? And, and other things?"

"You said you'd do anything." He didn't want to argue about every little thing with her.

"I will. Of course." She reached for her buttons and he felt a moment of panic.

"Wait until dark. You don't need to flash the birds."

She smacked his arm, hard enough to sting. He moved out of her reach.

"Why did you hit me?"

"Why do you have to be such a jackass?" Her hands were balled into fists. "It's hard enough for me to be here with you, doing what I am doing away from my family. I don't need you behaving like a jackass and making me feel cheap and stupid." The tendons in her jaw grew tight as she clenched her teeth.

Had he been doing that? He sure as hell hadn't meant to, but he was more concerned about her safety than her feelings. Feelings didn't amount to a hill of beans out here. Feelings were like a rat's fart in the wind.

"Don't throw that in my face. Just don't." He shook his head. "This is exactly what I didn't want."

Their mission was too important to fall into foolishness with her. He would leave her behind if she kept it up.

Olivia turned to her horse and he heard some fierce mumbling coming from her direction. He didn't care if she fussed at him or the horse.

He had a plan and he was sticking to it.

Olivia kept her mouth shut, partly because she was annoyed as all hell at Brody and partly because she was nervous. When the sun went down, she was about to cross a line, literally and figuratively, and wade into danger the depth of which she'd never known before.

He was right to try to scare her, but his bullying coldness infuriated her. When this was over, she didn't ever want to see him again, no matter what they'd done together. She couldn't stay with a man who didn't respect her.

Stay with him? Why was she even thinking about staying with him? There were no promises made between them, just pleasure shared. She might have had some silly schoolgirl dreams about being with him, but ten minutes on the trail had taken care of that problem.

She had to focus on Benjy and getting out of Mexico alive, with him at her side. There was no other thought in her head as important. She sat down and waited, quiet and tense.

The evening shadows lengthened, sprinkling pockets of darkness into the corners around them. Olivia's stomach grew tighter with each passing minute. She hadn't had enough time to think about what she was doing, or the consequences of what she had already done.

Waiting for night had given her that time. She was not happy about it either. It made her more anxious and worried she'd made a terrible mistake in forcing the ranger to take her with him.

"It's almost time." He appeared beside her as quietly as the shadows around them. "Did you, ah, take off the items?"

Her cheeks heated and she hoped it was dark enough that he couldn't see her blushing. "No, not yet."

"It's almost time to get moving. Get rid of them. Now." The gloom swallowed him up, leaving her with no one to yell at.

Instead, she maneuvered behind a tree and managed to take off her underthings. After a few steps, she was strangely aroused by the feel of skin against cloth. Her doggone nipples peaked within seconds.

She was again grateful for the darkness dropping around them.

Olivia placed her hand flat on Mariposa's neck and waited. She listened to the sounds around them: the buzz of insects, the occasional shuffle in the trees above, or the bushes to the right. An owl hooted and she about jumped a foot in the air.

"Ready now?" Brody's voice floated through the darkness to her.

"Yes." She wanted to say so much more but didn't. Later, after they were home with Benjy, she would tell the ranger exactly what she thought. Olivia would be content with tucking away in her memory all of the items she would lambast him with. Later. After all of them were safe.

"Walk her slowly through the water. Let her get her footing so she doesn't slip. The last thing we need is the horses to give us away." He stood beside her, the reins wrapped around his wrist. Gone was the Texas Ranger and in his place was a man cloaked in shadows with eyes glittering in the rising moonlight. Her heart slammed into her throat and for the first time Olivia knew a moment of fear with Brody.

Then it was gone. Thanks to his mouth.

"Olivia, if you aren't going to pay attention, I'm going to have to repeat myself. I don't want to do that." He pushed Mariposa's reins into her hands. "Hold onto her and walk slowly." He slowed his words, lowering his voice to barely a whisper. "Grunt if you understand me."

She actually growled at him, but it was apparently enough to make her meaning clear.

"Let's go."

Olivia wrapped her fingers around her mare's reins loosely, not willing to risk hurting the horse because of her own annoyance. They waded into the water slowly, as though they were strolling along the banks on a lazy summer day. They barely made a splash and the horses were quiet as could be. The river was shallow enough to walk across without a mishap.

As soon as they started up the bank on the other side of the river, Olivia's stomach tightened again. She had the urge to pinch herself to realize it wasn't a dream, or a nightmare. They were on Mexican soil.

A gentle breeze drifted across her cheeks. She turned to Brody, nothing more than a black blob in the thick darkness. "Now what?"

"We head for the nearest pueblo." His voice was barely louder than the tiny breeze. "Keep walking."

She knew they had to walk the horses for a bit, in case there was anyone close to the river watching or listening. Water squished from her soft-soled boots as she walked, chafing her heels, but there was no way she'd mention it to Brody. She also wouldn't tell him about how her wet clothes raised goose bumps on her skin. Perhaps she'd get lucky and her teeth wouldn't chatter.

The moon rose steadily in the sky as they walked on. Sure enough, her heels grew sore from rubbing against the wet leather of her boots. She should have stopped right at the riverbank and emptied them out. It might not have helped too much but it couldn't have hurt.

She wouldn't whine, though, not a smidge. Brody hadn't wanted her to come to begin with and if she whined, then it would prove his theory she didn't belong on the trail with him. Olivia could be as tough as he could. No matter if her heels were on fire.

The sounds of the night were not so different from those she heard at home. What made the soil beneath her boots Mexican instead of Texan? Twenty miles? It smelled the same, felt the same and sounded the same as the very ground she lived on. However, here she was an enemy, an interloper, one liable to be killed if she was found out.

It was a bad dream come to life, one with her brother in a starring role.

The encroaching night turned into an inky blackness only illuminated by the meager light of the moon. Stars were like pinpoints in velvet, tiny pricks of light so far away she wondered if they were real.

With the dark came the cool air, cutting through her damp clothes to her skin. The comfortable breeze turned into a cutting wind. Through force of will she kept her teeth clenched and didn't let them chatter. Who knew how Brody would react if she made any noise?

Hooves and boots moved easily in the soft sandy soil, a quiet whisper in the emptiness of the night. A coyote howled in the distance, followed by another, then another. Goose bumps raced up her skin and she pressed her palm against Mariposa's warm neck. The horse seemed to understand that Olivia needed comfort because she nudged Olivia's shoulder with her great head.

It wasn't much but it was enough.

Olivia was able to block the pain by thinking about family and home—the good times and the fun times, even a few hard times. All of it kept her mind occupied as they trudged through the night toward nowhere.

Hours later, Brody stopped. She almost ran into him and the horses shied away from each other, smart enough not to bang heads. Olivia was numb from the waist down and her legs wobbled so much she nearly fell face-first into the ranger's back.

"What the hell are you doing, Liv?"

"I was about to ask you the same question." She gritted her teeth. No need to remind him how annoyed she was at him. There was no point in fighting. She needed him and she wanted to think he needed her, at least a little.

"We're far enough away from the river that we can ride the horses." He was speaking low, near her ear. His warm breath sent shivers down her neck. "We are about two hours from the pueblo we need to get to. We're going to ride at a trot. Too slow or too fast and we'll call attention to ourselves."

Olivia nodded, although she realized he couldn't see her. "Then what?"

"You ask too many questions."

"I want to be ready if we run into trouble." She pressed her fist into her growling stomach. "I need to know what to do. When to pull out my pistol. When to run like hell."

He stared at her, six inches from her face. His breath smelled of coffee and something else she couldn't define. Olivia felt the urge to kiss him, not exactly an opportune time to do so. Some moments he was perfect, a man she could love so easily, and some moments she wanted to run from him.

"I need to know," she repeated. "Please."

His breath gusted past her cheek. Her body shook with all the emotions racing through her from head to foot. What was happening?

"I need . . ." She couldn't even find the right words to say what she needed.

"Me too." He cupped her cheek, his thumb rough against her skin.

This was loco. They were in the middle of Mexico, in danger and she was about to kiss him. Or he was going to kiss her. Either way, they shouldn't even be thinking about kissing.

His lips brushed over hers once, twice, three times.

She turned into a beacon of heat, her discomfort completely forgotten. His arms crept around her, pulling her closer, even as she leaned into him.

Yes, this was it. *This.*

His body was so warm, so hard. She sighed at the familiar heat between them, so easily sparked. He pulled her even closer, pressing his chest into hers. Her nipples peaked immediately, aching against the minimal clothing separating them. A moan crept up her throat, but she swallowed it back down.

Just as his mouth was going to close over hers, Mariposa pushed against Olivia's back, shoving her into Brody. He pulled away from her, his breathing uneven.

"Um, we need to get going." He cleared his throat and turned to his horse.

"Wait."

"What?" He sounded unfocused, so very unlike the stoic ranger.

"I still need to know what to do." She touched the pistol tucked into the waistband of her skirt. "Do I hide the pistol or keep it visible? What if someone talks to me? Do I answer in Spanish or English?"

He threw himself up onto his horse. "You ask too many questions. Just follow my lead and let's go."

This was definitely one of those times she wanted to simply run from him, to go home and be safe with her brothers and sisters and Eva. To escape from the incredible, intense way Brody made her feel.

It would be a cowardly thing to do. Olivia was no coward. She would stay and she would fight. Benjy needed her.

They traveled for hours in silence. That was what Brody wanted, for her to be quiet, so she was. And stewed in her own annoyance and fear the entire time. If only he'd just told her what she wanted to know, she'd feel more comfortable.

Instead, she had to wonder exactly what was in store for them and how she should act. She'd just have to watch him and hope she didn't make a mess of things. The murky shadows of buildings rose in the distance and Olivia's throat tightened at the sight.

It was almost time.

"Is that it?" She couldn't keep quiet any longer.

"Yes. It's Fogata."

"Bonfire" was an unusual name for such a dark, tiny place. She knew what lurked beneath the shadowed exterior could be a lot worse than the name Bonfire.

"Who are we?"

"I hope you're not asking because you've gone loco and can't remember." The man just couldn't seem to help himself.

"No, because I thought you might want us to be someone we're not once we get there."

Brody didn't answer, not a surprise. He kept the horses at a slow trot, even though she wanted to ride hell for leather toward the pueblo.

As she watched, heart pounding, mouth dry, they reached the outskirts of town. Olivia stared at the rough-hewn boards held together with rusty-headed nails. There were scrubby bushes around the outside, along with various sizes of succulents, rocks and dry grass.

Not so different from any town in southern Texas.

She managed to swallow dry spit although it tasted like dirt and anxiety.

Brody led them around to the end of the buildings, then turned left to ride into the town. Her damp palms slipped easily on the reins. She tugged to get a better grip, which made Mariposa shake her head in protest.

"Sorry, girl." She patted the horse's neck in apology.

The town appeared deserted except for the light spilling out onto the street from a single building. The number of horses out in front and guitar music marked it as a tavern. It was the only two-story building and the second floor was also lit, although not as brightly. She suspected the soiled doves were plying their trade up there while the drinking and carousing happened downstairs.

Again she was reminded of any small town in Texas, so familiar yet foreign. Brody headed straight for the tavern and she had no choice but to follow him, even though she wanted to go anywhere else.

As they stopped outside the tavern, each note of music plucked at her nerves. *Twang, twang, twang.*

"Stay at my side, no matter what." Brody spoke under his breath as he dismounted. "Keep your mouth shut unless I ask you a question."

Olivia was so nervous she couldn't be annoyed at him for his bossiness. She just nodded and dismounted beside him.

He tugged her hat down a smidge, and spread her hair out on her shoulders. A hysterical laugh bubbled up her throat when he spread her shirt open even further. Here she was getting half-naked again in front of him. What was it about Brody Armstrong that made her bare herself?

"Keep your gun tucked in under your blouse in your waistband. Don't take it out."

"Then why do I have it with me?" She shivered in the cool night air, realizing her feet still hurt from the water in her boots.

"Because you can't leave it with your horse." He stared down her shirt, his breath gusting onto her skin.

She could tell he was thinking he shouldn't have brought her with him. Olivia didn't know whether to laugh or cry. "Let's go."

Although her feet didn't drag, she felt as though she was walking through molasses anyway. As they walked through the door, she noted there were a great many spots on it that looked like knife marks. Just what she needed to see.

There came that crazy laughter trying to escape again. The normal Olivia had been left behind in the warm currents of the Rio Grande. This new woman, who had darkened skin and carried a gun, was someone completely new. She didn't know if she liked herself remade or not.

It was apparent Brody didn't like either version.

The interior was lit by a dozen lanterns scattered around the room, throwing pools of yellow light around the tables they sat on. There were at least a dozen men and three women, including an enormous man behind the bar and an equally skinny man with a guitar.

All of them turned to look at the newcomers.

Olivia opened her mouth to speak.

CHAPTER SEVEN

Brody knew he should have gagged her and left her outside. The damn woman couldn't take a simple order and obey it. No, she had to go ahead and do exactly what he told her not to. He suspected she did it deliberately to prove a point. If Olivia didn't have every last bit of detail about every last thing, she nagged until the other person's ears bled and they gave in.

He had refused to do that, choosing to keep his plan to himself. All she had to do was stand at his side and keep quiet. It was obvious that wasn't going to happen since she opened her mouth as soon as they walked in.

"Buenas noches, señors y señoritas." With a sway to her hips that made Brody's eyes widen, she stepped over to the bar. She looked every bit the seductress. "Whiskey."

The buffalo behind the bar spilled at least half a shot of whiskey because he was staring at Olivia. There appeared to be a line of drool coming out of the left side of his mouth too. Brody didn't blame him one bit. Olivia screamed for attention with every inch. Jesus.

"You lost, *hombre?*" A man in the back of the tavern spoke. He was dressed in black, similar to Brody, but his clothes were rougher looking. The stranger wore a black, flat-brimmed hat, which shaded his face. This was the man in charge, the one Brody had to watch. *"Tu chica es muy guapa."*

Pretty? Hell, Olivia was simply gorgeous. She had a natural sensuality that had been hidden by her smart mouth and prim clothes. Now she made his cock hard without even trying. He had felt in control before they walked across that damn river. Now he was hanging on by his fingernails, lost in a twister named Olivia.

"Sí, but she's *mine."* The words crept out through Brody's clenched teeth. Not only did they sound real, they felt real.

"Mmm, you shoot knives from your eyes, *señor."* The stranger took a tug from the bottle of whiskey in front of him. "I ask you again, you lost?" The man's voice was calm, not cold but very controlled.

"No. I'm looking for somebody. You Rodrigo?" As soon as Brody dropped the name, the entire mood in the room changed. Tension replaced uneasy curiosity and he had to hold back the urge to pull his gun. Instead, he just kept his hand on the butt, his gaze locked on the man he assumed was Rodrigo.

The name was the right one judging by the reaction it got. Olivia was murmuring to the buffalo but everyone else was staring at him, even the whores.

"You came here to die, *señor?* You walk in my tavern with a *pistola* and disrespect me?" The man got to his feet and Brody sized him up. The Mexican was obviously strong, with muscled arms and legs, shoulder-length black hair and one missing pinky finger. A man who had lived life on the edge

"I do not disrespect you." Brody managed to sound calm, although he knew at any second, he and Olivia could be stains on the floor amidst the dirt and grime. "I came to do business with you."

"Business? Who tells you I would do business with a gringo?" Rodrigo's laugh didn't have an ounce of humor in it.

"Jeb Stinson." As soon as Brody said it, the dangerous amusement in the stranger's face vanished. "I came to pick up where he left off."

There were so many things that could happen. Brody knew he'd gone far beyond what he was authorized to do as a Texas Ranger. Hell, he was so far off the map, he was literally and figuratively in another country.

The question he didn't ask himself was why. Brody could have stayed in Texas and waited for Chavez and the rest of the crew to make another run at a ranch. He could have waited for the court to decide Stinson's guilt. He could have asked for another assignment. But he hadn't.

Armstrong had been investigating five of the ranch attacks for eight months. The attacks always came when the hands were out on the range, so it was someone who knew the comings and goings of the ranchers. Therefore the gang was in Texas, not Mexico. Someone had been buying the land either left behind by the dead or sold by the ones who ran. The mastermind was Jeb Stinson, but two more attacks had been carried out since his arrest.

Hell, the man had had his own sister killed. Whoever he rode with was worse than anyone Brody had come up against.

That still didn't answer the question of why he had followed this case into Mexico. Was it just for Olivia? Or because whoever these men were, they killed women, took at least one if not two children, and burned what they could. These acts were cowardly and malicious, and darker than the blackest night.

Brody didn't think of himself as a hero, far from it, but

he would not let this type of crime go unpunished. It was a matter of honor and doing what was right. If his brothers had taught him anything, it was that. He carried their honor with him now and everything he did held true to their beliefs.

Rodrigo watched him like a predator, with the eyes of a man who sized up his enemies the same way he did his allies. After a few excruciatingly long minutes, he finally spoke.

"I hear of this Jeb Stinson. I also hear he is dead, hanged until his neck snap."

Brody kept his face still, showing no flicker of a reaction. "That's why I said I wanted to pick up where he left off."

"You would step over his body?"

"Someone has to." Brody pulled out a cheroot from his shirt pocket slower than a snail on cold dirt. As he lit it, he kept his gaze on Rodrigo.

"What do you know of Jeb's, ah, business?" From the other man's accent, or rather the lack of a thick accent, Brody would bet money he was not born in Mexico. His English was too smooth.

"I know where he hit, what he took, who he took, and where he brought it." Brody took a long tug from the cigarillo. "I need you to buy it from me now."

Rodrigo took another drink of whiskey. That's when Brody realized everyone was watching them. Olivia stood behind him, her hands on his chair. He dared not look at her.

Shit, he didn't even want to break wind.

"You and your *chica,* you stay here for a couple days and enjoy my hospitality." Rodrigo smiled at Olivia, his teeth white and shiny in the dim light. "We get to know each other and then we can discuss business."

Brody realized two things at once. One, Rodrigo had never confirmed he was the one doing business with Jeb. Two, the man had it in his head to bed Olivia.

Shit.

Although they had been welcomed in a fashion by Rodrigo, Brody felt far from at home. Two dark-haired, dark-eyed girls came through a door in the back with plates for the three of them. Olivia sat down between them, a trembling in her fingers the only sign she was nervous. Otherwise, she thanked the girls and Rodrigo and daintily picked at her food.

Brody made sure Rodrigo ate before he did. He wanted to be sure they hadn't put something in the food to make them sick or worse. It was beans, tortillas and rice, standard fare anywhere in Texas or Mexico. However, the food did have a nice kick to it and his grateful belly thanked him.

He'd eaten out on the plains, in jails, in battle, hell, he'd even eaten in a swamp once, but this tavern was a new experience. He was hungry but on edge, the spicy food dancing on his tight nerves. Rodrigo spent his time watching, or rather devouring Olivia with his gaze.

"Señorita, you are with this *cabron*, no?"

She touched Brody's hand. "*Sí, señor*. He is mine and I am his."

He had the crazy notion to wonder if she really meant it.

"You are from Texas." It wasn't a question and Rodrigo apparently didn't expect an answer. "But your skin is brown from the sun and your Spanish *es magnifico*."

"*Gracias, señor.*" She dabbed her mouth with her sleeve because she had no napkin to do so. However she did it,

Olivia maintained her dignity while using her shirt that way.

"I do not know your name, *bonita*." Rodrigo ran his fingers down Olivia's arm. "You must tell me."

To Brody's secret delight, she carefully removed the other man's fingers. To his surprise, she used her mother's name. "My name is Meredith. And you?"

"You wound me, Meredith. I just want to see if your skin is as soft as it looks." Another sly smile from Rodrigo. "Your man does not want to share."

"No, I don't want to share." She glanced at Brody and flashed her blue-green eyes at him. "I don't play that game."

"Ah, this is tragic. I would be good for you." Rodrigo winked at her.

Brody had to hold back the growl that threatened.

Who was he to get angry? Olivia wanted the same thing he did—to find her brother. If some two-bit Mexican warlord wanted to flirt with her, then so be it. If she wanted to bed the man to further her mission, then so be it.

If he wanted to tear the man's arms off for looking at her that way, then so be it.

"And your name, *señor*. You did not give it." Rodrigo took off his hat and placed it on the table beside him. He was a handsome son of a bitch.

Brody knew his name was unique enough that Rodrigo might have heard it, so he had to give one Liv would remember. "Stuart."

"Ah, this is a strong name for a strong man." Rodrigo smiled.

Brody just nodded, not willing to get into a discussion with the man about the name Stuart. All he needed was for Olivia to remember he wasn't Brody Armstrong.

"Didn't pick it. Parents gave it to me." Brody shrugged. "I could pick a different one but I'm used to it. It's a good name."

Olivia kept her gaze on her plate, but she answered, "It's a good name."

He understood the message and she obviously understood his. They had to tread lightly and keep as anonymous as possible. As far as Rodrigo was concerned, Brody was looking to go into business with him, nothing more.

Before he met Olivia, Brody had it all figured out. He had left the war a wounded man, inside and out. The Rangers gave him a new home, a new purpose, and he fully intended on living as one for as long as they'd have him. Now he found himself betraying the very thing he had sworn to be true to and all because of her.

That didn't make him any less culpable. He wanted to beat on his chest and declare his territory in the face of a charming, handsome stranger's flirtatious behavior. Olivia wasn't his, she wasn't anyone's. Brody had to keep reminding himself of that lest she get it in her head to take Rodrigo up on his offer to "share."

"Elena, *venaca*." Rodrigo summoned one of the whores from the corner where she sat.

The woman who walked toward them was nothing short of stunning. Brody hadn't noticed her because she'd been in the shadows. She had long, silky black hair shining in the lamplight. Her equally dark eyes were framed by long lashes, high cheekbones, ruby red lips and flawless skin. He could only stare at her while enduring a kick from Olivia under the table.

He might appreciate the way Elena looked but that didn't mean she stirred his loins. Matter of fact, they weren't even twitching at the sight of the most perfect woman he'd ever laid eyes on.

Brody didn't want to think about why just yet.

Rodrigo swept his arm toward them. "Elena, this is Stuart and Meredith, who are my guests tonight."

Brody didn't think they were guests in truth and he knew Rodrigo didn't either.

"You have horses, *sí?*" He'd probably heard them ride up but he asked anyway.

"Yep. They're outside at the hitching post." Brody assumed one of Rodrigo's men had already searched the horses and knew very well what they had and didn't have.

"*Bueno.* Elena, show them where to put their horses, then give them a room. Make sure they enjoy themselves." Rodrigo's smile appeared to be more like a baring of teeth. "In the morning maybe we do business."

Brody understood that now their meal was over, Rodrigo was dismissing them. It stuck in the ranger's craw, but he could do nothing but thank his host and follow the beautiful Elena out the door with Olivia on his heels.

He felt Rodrigo's gaze on him, watching as any predator would from the cover of the shadows. Brody would sleep with his pistol in his hand and ammunition in the other.

Olivia was in a bad dream. The delicious food sat like a rock in her churning stomach. She followed Brody and the incredibly beautiful Elena outside, wondering if she'd see the sun rise again.

Rodrigo made her skin crawl each time his gaze or his touch fell on her. He was probably in cahoots with the men who'd killed the real Stuart and Meredith, her parents. But it was more than that, it was something inside her that recoiled from him. Something instinctual, protective.

Now they were to actually sleep in this tavern, knowing he was downstairs with his men, ready to kill them
or something worse. It might be funny if it wasn't true.
She wouldn't be able to do anything but sit up with her
pistol close by.

She tried not to think about the woman ahead. Elena.
When she'd approached the table, every man's face
looked stunned. Even Olivia had been struck by just
how lovely Elena was.

That didn't mean she had to like the woman or the fact
Brody looked as if he'd been pole axed. Olivia would
not admit to him that she was jealous, but she was.

The night air cooled her overheated face a bit, but she
still felt hot and out of control. That had been the
strangest meal she'd ever eaten, with the strangest company. She kept reminding herself it was for Benjy and
that her own discomfort was minor compared to what
he had already endured.

"The horses can stay behind the tavern with the
others." Elena's English was lightly accented but soft as
butter. "They will be safe there."

Olivia didn't bother to tell her no one, and nothing,
would be safe in this pueblo. She didn't think it needed
to be said. This was not a place anyone would choose to
be. Perhaps not even Rodrigo.

They walked toward a small stable, which was nondescript but relatively clean. They brought the horses into
two empty stalls in the back. At least half a dozen horses
were already sleeping or munching on feed. Mariposa
didn't want to go into the stall and Olivia didn't blame
her.

After some careful coaxing, the mare finally stepped in
and let Olivia unsaddle her. The simple chore gave her
a few minutes of normalcy in an otherwise far from nor-

mal week. Brody was talking softly to his own horse in the stall next to her. It was comforting to have him near, much as she wanted to be angry with him. He was putting his life at risk the same as she was.

When she stepped out of the stall with her saddlebags, she was startled to find Elena right in front of her. She stared at Olivia as though studying her face.

"Your name is Meredith?"

"Um, yes, Meredith." Oh, how it hurt to say her mother's name.

After another few awkward moments, Elena turned away and Olivia was able to take a breath. The look on the other woman's face had been recognition. How was that possible? Olivia had never been to Mexico and she was fairly certain Elena had not been anywhere near the Graham ranch.

What did the recognition mean? Did Elena see something in her face that reminded her of someone else? Could she possibly have seen Benjamin?

Olivia wanted so badly to ask but knew it wasn't the time. If she even tried, no doubt the woman would stop talking to them and they might even be dead before the moon was high in the sky. No, it wasn't the time but her heart actually ached to ask about her brother.

She took a few minutes to swallow the frustration and fear before she walked into the other stall. Elena was there, her hand on Brody's arm. A surge of annoyance rushed through Olivia at the sight.

"Are you finished yet?" She hadn't intended to snap at them, but she did anyway.

Brody's mouth tightened. "Just about. Anxious, darlin'? You want to find our bed?"

"Of course, honey. I always want to find our bed together." She turned her gaze to Elena. "Can you take us back now?"

Elena looked between them before she nodded. "You must be married. Only married people fight like this."

Olivia was startled by the other woman's observation. Did they fight liked married people? She didn't think anything at all of how much they tussled verbally. Yet others must have seen something there. The question was, were they right?

Olivia didn't want to think her heart was involved yet, but she knew she was kidding herself. No matter how angry she got at Brody, he had wormed his grumpy way into her heart. He was smart, strong and honorable, the kind of man her father would have wanted for her had he lived.

Her heart was caught between pursuing what she felt for Brody and her love for her family. She had to find Benjy, to find the people who'd murdered her parents, before she could even think about what she might have with the ranger.

There was the possibility he didn't want anything to do with her. She had to stop thinking about the future and concentrate on the present. She was in a Mexican pueblo, at an outlaw's tavern, and now her horse was going to be left out of her reach, unsaddled and unprotected. There was definitely enough danger and fear to keep her occupied without thinking too much about other things.

If Brody wanted to bed the beautiful Elena, Olivia had no say in the matter. He was a grown man and she was not his wife or even his intended. She was simply the woman who had found passion in his arms. That was a bitter truth to swallow.

"Ah, Meredith?"

She realized she'd been staring at Brody, and he'd called her mother's name more than once.

"What?"

"You plan on sleeping out here?" He gestured to Elena, who hovered by the door, watching them with her dark gaze. "She's waiting for us. Are you ready?"

Olivia stared at him, as the events of the several days rushed through her mind. She trusted him. She *trusted* him. They would do what they'd come to do. They had to.

"Yes, I'm ready."

Walking back to the tavern was harder the second time. She knew who and what was in there. Her free hand shook and she clenched it into a fist to hide the trembling. She refused to let Rodrigo see how scared she actually was.

Elena's long braid swung back and forth across her back, following the gentle sway of her hips. Everything she did seemed graceful, an incongruous quality against the backdrop of the dark place she existed in.

Conversation was down to a murmur when they walked back in. If she had more gumption, she would have ordered a drink of whiskey. But she needed a clear head. Everything depended on whatever plan Brody had, the one he wouldn't tell her about.

By the morning, she would know. He could count on that. Olivia would not allow another hour to go by without having the truth from the ranger.

Elena nodded at the overly large bartender as she walked directly to the stairs. Every eye in the room was on them, like a pack of rats watching fresh meat march past. If they had Rodrigo's permission, they probably would have taken out their pistols and knives.

Rodrigo had put a spell around the newcomers, protecting them, for now. Olivia understood clearly that the outlaw's protection was a temporary thing that he could snatch away any second. Her pulse pounded through her as they walked up the stairs. Sweat tickled down her spine and between her breasts. It even pooled in her palm as she held onto the leather saddlebags.

It took only seconds to reach the top of the stairs, but it felt much longer. There was an open railing overlooking the tavern, allowing all those below to keep watching them. Olivia wanted to scream at them to stop staring but she focused on Elena's braid; the tick-tock motion held her gaze.

The pretty woman led them to the end of the hallway to the last door on the left. If they stayed in that room, they would have no way to leave without everyone seeing them. Rodrigo could choose to put a guard at the stairs, thereby completely cutting them off from even going to the outhouse.

Olivia's mouth dried up like Texas dirt in the summer. They were going to be prisoners in the outlaw's tavern. Was this Brody's plan? What was he thinking about when he devised it?

Her mind swam with questions she couldn't voice aloud. She pressed her lips together and kept walking. When they arrived at the door, Elena opened it and gestured for them to walk inside.

Olivia wanted to run in the other direction but she stepped into the room. Brody followed her in and when she turned around, she realized Elena had entered the room, shutting the door behind her.

Was she going to be an ally? Or was she their jailer to watch them for the night?

"Elena?" Brody sounded as confused as Olivia felt.

"I am to be sure you have pleasure." She stepped toward Brody and put her hand on his chest; then she turned her head to look at Olivia. "Both of you."

Olivia's education with regard to sex was limited to the two men she'd been intimate with and watching the animals do their mating. Nothing had prepared her for the surge of panic that burst within her now. She wasn't sure if it was part curiosity and part crazy fear, or more one than the other.

Brody stood very still, looking down at Elena with his face devoid of emotion. "We don't need help with our pleasure."

Elena shook her head. "You do not understand. I cannot leave this room until you are both satisfied. Rodrigo would be unhappy if I did."

With that, Elena reached for Brody's trousers. He tried to push her away but she would not be deterred. She dropped to her knees and had the buttons undone in minutes. His cock was half-aroused, yet when she wrapped her long fingers around him, it appeared to grow and harden instantly. Then Elena opened her lips and pulled his pulsing staff into the dark recesses of her mouth.

Olivia was frozen, stuck to the door as though an unseen force kept her there. She'd never seen anything like this, never knew people did such things.

When she and Brody had been together, they had both found pleasure, but was it the same as what he was experiencing at Elena's touch? She didn't want to know the answer to that question.

Her own body reacted to what she saw. Her nipples ached and grew taut while a low throb settled in her core.

"Jesus, stop. Stop." He pushed Elena's shoulders away

and stepped back. His cock bobbed up and down, wet and pulsing with life. Olivia wanted to shove the other woman out of the way and taste him.

The thought shocked her. It also sent a pulse of pure arousal through her.

Brody pulled his trousers up, pushing himself back in as best he could. *"No mas, Elena. No mas."*

Elena wiped her mouth with the back of her hand and stared up at him for a moment before she turned her head toward the door. Toward Olivia.

The other woman's eyes were darker than pitch. She got to her feet and approached Olivia. It was like a dream, unreal and unbelievable.

"Leave her alone." Brody's husky command didn't stop Elena's approach.

She took Olivia's hand and pressed a kiss onto the palm, her lips hot and moist. As Elena moved closer, her breasts pressed into Olivia's and she gasped.

Just as Elena's mouth brushed hers, suddenly the other woman was gone. Brody held her by the arm, righteous anger on his face.

"I don't know what Rodrigo told you to do, but she's not a whore and she sure as hell isn't going to fuck you." He glanced at Olivia. "Move aside, Meredith."

Olivia slipped sideways along the wall and tried to catch her breath. Her body hummed with both fear and arousal. She watched Brody push Elena out the door, then vaguely heard the lock tumblers scrape together.

They were locked in.

CHAPTER EIGHT

Brody's breath had stopped the moment Elena's lips touched Olivia's. He'd never been as aroused by a sight, not even purely naked women. Of course, his hard cock probably had something to do with it. Elena had a very talented mouth.

Olivia's eyes were wide as saucers in her face. Her mouth quivered slightly as she stared at him.

"What just happened?"

He had to stop himself from throwing her on the bed and fucking her until they couldn't see straight. His arousal was roaring inside, but he took a deep breath to tamp it down. Olivia was nearly in shock from what she'd seen and experienced. He had to focus on her, not on himself.

"What just happened?" she repeated.

Brody had to choose his words carefully. He forgot sometimes that she grew up on a family ranch. Her experiences had been limited until her parents had been murdered, then her world turned upside down. Now she'd stepped even further into the shadows of the dark corners and this time, she'd been unable to stay on her feet.

"Rodrigo told her to seduce us. Both of us. She wanted to see how we would react, if we'd take her up on the offer." He took her hands, which trembled like trapped birds in his. "She also wanted to search us, so she knows both of us have a gun."

He pulled her into his arms, noting her breath came in short bursts, warm against his skin. For now, he needed this contact as much as she did. They stood there for what could have been ten minutes or forty minutes. When he realized she wasn't shaking anymore, he stepped back and looked down at her.

"You need to tell me what you're planning. I don't like not being ready. If I had known she would, well, do that, I could have, well, I don't know what—" Olivia had gotten her wind back, that was for sure.

"I didn't want to risk your life."

She snorted. "I've been risking my life for a week with you. I asked you, begged, even pleaded, although I'm not proud of that, to tell me what your plan was. You didn't."

It was a raw truth but she was right. He'd left her vulnerable because he didn't trust her yet. Hell, she'd only been with him a short time. Not long enough to know if he could trust her.

That wasn't enough time for him to know her well enough.

He was lying to himself though. He did trust her. He felt more when he was with Olivia than he had in a couple of years. She'd brought him from the cold reality he existed in as a ranger and dragged him into living again. His brothers would've laughed at how much of a twist his tail was in. It was all due to Olivia.

"I, uh, I'm sorry." He barely choked the words out but he did.

Her eyebrows went up, but her expression was skeptical. "Do you mean that?"

"I don't do this. I don't know how to do this. Being with someone all the time is too damn hard." He sat down on the bed and leaned forward, resting his elbows on his knees. "I don't have partners. My life is solitary. When you wanted to be my partner, I didn't know what to do."

She sat beside him and leaned against him. "You don't have any family or friends?"

His heart pinched at the memory of what he'd lost. "My brothers died in the war. Didn't have anybody but them growing up."

"I'm so sorry. That's why you understand how I feel about Benjy." She kissed his shoulder, but he felt it through his shirt anyway. "You do have a heart, Ranger."

The aforementioned organ thumped hard. "I wanted to forget it but you wouldn't let me."

"I was never allowed to hide how I felt so I just let it loose on the world. For better or worse." She sighed. "I'm afraid I can be opinionated."

Brody didn't point out it was obvious she wasn't afraid to speak her mind. "You are a unique woman." Brody had no doubt he would never meet another woman like her.

He'd be a fool if he didn't try to keep her by his side. Brody thought maybe he was an even bigger fool because he couldn't find the words to tell her that. They were trapped somewhere inside him.

Olivia stared at him, but he didn't look her in the eye. He was no coward, but right about then he wanted to have more courage than he possessed.

"You are a hard man, Ranger." She pulled away from him and rose from the bed.

His heart cried out, battering against the bars that held it captive. Yet he said nothing, did nothing, just let her walk away from him.

He couldn't have a wife as a ranger, hell, he might not even be a ranger anymore. An outlaw certainly couldn't keep a wife and neither could a dead man. Until this thing was finished with Rodrigo and Benjy, and he could bring her safely back to Texas, he had to let her go.

Damned if his eyes didn't sting.

She sat down in the rickety chair in the corner. "Now that we've been all foolish and lovey-dovey, let's get back to business. Tell me your plan, Brody. Now."

He owed her that much. It was his plan that had landed them in this room, at the mercy of a man who would use them for sport with his own whore. It was an untenable situation and they had to work together to change it.

"An idea hit me when I was talking to Jeb at the jail in Austin. I realized no one had ever seen his partners and he refused to give up information easily." Brody wasn't proud of the way he'd pushed Jeb to talk, but he had been desperate to get something from him. He decided not to tell Olivia about that part of the conversation. "After some time, he mentioned Bluehound and that sparked my idea. I still didn't know who his partners were but I realized they didn't know me either."

She leaned forward. "You decided to take over Jeb's business."

"Exactly. I wanted to stop the supply chain from the bottom up. Finding whoever was buying the goods was going to be the hardest part. I thought at first I'd pretend to be Jeb, but when Bluehound already knew about Jeb's death, I had to think of something else." He gestured at her. "And with you along killing bad guys and pretending to be a whore, I had help."

This made her expression relax just a bit, but it was enough for him to know she would be okay. It was important because he was going to be brutally honest with her.

"I wanted to set up a deal with the buyer in Mexico and kill him. I can't operate as a ranger here in Mexico, but I have to do this, to bring down these monsters. My brothers gave their lives for what they believed in. I want to do the same."

Brody could hardly believe how much he'd just told her. For the first time in his recollection, he had spent time talking, just talking. The silence between them grew longer and he silently urged her to say something. Her blue-green eyes watched him steadily.

"I respect that, Ranger. You are doing what you think is right. That's why I'm here too. Because I had to do what was right, no matter what the consequences."

Brody didn't breathe a sigh of relief, or at least not out loud. It shouldn't be important to him that she accepted his motivations, but he'd be lying to himself if he said it wasn't. He'd never experienced such a thing before. He'd lost his parents young enough he didn't remember them. It wasn't as though his brothers didn't love him, but two teenage boys didn't know how to spread loving on a five-year-old.

As frightening as it was to admit, he had a sneaking suspicion he was falling in love with the rancher's daughter. She was the perfect woman for him, fearless, smart, gutsy and bossy.

Well, damn. That was a development he didn't expect. It could be dangerous for both of them.

"What do we do next?" A small smile curved the corner of her mouth.

Brody found his own lips twitching to return the grin. "We use Rodrigo to find the buyer and nail the son of a bitch."

She rose from the chair and sauntered toward him. "I think she locked the door behind her. We're not going anywhere tonight."

Brody's lust roared back to life. This time it was more than physical. It was pulling at every fiber of his body. He wanted Olivia. No one else.

"We shouldn't do this." His protest was halfhearted at best.

"We have to do this. I have to." Olivia stopped in front of him, her breasts inches from his face. "I need you to wipe her touch away. Please."

He understood that more than she knew. Oh, Elena had a talented mouth, but she'd left behind a residue he needed gone.

"Let me wash up first." He got to his feet and pulled her close. Her soft curves felt perfect against him, exactly where they were supposed to be. He leaned down and captured her mouth in a hard kiss. "I need to wipe her away too."

"Then let me do it." Olivia stepped back and went to the rickety washstand in the corner. She peered into the pitcher, then stuck her hand in. "There is water but it's not warm."

She poured water into the basin and glanced around for a cloth. Brody pulled a clean neckerchief from his pocket and tossed it to her. She caught it and smiled. His cock twitched with anticipation.

"Take off your clothes." Her soft command felt as though she'd shouted it. He obeyed without a peep of protest. To his surprise, she took off all her clothes too before she approached his overly anxious naked self.

She stopped with the basin in hand and looked at him, her gaze traveling up and down his body. Her eyes drank him in as though he was a feast before her.

"What?" He would not cover himself, although he sure as hell felt odd being ogled.

"You are a good-looking man." The simple compliment made any embarrassment fade. She was the most genuine woman he'd ever met.

This time when a woman knelt in front of him, he wanted her there. She dipped the rag in the water and wrung it out, then began washing him. Her scent surrounded him, her touch excited him. She worked her way down his body, leaving behind a trail of goose bumps he couldn't hide.

By the time she made it to his cock, it was standing up like an oak tree. Hard, aching and pulsing with each rush of blood through his veins. She rinsed the rag again and took the unruly staff in hand.

He closed his eyes and sucked in a breath through his teeth. So good, so damn good. She washed his cock, then moved to his balls, much to his delight. Her nimble fingers cupped him, made him want to fuck her hard right then and there. But he had to hold back; restraint was called for and he could do that. He would do that.

When her mouth touched him, he cursed loudly. She sat back and looked at him with wide eyes, her expression wary and unsure.

"Oh, honey, you don't have to do that." It was the most unexpected thing she'd done and that was saying a lot. Not that he didn't want her mouth on him—he'd had dreams about it, but he didn't want her to do it because she felt she had to.

"I want to. Please." Her throaty whisper made his cock twitch.

"Oh, God, Olivia." He lay back on the bed and waited. She was hesitant at first, hot and wet on his flesh. She

swiped him with her tongue and his leg muscles tightened. When her mouth closed around him, a rush of
pleasure shot through every pore of his body.

"Jeeeesus," he gasped.

She lapped at him more, her soft tongue blazing on his
already overheated cock. He knew there would only be
a minute or two of the delicious feel of her mouth on
him because he refused to come in her mouth. There
was no way he could last any longer than that.

When his cock touched the back of her throat, he sat
up and she released him. His wet cock slapped against his
stomach, howling for more of the angel's touch.

"Ride me, honey. Now."

Olivia stared at him, her lips red and moist. Her nipples were hard and her eyes heavy with lust. He'd never
seen anything so arousing or beautiful in his life.

She got to her feet and threw back her hair. It was
Brody's turn to look at her naked form. Her body curved
in all the right places, soft and loveable. He grabbed her
hips and pulled her forward, then planted a kiss on her
belly, which tightened beneath his touch. Another time
he would return the favor and lick her until she came,
but now he needed to be in there. He smelled her musky
arousal and slipped his finger into her folds. She was so
wet, he shook with the knowledge he would be inside
her in moments. God, how he wanted her.

He kissed her belly again and pulled her down until
she straddled him. Her heat caressed his skin as she drew
closer to his cock. She fumbled to find the right angle to
take him in. He took pity on both of them and took
hold of his staff. Like a divining rod, it found the opening of her wet core.

As she slid down his length, he took one of her nipples into his mouth and sucked. She gasped as he bit her and buried himself inside her. He paused, his fingers gripping her hips tightly. She was tight, so tight.

"Oh, God, Brody." She gasped against his cheek. "Oh, God."

He knew exactly what she meant. The wet slide of them together was incredible. He pulled her up just a few inches, then down, again, then again. Soon she had the rhythm and took over. He lay back on the bed, watching the amazing sight of Olivia fucking him. She rode him, her breasts swaying, her hair brushing her nipples, her face a study of pleasure unbound.

It was the most erotic moment of his life.

He reached up and tweaked her nipples, earning a gasp from her. Her tight passage squeezed him with each pinch, so he kept doing it. Her pace increased and he found himself pushing up as much as she pushed down.

His balls tightened and he knew he would not last much longer. There was no way he was going to find his own release without her finding one. He focused on her beautiful face and reached for her clit with one hand, while the other continued to pleasure her breast.

He found the nubbin in her swollen folds and squeezed it with his fingers, rubbing them together. Her body jerked and his cock howled with pure joy.

"Do that again."

Oh, was he in trouble if he found himself falling in love with a woman who ordered him while she fucked him. But he was and he knew it. She was the right woman for him, the only woman for him.

He obeyed his bossy partner and flicked, squeezed and tweaked her. Her pace increased as she neared her peak. He found himself watching her, fascinated by the sight of her unfettered pleasure in making love. She enveloped him, pulled him into a realm of raw ecstasy he'd not known before her.

Brody felt her orgasm hit him with the force of a twister. It wound through him, leaving pulses of passion in its wake. Her body contracted around him, milking him, prolonging their mutual pleasure with each pulse of her own orgasm. He heard himself call her name as he spilled his seed deep inside her. Stars exploded behind his eyes as he reached the ultimate ecstasy with the woman he had found to be his mate.

His woman. His Olivia.

The gray light of dawn peeked through the meager curtain on the small window. Olivia had sat up most of the night with her mind whirling. Brody had been right, they shouldn't have had sex, but she wouldn't regret it even though he had planted his seed within her. After being touched by Elena, she'd needed to feel him, not her, on her skin.

She listened to his even breathing beside her. Funny how she'd never been awake when he wasn't. His face was more relaxed in sleep, even though his dark whiskers cast a somewhat menacing shadow over his angular jaw and cheeks. Brody wasn't classically handsome but all the pieces fit together well. He clenched that same jaw when he was angry or annoyed and she'd come to recognize the tic in his cheek when he did.

Olivia watched him sleep, wondering if they'd make it out of Mexico alive, or even out of Rodrigo's tavern. She was glad they'd made love the night before.

Make love. Was that what they'd done? It hadn't been like the other frantic couplings they'd had previously. No, this had been slower, more deliberate. She wouldn't admit it out loud to anyone, especially him, but she was in love with the ranger. He was what she needed, wanted, although not what she'd ever expected. If God were kind, she would be able to live the rest of her life with Brody. If He were merciful, that life would include Benjy and the rest of her family.

She heard shuffling outside the door and before she swung her legs off the side of the bed, Brody was on his feet, gun in hand. Her mouth dropped open at the speed of the man. He'd been sound asleep! How did he manage to wake, get out of bed and draw his gun in less than a second?

He met her gaze and mouthed the word "gun." She nodded and pulled it from the folds of her skirt where she'd had it hidden. To her surprise, he smiled fiercely.

"That's my girl." His words were barely a whisper but she heard him anyway.

It made her heart skip a bit.

The key scraped in the lock, loud in the quiet room. When it swung open, Elena stood there. She glanced at their guns, then at their faces.

"*Desayuno.*" With that, she walked away.

"I guess we're commanded to go eat breakfast." Olivia got up, wincing at the tenderness throughout her body. The time with Brody had been exceptionally hard on her lower half.

"Make sure he eats first. I don't want them giving us some desert poison in our *huevos* that puts us in the crapper for a week." Brody picked up their saddlebags.

Olivia had to work to contain her surprise. Not only had she not expected to hear "crapper" from the taciturn ranger, but it came out almost funny. Either she wasn't paying attention earlier, or he was changing in front of her eyes.

She shook off her momentary amusement and focused

on the situation they were in. At least they were no longer locked in the room. "I'll make sure I do that. I saw you watch him last night too. I never thought of poison."

Thank God, he had been thinking of something so sinister. She was a novice at hunting criminals, but she was learning quickly just how far people would go.

They stepped out into the hall and she noted the tavern was deserted. There were no bustling patrons, clinking glasses or guitar music this morning. The burly barkeep was absent as well. She wondered if they all hid during the daylight hours, or perhaps had just gotten to their beds. Either way, she was glad to see there was nobody about. The experience last night had been uncomfortable enough.

At the bottom of the stairs, Elena waited, her hands folded neatly in front of her. Her expression didn't reflect annoyance, but Olivia saw something flash in her eyes before she turned away, gesturing for them to follow.

She walked to a swinging door behind the tables and went through. Olivia was pleasantly surprised by the cleanliness of the kitchen they entered. Its tidiness, combined with the delicious odors, made it feel almost homey.

She had to remind herself again that this was not a friendly kitchen. It was an enemy's domain, no matter how appealing or friendly they seemed. Elena pointed to a round table on the left and walked over to the large black stove in the corner.

Rodrigo sat at the table, a mug in front of him. The hat was gone, as was the black clothing. He wore a plain white shirt open at the collar and his dark hair hung in waves to his jaw. Olivia was struck by just how young the outlaw looked; he couldn't have been more than twenty or twenty-one, the same age as she was.

"Buenos dias, señorita. Tu eres muy guapa esta dia." He gave her a lazy grin.

"Buenos dias, señor." Olivia glanced at Brody as she sat down. His jaw was clenched and the tic jumping madly in his cheek. She didn't respond to the compliment and she didn't think Rodrigo expected her to. Telling her she looked beautiful was almost ridiculous in the current situation.

"Rodrigo." Brody sat down, dropping the saddlebags beside him on the floor. "Didn't appreciate being locked in."

"It is for your safety. People in Forgata don't like gringos." Rodrigo sipped at his coffee.

"I had to take a piss and couldn't." The ranger was intent on being ornery.

"There was a chamber pot below the bed." Rodrigo turned back to Olivia. "You like coffee?"

"Yes, please." Olivia decided to use her manners. Brody flashed her a warning with his eyes. She would heed it. There wasn't a chance she would put herself at risk for coffee.

Elena came over with two empty tin cups and a coffeepot. She set the cups down and poured, careful to hold the handle with a rag. Her gaze met Rodrigo's for a second before she poured more coffee into his cup.

"We have no sugar for coffee." The outlaw sniffed at the brew. "But real men don't need it, eh?"

Brody didn't answer. He picked up his own cup and pulled in a gulp.

Olivia drank her coffee, but she was on pins and needles wondering if whatever they were served next would be poison. If it wasn't for their protection, she might have been annoyed at her lover for putting the idea in her head.

Lover.

That was a new word just bursting in her head. Brody was her lover now, for better or worse. One day he might be more, but for now she felt good thinking of him as her lover.

"I've asked people about Jeb's death. Did you know him?" Rodrigo directed the question to Brody.

"Yep, I knew him. I took his business and his woman away from him."

Now they both looked at her again.

"Ah, the pretty *señorita* was Jeb's *mujer*, eh? Is this true, *chica*?" Rodrigo almost petted the rim of his cup. She watched the slender, olive-toned fingers move—he was quite graceful.

"Yes, I was his before I met Stuart." She'd almost said Brody. Thankfully her brain stopped her tongue from killing them.

"Did you love him?" Rodrigo's eyes were at half-mast but they were sharp as knives.

"No, but I liked him. He was easy to know, easy to like. Folks took to him. It's how he was able to do what he did for so long without anyone knowing." Olivia stopped and sighed. "I do miss him a little." It was true, unfortunately; she did miss the charming Jeb she'd known as a neighbor.

"Jeb was lousy at a lot of things." Brody pressed Rodrigo. "That's why Jeb got himself killed. He didn't have a head for business; he was greedy and had crossed people for money. I won't make the same mistake. I set up the buy before I take a thing. I don't want merchandise I can't get rid of."

Rodrigo regarded Brody for a full minute before he

spoke again. "I like your business attitude. You are right, of course. If you take what you cannot keep or sell, then you are an *idiota*."

Elena set down plates of steaming eggs, tortillas, peppers and onions. The smell was heavenly and Olivia's stomach growled on cue.

Rodrigo chuckled. "Elena is a good cook. She learn from her mama, who owns her own, ah, tavern in another town." Rodrigo took a bite of his eggs and spoke with his mouth full. Olivia had all she could do not to admonish him as she would her younger siblings. "This is where we will go today."

"To see Elena's mother?" Olivia blurted. Both men sent her an annoyed look. "It's an honest question."

"Is the buyer there?" Brody took another gulp of coffee.

"*Sí*. This is where we need to go." He twirled his fork in a circle before he pointed it at the ranger. "I will take you to meet the buyer, but I tell you this now. If you play me for a fool, gringo, I will make sure you suffer before you die."

The air crackled with the threat. The small hairs stood up on Olivia's arm as the two men stared at each other.

"Fair enough. I'll make you the same promise." Brody held the other man's stare until Rodrigo's smile returned.

"Is good. Is good. Now eat and then *vamanos*."

They ate an uneasy breakfast, and although the food was good, Olivia could not shake the feeling that something very bad was going to happen. They were taking the word of an outlaw that they would find what they sought—a buyer for children and women. It would be foolhardy to do so, but they didn't have a choice.

* ★ ★

Brody ate what was put in front of him, but he didn't taste it. The battle lines had been drawn and his plan was now officially in play with Rodrigo. This was his opportunity to find the people he hunted, no matter the consequences to himself. The consequences to Olivia were another matter.

Although she'd assured him her eyes were open and she knew the dangers, he didn't want anything to happen to her. There wasn't a doubt in his mind that Rodrigo would do everything he promised and more. It was Brody's job to make sure that didn't happen.

Elena cleaned up the kitchen in a blink, and then they followed Rodrigo out of the tavern to the barn to get the horses. Elena walked beside Brody, the quiet seductress who probably had killed for the man she served.

"Cuidado, señor," she whispered as they walked behind Rodrigo and Olivia, who were talking about horses ten feet in front of them.

Brody's instincts reared to life. The woman who'd tried to seduce him was warning him of danger. *"¿Porque?"*

"You are working with people who would kill you in a second and not care. I know why you are here. I know why she comes."

"What are you talking about?" He didn't want to even consider that they had been found out already.

"Her eyes." Elena glanced at him. "The boy had the same color."

"The boy?" Brody's stomach flipped, full of the heavy Mexican breakfast. Oh, God, could Benjy have come through the tavern?

"Sí, el hijo. He was here months ago, but I remember his eyes. He cried for his mama and for someone named

Eva. Rodrigo told me to tie him up and gag him so he not hear him no more." Elena nodded at Olivia. "You look for him, *si*?"

"I don't know what you're talking about." The last thing Brody needed was to confirm they were looking for Benjy.

Elena nodded. "*Entiendo*. You keep your woman safe. Is good. Remember what I say. Do not trust anyone, especially *mi mama. Cuidado, señor*."

They reached the barn and Elena disappeared into a stall to saddle a horse for herself. Brody could hardly believe the conversation he'd just had. As he walked into his horse's stall, he noticed that Olivia was watching him. She must have seen Elena whispering to him. He wanted so badly to tell Olivia what he'd found out but knew it was far too risky to do so now. He would just have to count on catching her alone for a few minutes later.

After saddling the horses, the four of them got started across the scrubby desert. The sun had risen enough to warm their backs as they rode west. Rodrigo seemed to love to talk and he chatted with Olivia as though they were bosom friends. Brody wanted to punch the outlaw and carry her away on his shoulder. Stupid, he knew, but he couldn't keep himself from feeling that way. The odds were stacked against them to survive, so wishing for it was even more foolish.

"Tell me about you, Meredith." Rodrigo had an easy seat in the saddle; clearly, he was a man who had spent many hours riding.

"Oh, there's not much to tell. I lost my parents when I was thirteen." She looked out toward the horizon, her gaze distant. "I still miss them, even now. I worked the jobs I could get, um, for money. Jeb found me a couple years later and took care of me. He was nice most of the time."

"Then you leave him for Stuart's dick, eh?" Rodrigo laughed at his own wit. "It must be bigger and better. This is good because you are a woman who knows what she wants." He licked his lips and Brody saw Olivia twitch.

Brody didn't care for the outlaw's implication. "Meredith is a smart woman. She knew Jeb was going nowhere in a hurry."

"You give her what she needs then." Rodrigo had put on his familiar flat-brimmed black hat. "You keep your woman satisfied."

"We get along just fine."

Rodrigo laughed. "I hear you getting along just fine last night. Meredith, she is passionate, no? I look for that in a woman too. No cold fish in the bed. Is boring! I look for fire and spark."

He had the right of it, damn his rotten hide. Olivia was passionate, full of fire and spark. She was his woman now and if he were smart he'd hang onto her with both hands. If he could survive the next few days, he would do just that.

"Elena has the bedroom skills. I like this too. She could teach Meredith good things." Rodrigo had already attempted to have Elena teach Olivia things, but they weren't good.

Brody had to change the subject before he lost his temper and beat the life out of the man. "How far is the pueblo we're going to?"

"A few hours. We will be there by dinner." He gestured to the wide-open desert. "For now we have all this fine land to ourselves and a nice day to ride."

Everyone was quiet for a few minutes, but it was not to last. Olivia's breasts seemed to fascinate the Mexican and his gaze kept returning to them. Brody gritted his teeth to keep quiet, his hands fisting on the reins, wrapping tight. His horse didn't like the pull on his bit and let Brody know by turning around and biting his leg.

"Ow, cut that out." He loosened his grip, unwilling to let anyone see what he'd been doing.

"Your horse is how you say, ornery, hmm?" Rodrigo's laugh grated on him like a hot, jagged rock.

"Sometimes he is. Maybe he don't like all the chatter." Brody couldn't help digging at the man. He had to shut up Rodrigo somehow.

Another laugh. "Too bad he is a *caballo* and cannot speak for himself. I like to talk to Meredith more. It is a long ride and we can become friends, *sí?*"

Olivia didn't look at him. "I don't think we're here to be friends, Rodrigo. We're here to do business."

"That means we cannot talk?" Rodrigo shook his head. "I thought we were *amigos*."

The dark undercurrents in his voice gave Brody pause. They had to keep up their disguise as outlaws, but they also had to keep Rodrigo happy enough to bring them to the buyer for the human chattel Jeb had been selling. All that meant was they had to be nice to Rodrigo, talk with him and remember he could have an ambush planned another mile up the road.

Brody couldn't tell Olivia everything he was thinking but he had to make her understand what they had to do, like it or not. "We can talk. Meredith is a little grumpy because she didn't get enough sleep."

"Ah, *entiendo*. You kept her busy, *sí?* You are the man she wanted more than Jeb Stinson." Rodrigo didn't appear to be too ruffled by Olivia's cool remarks.

"She is a good woman."

"*Sí*, I can believe that. She take care of you and not complain about it." Rodrigo glanced at Olivia. "I would like a woman like this."

She didn't turn her head but a small grin kicked up the side of her mouth. "I'm not interested, but thank you."

Rodrigo threw his head back and laughed. "She is funny too. Meredith, Meredith, Meredith, Meredith." It was almost sing-songy and quite bizarre.

"What is your mother's name, Elena?" Olivia must have felt the same sort of discomfort at the outlaw's amusement. It was disturbing and it set the small hairs on his neck standing up.

Rodrigo was still chuckling as he flapped his hand in the other woman's direction. *"Puedes hablar, Elena."*

Ah, even more interesting. Elena had to wait for Rodrigo's permission to speak. No wonder she'd whispered to Brody back in Forgata. He had to find an opportunity to talk to her in private again. No doubt the quiet, strange woman had more secrets to share, knew the darkest tales from the outlaw's life.

"Her name is Lucinda." Elena's quiet voice broke the silence.

"She owns her own business then? Unusual for a woman." Brody didn't want to insult her by asking if it was a brothel because she could own a seamstress shop. However, given the caliber of the people they were dealing with, it was unlikely.

"It is a place for pleasure, *señor*. She has women and liquor. People come to see her every day." Elena didn't elaborate on why people came to see her mother but it was obvious. Taverns made money on liquor and women.

"It must have been hard to leave her." Olivia turned to look at her. "You must love Rodrigo very much."

The expression on Elena's face was carefully controlled, but Brody could almost see the truth in her gaze. She didn't love Rodrigo. Hell, she probably didn't even like him. Nor did he think Elena was willingly with the outlaw. He suspected she'd been sold, or maybe even used to pay a debt. It was an unfortunate fate for many women who were more children than adult.

"I am loyal." Elena's response was what he expected, cryptic.

"I'm sure he appreciates your loyalty." Olivia shot Brody a scowl, as though he'd been the one to pull the words from her mouth. "Thank you for coming with us. I'm sure you want to see your mother too."

This time Elena didn't answer.

Everyone was quiet for a few minutes, for which Brody was grateful. He needed a few minutes to think about the information he'd been given. He kept his gaze on Olivia until she looked his way.

"Be nice," he mouthed.

She scowled again.

"We need him," he mouthed.

She rolled her eyes and turned away from him. He hoped like hell she understood what he was trying to tell her.

Olivia sighed but then finally spoke. "What about you, Rodrigo? Do you have any family?"

"I have a broken family, *amiga*. It is scattered like the tumbleweeds." Rodrigo didn't sound particularly sad about it.

"I'm sorry." Olivia had such a large family, she probably did feel sorry for him. "That must be hard."

"I have all I need." Rodrigo smiled at her. "My tavern, a woman, my men. One day I will be a *caudillo*."

Brody had wondered if Rodrigo had plans to become

a *caudillo,* a warlord in Mexico. He was well on his way: a dangerous man with dangerous plans.

"I was born in Texas, you know. My mama, she worked a big hacienda and then she had me. But I was not home until I came here. This, *this* is my home."

For the first time since they'd met, Brody heard honesty in the outlaw's voice. There were plenty of hacienda owners who got children on their hired help, but never acknowledged them as their offspring. They were half-breeds to many, bastards to others. Rodrigo was probably better off in Mexico than Texas.

If Rodrigo had stayed where he'd been born, he would have had nothing. Now he had his own little corner of the world with dreams of something bigger. But if Brody had anything to say about it, Rodrigo's dreams wouldn't come true.

CHAPTER NINE

As the sun rose high into the afternoon sky, the small group of four riders neared another pueblo. This one was much larger than the one they'd just left. There were at least five times as many buildings, some even three stories high.

Olivia had been uncomfortable entering Forgata, but this place made every hair on her body stand on end. They were Texans deep in Mexico with no one to help them or back them up.

If anything went wrong now, they would be dead. There was no doubt in her mind about that. Given the last twenty-four hours, she was prepared for just about anything, and yet her stomach burbled with fear. Not just for herself, but for Brody and for Benjy, wherever he was.

She had to be strong and that meant not showing fear. The town grew larger and larger as did her anxiety over exactly what Elena's mother, Lucinda, was like. If she ran a brothel and a tavern, she must be smart, but Elena had had nothing to say about her mother. It added to her misgivings about the quiet beauty. Olivia's mother was gone forever; Elena's mother lived, yet she ignored her.

"We go straight to Lucinda's, *sí?*" Rodrigo didn't appear to actually be asking a question because he led the small party into the main street and toward the largest building.

This town reminded her of home; it was not so very different from where she would go every Saturday with Matt and the rest of their siblings. While the younger ones would play checkers, they would do their shopping, get supplies and conduct their business in town. Her throat tightened at the sight of three little girls playing on the side of the street, laughing and whooping as they ran in a circle. The reminder of her siblings, of safety and love hit like a mule kick.

The buildings were mostly of wood construction, with some adobe ones as well. There were a few wooden sidewalks, but not many. She expected it didn't rain much in this dry land, therefore not much mud, and no need for sidewalks. A few people turned to look at them, then moved quickly away or averted their eyes. She knew it wasn't because of the two gringos but because of Rodrigo. It appeared the young man with big dreams had already conquered part of the land he loved.

She'd been surprised to discover he was Texan, but chose to be a Mexican. There were so many haciendas scattered around southern Texas, owned by wealthy men who had made their money on the backs of others. She wondered if his father was such a man, or if Rodrigo had imagined him that way. It shouldn't matter to her, but it seemed neither Rodrigo nor Elena knew a true family's love and for that, she pitied them. The most important thing in the world to her was family.

They pulled up in front of a three-story building made of wood. Many of the boards were new, or had recently been replaced. There were at least eight windows and a terrace on the second floor. The sign had been painted in bright red letters, using bold strokes: LUCINDA'S.

It was an enormous building by anyone's standards and to find it here in the middle of nowhere sent a chill up Olivia's spine. How did Lucinda have so much money? Was the blood of innocents fueling the building of this place?

"*Estamos aquí, amigos.* Now that we are here, let us have a drink to quench our thirst." Rodrigo dismounted and waited for the others to do the same. He tossed his reins to Elena. "Put them in the barn."

Elena nodded and held out her hand to Brody and Olivia. The ranger took off his saddlebags and gave Elena his horse's reins.

"She needs a good rubdown." Olivia took her time dismounting and taking off her saddlebags. She didn't care to hand over her mare to the woman but there was no choice. "And some feed if there is any."

Silent still, Elena tugged the horses' reins lightly until they started following her. She walked to the side of the building and disappeared. Whatever hold Rodrigo had over her, it was strong, very strong.

"Does she need help?" Brody scowled at the spot where she'd been. Olivia was curious why he cared enough to ask. That woman had tried to force both of them into having sex with her. She was definitely not a friend.

"No, Elena is very good at doing what I say." Rodrigo gestured to the door, which had also been painted red. She'd never seen such a color or so much of it. "*Bien-venidos a* Lucinda's."

He opened the door and Olivia took a deep breath and stepped inside. The inside was plain, much to her surprise. There were a few tables here and there, with one old man sleeping at one, but there was no crowd of people, no brightly dressed loose women lounging about.

She'd expected to see a great deal of debauchery and whiskey, but there was none. The place was almost empty.

She smelled a mixture of things, including a sweet, spicy aroma mixed with a musky overtone and another pungent odor, perhaps the old man. Beneath all of them, a dark scent lurked.

"Kind of quiet in here." Brody glanced at the man and all around the room, as though memorizing it.

"It is *siesta* time, *señor*. People will come later." Rodrigo walked toward a curtain at the back of the large room. "Follow me."

Brody took her hand and squeezed it. She wouldn't admit this to him, but it made her feel better. They had been together physically of course, but not like this, not in comfort. It meant a lot to her that he considered she needed a bit of reassurance right about then.

The curtain was a coarse brown material but well made and thick. Brody held it aside so she could walk into a huge kitchen. Lucinda's was a restaurant?

An older woman stood at the stove frying something that smiled heavenly. She had thick silver hair braided down her back, reminding Olivia of Elena. Perhaps this was her mother.

"Mama." Rodrigo came up behind the woman and kissed her cheek.

She turned and spread her arms wide. *"Mi hijo!"*

When he picked her up and spun her around, she squealed like a little girl. Olivia was surprised by the gesture, and it skewed her perception of the outlaw.

The woman spoke in rapid-fire Spanish as he set her down. Olivia followed some of it, but the dialect was unlike anything she knew. Then the older woman spotted the two of them in the kitchen and she stopped speaking. The woman was beautiful, strikingly so. Her skin had wrinkles but not a significant amount. Her cheekbones were high and pronounced, balanced by a strong jaw and chin. Her eyes were dark as pitch, and they stared with the sharpness of a dagger.

"*¿Quien es los gringos?*" Her voice had dropped to a quiet monotone. Of course she would question who they were, but her tone made Olivia tighten all over.

"*Mis amigos,* Stuart and Meredith." He smiled at them. "They have come to do business, but first, we must eat."

The woman stared at them for what felt like an exceptionally long time before she turned back to the stove. Olivia recognized that whoever this woman was, she held the power in this building. She was no ordinary cook or just someone's mother. This had to be Lucinda.

Rodrigo hung his hat on a hook on the wall and gestured to the square table in the corner. Brody took off his hat and held it as they sat down. A charged silence filled the big kitchen.

Olivia folded her hands on the table and tried to appear casual. She'd darkened her skin to appear to be someone she wasn't and at that table, she felt like someone else. Instead of being at home, safe and comfortable, she was in a strange place, dusty, scared and surrounded by strangers who could kill her for just being a *gringa.*

Brody was as still as a statue beside her, his gaze constantly roaming the room, yet landing on the woman and Rodrigo with regularity. He looked calm, but she wondered how he felt on the inside. She knew what he planned, but how could they possibly find out what they needed to know when only Rodrigo spoke to them? At least in his small place in Forgata, the barkeep had talked to her after he found out she spoke Spanish. Here, she was even more out of her element and afraid she didn't know what to do.

Perhaps they would get a few moments alone so she could talk to Brody. The last thing she wanted to do was make a mistake since they were literally in the lion's den.

The older woman brought a plate of steaming food and set it in front of Rodrigo with a fork.

"Mama, comida para todos." His voice was gentle, another surprise, although he was ordering her to serve food to everyone.

"I don't want to make her—"Olivia started to say.

The woman's gaze snapped to Olivia's, cutting her off in mid-sentence.

"You are in my house and I will decide what is done." The woman spoke nearly perfect English with barely an accent. "You may be Rodrigo's 'friends' but you are not mine."

Olivia realized she'd offended the woman—just what she'd hoped not to do. "I apologize."

The woman made a quick motion with her hand and turned back to the stove. Brody glanced at her and she tried to apologize with her eyes. He turned his attention back to the old woman and did not take his eyes off her again.

To Olivia's surprise, Lucinda set down plates in front of the two of them. It was meat, peppers, onions on top of a big tortilla layered with beans. Not only did it smell delicious but after Olivia took her first bite, her tongue confirmed it was delicious and spicy. She groaned before she could stop herself.

"You like spicy food."

"Sí, señora. I grew up eating it." A full truth at last.

The old woman sat down across from her and watched

as they ate. No matter the strange circumstance, Olivia was ravenous, and dug in with gusto.

"Why are you here?"

Olivia's fork hung in mid-air and she set it down slowly before she dropped it. Brody set his down deliberately and wiped his mouth on his sleeve.

"To do business."

She steepled her fingers under her chin, her dark eyes sharp. "Rodrigo brings you so he must think you are a businessman."

"I am a businessman. I've taken what I wanted and now I want more." Brody had slipped into his cool ranger persona, unflappable and controlled.

"You wish to do business with me?" She narrowed her gaze.

"I wish to find a buyer to do business with. If that's you, then yes." He didn't even blink as he spoke.

She turned to Rodrigo and spoke in that rapid-fire Spanish again. Olivia tried to follow the conversation but only picked up words here and there. After a few minutes of dialog with the outlaw, the woman got up and walked to the curtain. With one last probing look, she left the kitchen.

Olivia picked at her food while the men continued to eat as though nothing had happened. She wanted to know more about who this woman was, what Lucinda knew about the buyer and most important, if she knew where Benjy was. It wasn't easy being patient when she was used to pushing until she got what she wanted.

"Are we leaving or staying?" Brody finally asked.

Rodrigo sipped at the glass of liquid the old woman had given him. It had a powerful enough scent that Olivia knew it was liquor but she had no idea what. It didn't smell like whiskey.

"Staying. Mama wants to think about your offer. She does not go into business with everyone, *señor*. That would be stupid and she is very smart." Rodrigo threw back the rest of the liquor and smacked his lips. "She has good tequila too."

Tequila—that's what he was drinking. Olivia did not want to know what it tasted like. Too much was riding on keeping a clear head. Although right about then, a stiff drink might've helped her nerves.

"Was that Lucinda?" Olivia couldn't help asking.

Rodrigo smiled at her, looking almost boyish with his tousled black curls and wide grin. "*Lo siento, amiga. Sí,* she is my mama, Lucinda."

"Wait, does that mean Elena is your sister?" Olivia wasn't expecting that bit of news. Who treated their sister the way Rodrigo treated Elena? Like a slave born to serve him and commit salacious acts at his command. The very idea horrified Olivia.

"*Sí,* she is *mi hermana.*" Rodrigo's smile faded. "I was born of the *jefe* of a big hacienda. Elena, she is a mongrel born of a *vaquero's* lust for a woman who took his money."

Olivia didn't know how to respond. Not only had he confirmed the beautiful seductress was his sister, a disturbing piece of the puzzle that was Rodrigo, but his mother was Lucinda, who was apparently a whore. What a family life they had. It was apparent Rodrigo thought himself above his sister and treated her accordingly.

Brody kept on eating as though the information was of no import. She wanted to kick him and slap Rodrigo.

"Is there a place Meredith and I can take a siesta?" He asked as he scraped the last bite into his mouth.

Rodrigo's grin wasn't genuine this time. It was lascivious and dark. "Ah, time to ride your filly again, eh? I don't blame you. I would fuck her as many times a day as I could." Olivia knew if Brody wasn't with her, Rodrigo would probably try to do just that. She promised herself never to be alone with the outlaw.

Brody didn't respond to Rodrigo's crude taunt. This time his silence aggravated Rodrigo, judging by the look on his face, which gave Olivia a certain measure of satisfaction. She wasn't the only one annoyed by the taciturn ranger.

"*Sí*, I will put you in one of the rooms upstairs." Rodrigo got to his feet. "I have my own business to do up there."

Olivia wondered what lucky woman would be the recipient of Rodrigo's business. Then again, she didn't want to know. The man was as twisted up as any person she'd ever met.

They left the kitchen through a staircase in the back. The smell of the house changed from the warm, spicy foods to something entirely different. Sweet perfume, human body odor and again that underlying scent of something dark. She wondered if Rodrigo would be offended if she covered her nose.

Something lurked within this building, something that stayed in the shadows, keeping out of sight. She felt it, knew it was there, and was worried it would reach out and snatch away any chance they had to find Benjy. Olivia didn't think she'd be closing her eyes for a siesta—her inner warning bells were ringing so loudly, her ears hurt.

Brody paced the small room, his boots too loud in the eerie quiet that had fallen over Lucinda's building. The entire town seemed to take their siesta seriously. Olivia stood at the window, staring out onto the deserted street.

He needed to make a deal with Lucinda and find out

exactly who her buyers were. Or at least enough information to track down Benjy Graham and the rest of the missing folks. He had to keep reminding himself that he wasn't there just for Olivia. Although, she bossed him around enough one would think he was.

Brody expected some dark people to enter his life, but he hadn't expected her. This situation had gotten so far out of hand now, he didn't know how to stop it, or save them. He knew they were risking their lives, knew they were helpless and at the whim of a Mexican outlaw. A loco one at that. The man whored his sister, for God's sake.

It chilled him to see just how little Rodrigo valued except for himself and the profit he could make. Brody suspected the buyer he was looking for was actually Rodrigo. The man delighted in playing word games and spinning things around until he made his opponents dizzy. Brody knew he was dangerous but didn't think he'd seen the full extent of the threat just yet.

"What do we do now?" Olivia asked in a hushed voice. She turned to look at him, her beautiful blue-green eyes full of worry and fear. It was probably the first time he'd seen that particular emotion from the prickly rancher's daughter and he didn't like it. She needed fire and sass there, not fear. The weight of their situation weighed even more heavily on him.

"We wait. We are in their world now, Liv. If we go snooping around here, our bodies will never be found." He didn't want to be anything but frank with her now. There was too much at stake to tell half-truths.

She blinked rapidly but she didn't flinch. "What do they do with the bodies?"

He didn't expect the question. "Leave them for the vultures and critters probably."

This time she did flinch. "Tell me what Elena said to you back in Forgata. Now." Her normally demanding voice had shrunk to a shaky whisper.

Brody sat on the bed and patted the spot next to him. "Sit down and I'll tell you."

With reluctance in her step, she sat down beside him and crossed her arms. She might just as well have put up no trespassing signs.

"She recognized you. Well, your eyes anyway."

Her expression exploded and the arms fell away. "She's seen Benjy."

He winced at the hope in her voice. "Yes, she said he'd been through here months earlier. He'd been difficult and kept calling for your mother and Eva. She said they'd taken him away with the others, but she remembered him. And she knew why you had come."

"He was alive then, at least." She pressed her hands to her eyes, her fingers trembling. "Is it good or bad that she recognized me?"

"Both I suppose. Elena now has information that can buy her favor from Rodrigo and Lucinda. But she also didn't say anything, as far as I know, to her brother, and that could mean she might not." Brody couldn't read Elena. He needed to get her alone. "I need to talk to her again, but in the meantime, I want to set up a business arrangement with Rodrigo and his mother."

Olivia blew out a breath. "What should I do?"

"Keep pretending to be my woman, keep your eyes open and your mouth shut." It was futile to tell her to be quiet, but he would at least try.

"I want to talk to Elena." She took his hand and squeezed it, her palms damp. "Please, I have to."

Brody knew there would be trouble if the two women were together, alone. "No, let me do that. You are too emotional about this. I'm here to do my job, not to rescue my little brother."

"Please, Brody. I can't do nothing." She got up so fast, he almost fell sideways. "I have always pitched in, done what I could, haven't I? I have to help."

"It's too dangerous."

"I helped in Rodrigo's place. I distracted everyone so you could talk to him." She crossed her arms again, frowning fiercely. "You are not my husband or my employer. I can do what I feel necessary."

Brody got to his feet slowly, cool anger flowing through his veins. He stuck a finger in the air, inches from her. "You will not risk our lives because you can't be patient. This isn't going to happen in ten minutes. It's going to take time. If you cause trouble, you will get us both killed."

"I wasn't going to cause trouble, I was going to flirt with Rodrigo or Elena and get what information I can from them."

Brody's mouth dropped open. "What did you just say?"

"You heard me. You thought it was fine when I acted like a whore with Sanchez. I will do what I have to for my family." She stuck her chin in the air in challenge, daring him to act.

He stuck his nose right against hers. "You will *not* do any such thing."

"You can't stop me." She whirled around and headed for the door.

Before he could reach her, she'd flung it open to find a burly, unshaven man outside the door. His face was scarred with what might have been a pox or acne, his eyes black holes in his face.

"*Hola,*" Olivia said breezily, but Brody heard the undercurrent of dismay beneath. *"Me llamo Meredith. ¿Como te llamas?"*

"Manuel." His heavily accented English was thick and deep.

The last thing they needed was a babysitter, but apparently they had one. The man was a wall of muscle in nondescript brown clothes with a knife strapped to his left thigh and a pistol on his right. No doubt he did whatever Rodrigo or Lucinda bade him to do. This would definitely put a crimp in his plans to snoop later on. He wouldn't have told Olivia what he was doing since she would insist on coming along and he couldn't risk it.

"Is siesta time over?" Olivia held onto the doorknob with whitened knuckles.

"Sí, come downstairs now." He turned sideways like a human door and Olivia stepped out.

When she turned to look back at him, he saw a glimpse of defiance in her face, then she schooled her features. Brody followed her and hoped like hell she wouldn't start something that would finish them.

As they walked back downstairs, they entered the main area again; this time, there were a few ladies lounging about. Each one was dressed in a plain cotton skirt and peasant blouse, their cleavage clearly displayed. Dressed for customers, their faces, however, reflected boredom.

Lucinda stood at the bar, this time wearing a form-fitting green gown that hugged her ample curves. Her silver hair was piled into a mass of curls, tendrils hanging down over her shoulders. Her lips were painted the same shade of red as the sign outside.

She was not nearly as old as he'd thought, given her performance earlier. But it was just that, a performance for two gringos. She thought to be a simple kitchen woman and watch them unawares. It was clever of her to do so and although she was obviously a criminal, Brody did appreciate a keen mind.

Olivia pinched his arm and he realized he'd been staring at the formidable Lucinda like a village idiot.

"Did you enjoy siesta?" Lucinda cocked one brow at them.

"It wasn't restful but we enjoyed it." Brody took Olivia's stiff arm and wrapped it around his own.

"You didn't enjoy it enough and neither did she, I think." Lucinda shook her head. "I ask about you in the pueblo and no one knows you, Stuart. You are nobody then, eh?"

Brody wasn't surprised to learn she had been busy trying to figure out who he was while he'd been upstairs pacing. Hell, she probably knew he had been pacing. This was a family of predators, a snake's den.

"I am nobody now, but I plan on being somebody. If I can find the right buyer for my merchandise." He was careful to keep his face blank, and his tone even.

She nodded. "*Bueno*. We talk business then." She gestured to the table nearest to her.

Brody glanced around pointedly at the whores staring at them. "I won't do this with an audience."

Lucinda cocked one brow, then clapped her hands. The other women wandered to the far end of the room, out of hearing distance. It would have to do.

Manuel loomed behind them like a wall that hovered in mid-air. He stood closest to Olivia, which annoyed Brody. His big body couldn't be more than six inches from her smaller form. Hell, her flyaway hairs were touching the man's arm.

Brody felt a surge of jealousy and swallowed it back with difficulty. The man could probably knock him out if he chose to do so, long before Brody could reach his gun. It didn't matter if Manuel got too close to Liv—it was his job to do that.

Foolish, lovesick man.

The idea that he was in love with Olivia made his stomach flip twice. He definitely didn't want to be in such a state, and he sure as hell didn't know what to do about it. Definitely one of those times he wished his brothers were here so he could ask them. They'd taught him how to pleasure a woman, but they'd never taught him how to love one.

"Talk, gringo." Lucinda watched him with her sharp, probing gaze.

"We can get merchandise out of Texas, but we can't sell it there. I was with Jeb's men when he was doing the same, but he was sloppy about it, which is how he got caught."

"Jeb Stinson? This is who you speak of?" Lucinda sat up straighter.

"Yep, that's him." He noted the play of emotions on her face and wondered if Jeb had spent some time in Lucinda's bed.

"Is he dead?" Her brows drew together and formed a dark V on her forehead.

"Yes, ma'am. He was strung up last month."

She closed her eyes and paused for a few moments. Olivia reached out and put her hand on the older woman's. Lucinda's eyes snapped open and she snatched her hand away.

"Too bad. I liked him." Lucinda sighed and turned to Olivia. "He was your man?"

Olivia's face crumpled just a bit, enough that Brody wasn't sure if she was acting or not. Damn. What a situation he found himself in.

"Yes, for a while. At least I hoped he was." Olivia glanced down at her hands. "Until he was arrested."

"Ah, yes, I hear the rangers got him." Rodrigo appeared from the shadows, his dark hat shading his eyes.

At the mention of the rangers, Brody's heart picked up but his face didn't even twitch. If the outlaw had discovered who he really was, he'd already have a bullet in his heart.

"That's what I heard too. I found Olivia hiding at this little shack where he stored the goods he took." He turned a feral smile on her. "Then I took her."

Olivia found the muster to grin back at him. "I wanted to be taken or you wouldn't have had a chance."

Lucinda looked between them and then waved her hands. "I don't want to know about this. Tell me about the business now."

The danger seemed to have passed and Rodrigo sat at a stool behind them near the bar. His presence didn't complicate things so much as annoy Brody. The outlaw had flirted with Olivia and sent Elena to seduce them. He was as dangerous as his mother.

"I need a buyer. If I have one, I can take orders for specific types of, ah, merchandise, and bring the types likely to fetch the highest bid."

Lucinda leaned forward and a small grin played around her mouth. "Let us talk about specifics."

Olivia felt rather than heard Rodrigo step up behind her. Every nerve ending jangled at the close proximity of his body to hers. His breath tickled her ear.

"*Querida,* they will be talking for a while. Why don't we have something to eat?" He pulled her toward the kitchen, and Brody was so deep in conversation with Lucinda, he didn't even notice.

It was enough to convince her she needed to do what she could to find information. No matter what Brody said, Olivia was capable and strong. She would use whatever means necessary to get details from the outlaw. Rodrigo was smart, but she was smarter.

She let him lead her into the deserted kitchen. As he walked toward the table, she mustered up enough courage to stop in her tracks. He turned to look at her, surprise on his face.

"What is wrong, Meredith?"

The sound of her mother's name was enough to push her into what she needed to do. This was for her family, her brother and the future of the Grahams. She would be a warrior for them.

Olivia stepped closer, pressing her breast into his arm. The surprise on his face turned to curiosity and interest.

"Does your Stuart know you play with me in here?" He turned until she was chest to chest with him, a hair's-breath away from actually touching his body. The heat between them slithered up her skin, making her shiver.

"I don't play." She ran her finger down his chest, not surprised to find it as hard as granite. He was every bit as muscular as Brody, but instead of quiet fierceness, Rodrigo exuded dangerous sexuality.

He captured her hand and brought it to his mouth. As his lips closed around her pointer finger, Olivia's stomach quivered. The wet slide of his tongue against her finger made every inch of her want to run in the other direction.

But she didn't. She simply watched as he pulled the digit out of his mouth, then blew on it. A chill raced through her.

"Oh, yes, you play." His grin appeared to be designed

to melt her resistance, but there was no chance she would fall prey to his wiles.

He had to fall prey to hers.

She extracted her hand and reached out to cup his face. His grin deepened as he waited. Her heart thumped harder than it ever had as she pulled his lips down to hers.

His mouth was softer than Brody's and tasted faintly of an exotic spice. She nibbled from side to side, then ran her tongue along the seam of his lips. He chuckled softly as his mouth opened to hers.

Even as her tongue slid against his, she closed her eyes to forget what she was doing. She could barely acknowledge that she was betraying the love she felt for the man in the next room. It was necessary for her to do what she did. No matter how much it hurt.

She sucked his lower lip into her mouth and slowly let it out before she pulled back.

"I don't play."

"I can see that, *querida*. What do you want from me?" He cupped her behind and rubbed his cock against her mons.

She was startled to realize she'd made him hard by kissing him. She had wondered if she could arouse him. Now a surge of confidence battled with the uncertainty and fear churning in her gut.

"I want a little boy." Now that the words were out of her mouth, she wanted to swallow them back. Judging by the way Rodrigo's eyebrows shot up, she had rushed her request.

"In your bed? I did not think you were that dark, but perhaps I was wrong."

"No, not in my bed." Her stomach threatened to regurgitate her food at the thought. She tried not to show him the disgust she felt that he had jumped to such a twisted conclusion. "I lost my boy last year. He was five and Stuart has promised me another one, but he hasn't let me keep any we took."

His eyebrows now lowered into a scowl. "You lost your boy? You are a mama?"

Olivia let her grief well up and her eyes stung with tears. "Elliott died from a fever. I've missed him every day since." Using Benjy's middle name made her heart pinch so hard, she gasped at the pain.

"Why don't you make another boy?" Rodrigo's hard staff had waned and she knew her window of opportunity was shrinking.

"I can't. Elliott's birth was too tough on me." She pushed her breasts into his chest. "I want another boy like him. If Stuart can't or won't, I need you to."

His face reflected no emotion as he stared down at her. She ran her hands up his arms, not surprised by the width of his shoulders. His scent surrounded her, making her all too aware he was not Brody.

"You have beautiful eyes, Meredith. Such a strange color." He wrapped his arms around her so tightly she couldn't move and it was almost hard to breathe.

"Th-thank you, Rodrigo." She managed a small smile. "Now where were we?" She lapped at his neck, the taste acrid on her tongue and lips.

His cock pulsed against her and she knew she had distracted him from her foolhardy attempt to buy a child from him. She knew it was likely impossible that Benjy was not already sold to the highest bidder, but she'd had to try.

In a split second, Rodrigo was yanked from her and Olivia stumbled at the sudden change. She heard flesh against flesh and grunts. By the time she was able to regain her balance and look up, she saw Brody locked in battle with Rodrigo.

"No!"

The two men were grappling for control, even as Brody landed a punch to Rodrigo's jaw. She tried to grab the outlaw's arm as he pulled back to retaliate. Instead, he punched her and she fell backwards. She landed hard on the rough wooden floor, her teeth clacking together enough to vibrate through her skull.

Her cheek throbbed from the fist, but she got up, ignoring the pain and tried again to intervene. An elbow landed in her shoulder and her foot was smashed beneath a boot, but she managed to wiggle between them.

"Stop. It. Now." She reached up and pinched both of them under the arm.

"Jesus." Brody jumped back and glared at her.

"*Puta,* you do not dare touch Rodrigo like that again." The outlaw had changed into a different person. Gone was the seductive grin and gentle tones. He looked more like a thundercloud with dark rage covering his face.

"Don't call her a whore. And if you ever put your hands on my woman again, I will fucking kill you." Brody punctuated his threat with one finger to Rodrigo's chest.

The sound of a gun cocking was the next thing Olivia heard over the roaring in her ears.

"You dare not touch Rodrigo like that again." Lucinda repeated exactly what her son had just said, in her own quiet, deadly way. She put the gun to the back of Olivia's head, the muzzle cold and hard against her skull. A trickle of sweat rolled down her back.

Her mouth went cotton dry and the reality of the situation hit her square between the eyes. Ignoring Brody's warning and pushing ahead to find information about Benjy might have cost them both their lives.

"I will kill her and then you if you do not step away from *mi hijo* right now." Lucinda pushed the gun even harder into Olivia's skull, enough that she sucked in a breath of pain.

"Don't hurt her." Brody wasn't asking and he sure didn't look scared. Heck, she was scared enough for both of them. This was all her fault, every heart-pounding second of it.

It could cost her the man she'd come to love and the brother she ached to hold again.

Stupid, stupid, stupid.

Lucinda clucked her tongue. "Get down on your knees, big man, and put your hands behind your head." Her thick accent was gone, her voice steely flat. Perhaps she wasn't Mexican born either.

Olivia had no idea who either of these people were, or even who they pretended to be. She had stepped into a world of shadows and deceit. Brody had been right about her—she had no idea what she was doing. She caught his gaze and saw nothing in his eyes but anger as he got to his knees.

Olivia's eyes pricked with tears and she had to stomp down the self-pity that rose within her. She was big enough to admit when she'd made a mistake, a huge one.

"I'm sorry," she mouthed.

He shook his head and looked away, his hands locked behind his head. Rodrigo snatched the gun from Brody's holster while Lucinda took Olivia's from her skirt pocket.

Lucinda punched Olivia in the back and pain radiated from the spot. She dropped on her knees and fell forward, landing hard on her wrists; pain shot up her arm.

Olivia bit her lip to keep the moan of agony locked inside as she straightened up. She refused to give them the satisfaction of seeing her suffer.

"I can kill you both right now and no one would care." Lucinda knocked Brody on the side of his head with the butt of the pistol. It wasn't hard enough to knock him over, but she drew blood. A few drops welled up at the spot, which was already turning red.

"Whoever had to clean the floor would care." Olivia hardly believed she'd had the audacity to say that.

Rodrigo chuckled in that low, unusual way of his. "I like you, Meredith." She noted he wasn't calling her *querida* any longer. Perhaps Brody's threat had meant something to him after all.

"Then let us up and you can do business with Stuart." She clenched her teeth to keep them from chattering. Panic wasn't pretty and it certainly wasn't going to help the situation.

"You like her because she is a *bruja* with a big mouth." Lucinda kicked Olivia in the knee. "Not many women dare to talk back to you."

Rodrigo smiled at her and in his face, she saw her own death. He would have no compunction about killing her or using her before he did.

"Put them downstairs and tie them up," Lucinda ordered and Manuel appeared by her side, rope in hand.

Olivia had to do something to stop this.

CHAPTER TEN

Brody wanted to spank Olivia at the same time he wanted to put her behind him and beat his chest while he roared. She brought out a jealous side of his nature he didn't even know he had.

His entire body still shook with the rage that had coursed through him when he saw her in Rodrigo's arms, his mouth on hers. He'd seen red and every smidgen of his training as a soldier and a ranger had left him. He'd been a primal being, not a man.

Even now he had trouble controlling himself. Manuel, Rodrigo and his bitch of a mother pushed them through a trapdoor in the kitchen floor. It led down a set of narrow stairs into what appeared to be a hiding spot. Likely it was used when they were hiding from the army or other outlaws. They might even hide goods, or people down there when needed.

It was dark, pitch black, and several scurrying sounds alerted him to four-legged critters crawling around the dirt floor with them. Rodrigo pushed just enough to make Brody tumble down the last two steps and land on his knees, unable to stop his fall with his hands tied behind his back. The bastard's laugh was like rusted nails on his skin. He held up the lantern and *tsked* while Manuel

stood by holding Brody's gun, his big face never reflect-
ing a single emotion.

"*Pobrecito*. The big gringo is weak and frail, Mama.
He can't even stay on his own feet." The outlaw just
smiled as he walked around Brody, the pistol in his other
hand. He gestured to Olivia, who stood a few steps from
the bottom, her hands also tied. Her eyes were wide
with fear and anger. "Your hero, *señorita*."

She walked to his side, her back straight and shoulders
squared. Olivia was a soldier whether or not she knew
it. Awkwardly, she reached down and pulled under his
arm until he got his footing and rose.

Brody was proud to stand next to this woman. His
woman.

"We came here to do business."

"You came here to sniff around," Lucinda said from the
step where she stood. "I do not like gringo*s* who lie."

"Everyone lies. I told you the truth about doing business." Brody's hands were starting to go numb, but he
didn't react to the pain. "We need a buyer for our goods."

Lucinda shook her head. "I do not think that is all you
came for. We will find the answer one way or the other."
She shared a look with Rodrigo before she disappeared
back up the stairs.

Rodrigo held the lantern up. "You stay here until you
tell us what you want. What you truly want."

When the outlaw moved toward Olivia, a growl
sounded and Brody was surprised to realize it had come
from his own throat. He had just snarled at another man
for moving toward his woman.

Damn, that felt good.

He still wanted to pound the shit out of him, badly
enough he could taste it.

Rodrigo held up his hands and chuckled again. If there was one thing Brody promised himself, it was to stuff that obnoxious laugh down the bastard's throat.

"I won't touch her. For now." With one last wink at Olivia, Rodrigo turned. "*Vamanos*, Manuel." The outlaw bounded up the steps with the lantern, followed by his hulking man. The thud of the trapdoor closing made Olivia jump beside him. Total darkness closed around them.

For a moment, the only sounds were their breathing and the occasional scuttle from the corner.

"Well, shit," Olivia snapped.

At first Brody could hardly believe his ears; then he started laughing. He couldn't help it. The situation was grave as hell, but knowing she was still fighting, and now cursing, gave him a fresh burst of fight.

"Shit is right. We're in it up to our noses and now we've got to get out of it." He twisted his hands but only succeeded in tightening the already too-tight rough rope. "Turn around and let me see if I can loosen your knots."

She bumped into him, her trembling hands cold as ice. He knew she was scared but he held his tongue. Her impulsive streak had led both of them to this. Trying to find a buyer was risky enough, but bringing a woman with him into Mexico had to be the dumbest thing he'd ever done. It didn't matter if he was falling in love with her or that he had been the one who'd announced she was his partner. If he could rewind the clock, he would have left her behind.

At least she'd still be safe.

Instead, she was tied up in a dark root cellar in Mexico. They would both probably be dead within a day. His fingers were going numb and all he could do was pluck at the knots.

"Damn. I can't even feel my hands anymore." He gritted his teeth.

"Did you see anything down here we could use to cut the ropes?" She tugged at the knots on his wrists while she talked.

"There's nothing down here but dirt and rat shit." From what he saw, Lucinda kept nothing down in the cellar. Likely so she could use it for situations like this. Maybe there were even bodies buried beneath the dirt under his feet.

"Did he have to tie the knots so tight?" she growled and a second later, he felt her tugging at his knots, *with her mouth.*

"What are you doing?"

He didn't know whether to be proud of her or tell her to stop. The rope was rough on his skin. It would tear up her mouth. Her lips grazed his palm as she snarled at the knots and the wet swipe she left behind could have been spit, snot or blood.

"Stop, Liv."

"No." She kept at it, the wet spot growing larger.

The idea she was bleeding on him to loosen the knots was impossible to accept. He was a man, a Texas Ranger, for God's sake, and his woman was sacrificing herself for him. What the hell kind of man was he? He needed to be the one to save her—she'd already saved him more than once.

"Stop." His voice had turned colder than the air, harder than the steel in her spine.

Olivia ignored him. Again. Frustration roared through him.

He started to step away and force her to stop when she gave one more huge tug and groaned loudly. To his surprise, the rope loosened. Olivia finally let go and he heard her rear end hit the dirt floor.

"That tasted disgusting." She spat somewhere to her right.

"Dammit, Olivia. I told you to stop." He feared that Manuel was stationed at the top of the stairs, but his voice came out as a low growl. How dare she not listen to him and continue doing what would hurt her? Women were not supposed to behave like she did. Yet she continued to do it.

What did that say about him? He was either half a man or he was lucky enough to have found the one woman in the world who acted like a man, but looked like a woman. With soft skin and a steel spine, she was still his conundrum. One who drove him absolutely loco.

"Too bad for you. I did what I had to." She grunted and pushed against his leg. "Now help me up so you can untie me."

He yanked at the rope until he was able to free his hands, then reached down and pulled her to her feet. He wanted to be rough with her because he was furious, blinded by his pride and his frustration.

But he wasn't.

Instead, he wrapped his arms around her. The thump of her heart against his diffused the righteous anger churning inside him. She pressed her forehead into his neck and blew out a breath, the gust cooling his overheated skin.

"Can you untie me, please? I promise I'll say I'm sorry if you do." She made an odd sound and tried to move out of his arms.

"Not yet." He held on tight, unable to let go. A rush

of emotion almost overwhelmed him and he needed to hang onto her. So much of his life had been spent in blissful ignorance of emotions. Until Olivia had to spoil it for him.

Now he was caught in her net, stuck in her web, or whatever else he could think of to call it. He was worried about her, being angry, amused, annoyed, hell, even in love with the damn woman.

What had she done to him?

He swallowed the lump that had appeared in his throat, another nuisance brought about by the infuriating woman in his arms. There had to be a way to save her, regardless of what happened to him. Brody could not watch her die.

"If you don't untie me, I'm going to kick you in your man parts."

Brody found himself wondering if she really would kick him and realized he already knew the answer. Of course, she would. He reluctantly let her out of his arms and spun her around.

After untying her, he rubbed her hands to get the blood back in them, and his. A small moan sounded from her and it sent a zing through him, at a completely inappropriate time. He sent his stupid cock a stern order to stop listening to Olivia and released her hands.

"Now we need to get out of here."

"And how do we do that? Manuel is likely sitting on the trapdoor." She moved away from him in the dark.

"What are you doing?" He was having trouble thinking straight.

"Looking for something to help us. What are *you* doing?" Rustling sounds and shuffling sounded from the other side of the cellar.

"Trying to figure out why you scramble my brain."

"That's not helpful, Ranger. We need to get out of this place before they decide to bury us down here."

Apparently, she'd had the same thought as he about the dirt floor beneath them. As he listened to her feel her way around the basement, he couldn't help wondering what any other woman would do in the same situation. Probably fall to pieces.

Not Olivia. Not his woman.

His mind took that moment to start working again.

"Oh, dear God, what was that? I'm going to need to wash my hands." She stopped moving. "Are you going to help?"

"No." He walked toward the stairs.

"No?" She shuffled back toward him.

"No. We don't need to find a weapon. We need to get Manuel down here." He held out his hand and somehow her small hand slid into his. Yes, *yes*, that was exactly where she belonged.

She squeezed his hand. "What's your plan?"

He grinned into the darkness. "We're going to trick him. Do you remember showing your wares for the outlaw back in Texas?"

She chuckled. "So I get to bare my assets again?"

Brody squashed a spurt of jealousy. "They're certainly pretty enough."

"You think they're pretty?" To his surprise, he heard doubt in her voice.

"Jesus, Liv, I can't stop thinking about them." He reached down and cupped one breast. "They are just like the rest of you. Beautiful."

Her breath caught and the silence was thick between them.

"Thank you." For Olivia, humble was a first.

He kissed her hard. "You're welcome. Now let's seduce Manuel."

Olivia's throat was dry, her heart pounded and her stomach quivered. It wasn't because of the danger, or the fact she was currently unbuttoning her blouse. It was because Brody had told her she was beautiful. *Beautiful*.

It made her a bit giddy. And apparently stupid because what she should have been thinking about was Manuel and getting out of there, not what the ranger thought of her.

When he reached for her blouse, she reminded herself he was just helping her get ready. His nimble fingers made quick work of the top half of the buttons and soon the dark, damp air caressed her skin. It was likely a good thing he couldn't see very well or he would have noted how hard her nipples were.

"Did you loosen your hair?" His voice wasn't romantic in the least as he spread open her blouse.

"Doing it now, boss man."

"For once could you stop fighting me and do what I ask?" He stopped and his hot breath blasted across her cheek.

This was her opportunity, the moment to tell him what she thought, felt and needed.

She could be rejected.

She could be insulted.

She could be laughed at.

Despite all that, Olivia reached down deep inside and summoned up the courage to speak.

"If you would ask me, I would follow you to the ends of the earth, barefoot. But you don't ask." She reached out blindly and found his whiskered cheeks, cupping the rough-hewn jaw she knew so well. "You bark, order and tell me what to do. In case you hadn't noticed, Ranger, I'm already in love with you. All you have to do is *ask*."

Oh, Lord, her stomach picked that moment to get antsy. How embarrassing it would be to vomit on him after telling him she loved him.

The silence between them ticked by with the beats of her heart. Finally, she felt another gust from him. This time, it was a sigh.

Her heart cracked and she caught her breath against the sudden pain. It hadn't been worth the risk. She had thrown herself wide open for him and he had rejected her. Her luck with men was lousy. There was something about Olivia that made them sample the goods but not stick around to sit at her table.

Intent on forgetting what she'd just done, she removed her hands and made to finish her hair. He grabbed her wrists, stopping her cold. Her aching heart thudded against her ribs as she waited for him to speak.

She waited ten long seconds before she gave up again and tried to pull away from his hold.

"No. I mean, no, please." Brody sounded different, softer and unsure. This was not the ranger voice she knew. Could her little speech have meant something to him? Dared she hope?

"Brody?"

He pulled her hands toward him and to her surprise he kissed them, his lips warm against her skin.

"I ain't good with much, but I'm good at being a soldier, at being a ranger." He slid her hands into his and held tight. "I ain't very good with people either and don't give much thought to anything but what needs doing. I'll try to remember to ask instead of tell."

It wasn't the confession of undying love she wanted, but it was enough to make her eyes prick with emotion. He did care for her. She knew that now. He didn't know how to tell her, so he offered to show her.

By asking because she wanted him to.

It was enough for now. She would take it like the gift it was and be patient for more. Or at least as patient as she could be.

"Thank you, Brody." She leaned in and found his lips for a soft kiss.

He stood up, bringing him with her and found her mouth again. This wasn't soft and it wasn't quick. He plundered her mouth, his tongue rasping against hers, even as he ground his hips against hers. This wasn't the time to be losing themselves in a kiss, but she didn't care.

She wrapped her arms around him and pushed her already hard nipples against his chest. Her body was alive, pulsing with a thousand points of light. This was what she found with him, what made them a match. Her former fiancé had never moved her to heights with a simple kiss.

Brody groaned low in his throat, an animal sound that vibrated through her. She scratched at his back, eager for more, to join with him.

Brody tore his mouth away and sucked in a breath. "Much as I'd like to take you right here, right now, I can't." He started to pull away from her and she heard herself mewl.

Mewl?

Olivia didn't remember ever making such a noise. Then again she had never ached with such a need before. Her entire body thrummed with the intense desire to spread her legs and bring him inside her. She needed it. Now.

She reached for him and found his cock hard and pulsing beneath his trousers. As she squeezed, he hissed out a breath.

"We can't."

"Please." She yanked at his buttons, needing him. Now.

He halfheartedly tried to push her hands away. As soon as she released his staff, he stopped pushing away and instead thrust his cock into her questing fingers.

She leaned down and licked at him, his taste salty mixed with his own unique flavor. Her need was desperate, to possess him and be possessed by him.

"I can't last." He reached down and picked her up. "Spread your legs. Uh, please."

Olivia couldn't stop herself if she tried. She was already wet, throbbing with need, the moisture already coating her folds. She opened her legs wide, wrapping herself around him. He leaned her up against the wall and fumbled to find her in the pitch black.

"Hurry."

"I'm trying, dammit."

She squirmed against him, hanging onto his shoulders, her entire body on fire. He pressed at her entrance and her nails dug into his back.

"Yesssss." Pure pleasure coursed through her and he joined with her in one hard thrust. Oh, yes, yes, yes, this was what she needed. *Needed.*

His mouth found hers. "You've got to be quiet or we'll have company before we're done."

Olivia had forgotten where they were but his reminder didn't put a damper on her need. She squeezed his cock with her inner walls, enjoying the shudder that went through both of them.

She whispered in his ear. "Then fuck me fast and hard. Please."

If anyone heard her now they wouldn't believe it. Olivia Graham had become a wanton.

And she loved it. She loved him.

She spurred her man into action by squeezing him again. She reveled in the feeling of having him embedded within her. She'd never felt so perfect, so right, anytime in her life. Brody had been made for loving her and she had obviously been made to hold him inside her. Perfect.

He grasped her hips. "Get ready, honey."

Olivia hung onto his shoulders, her nose pressed into his collarbone, breathing in his scent. He filled her in every way possible, from her heart, to her body, to her head. Brody became part of her in that moment.

As her body began to reach its peak, she pressed her mouth against his neck, tasting him. The salty tang on her tongue sent her over the edge. She moaned into his skin and she felt an answering moan from him against her temple. He slammed into her, sending her into a whirlpool of pleasure.

She closed her eyes tightly, stars exploding behind the lids. He whispered her name as his seed pumped into her, his cock still as hard as stone.

"Jesus, woman, what have you done to me?" His shaky question made her smile.

"I'm fairly certain the same thing you just did to me."

He chuckled, the gust of air cooling her overheated skin a little. "We shouldn't have done that."

She found his mouth and bit his lip. "What did you say?"

A beat passed, then another, before he spoke. "I'm glad we did that."

This time she kissed him. "Me too."

She squeezed him one more time, sending tingles

straight from her core out to every nerve ending. With regret, she lowered her legs until her feet touched the dirt floor. He pressed a piece of cloth into her hand without a word.

Again, she was touched by the unspoken way he expressed himself. Although he didn't say the words, she knew he cared. She cleaned herself up and straightened her clothes. When she took a step forward, her legs shook. Hell, her entire body shook from not only the effort to hold herself up but from the sheer bliss she'd just found with Brody.

He pulled her into his arms. His heat surrounded her and she leaned into him. Brody kissed her forehead. "Are you ready?"

"Yes. I'm ready." The steady tattoo of his heart beat against hers and she knew then everything would be okay. They had to stay together and work together, but that certainty was enough for her to find another burst of energy and strength.

Time to seduce Manuel.

She pulled away from Brody and ran her fingers through her hair. "You need to lie on the floor."

"What?" His tone told her there was a deep scowl on his face.

"This won't work if you question my plan." She turned toward the stairs. "Lie on the floor, please."

She felt rather than heard him cursing under his breath, but it was followed by shuffling as he got on the floor. Olivia had no time to enjoy her triumph. She had to get Manuel downstairs, which was easier said than done.

The plan would fail if he wasn't there or worse, if he ignored her. She had to convince him to get back down there somehow.

Olivia dug down and remembered how she'd felt

when she'd come home to find the carnage at her home. The terror and pain at the knowledge her parents were dead and Benjy gone. She tasted all the horror and her stomach roiled at the memory.

Then she put her hands behind her back, opened her mouth and called for help.

"¡Manuel! ¡Ayudame, por favor! ¡Ayudame!"

Tears rolled down her cheeks without even calling them. Memories were powerful enough to evoke the kind of raw emotion she found coursing through her. Perhaps it was due to the fact she'd just confessed to Brody how she truly felt or her very real fear they would die.

It didn't matter the reason. She heard terror in her own voice, and no doubt the big man upstairs heard it too.

Heavy thumps sounded above her and she repeated her cry for help.

"¡Manuel! ¡Ayudame, por favor! ¡Ayudame!"

The trapdoor opened a sliver, sending a painfully bright shaft of light down into the inky blackness. The sting in her eyes lent more tears to her eyes.

"¿Que paso?" Manuel sounded unsure. Step one, complete.

"Necessito ayuda, por favor, señor. Mi hombre es muerto."

Olivia wondered if Brody's eyebrows had gone up when she'd told Manuel he was dead.

"¿Muerto?"

"Sí, muerto. Por favor, Manuel, ayudame." A small sob bubbled up and she let it loose, then stepped into the shaft of light so he could see her.

She wondered what he saw. A woman with wild hair, a blouse open to her breasts, swollen red lips, tear-stained cheeks. She could only pray he found her appealing or her plan wouldn't work.

A full minute passed before she heard Manuel curse and open the trapdoor completely. His heavy footfalls down the steps made small dirt clods vibrate on the wood beneath him.

Step two, complete.

Olivia backed up so he could still see her but she was out of the direct light.

"*Gracias, Manuel.*" She gestured to Brody's prone form with her shoulder. "*Aquí.*"

Manuel didn't turn to Brody. He licked his lips as his gaze traveled down her body, then back again, stopping on her breasts. Without any underthings, they were clearly visible and her nipples were clearly hard. Stress or leftover passion may have been the cause, but either way, the sight drew him like a moth to flame.

"*Señorita, puedo darle el placer.*"

I can give you pleasure.

Olivia opened her eyes wide and prayed Brody was as fast and as capable as she thought he was.

"*Señor, mi hombre necessita ayuda.*"

Manuel stepped toward her, apparently uncaring that her man needed help.

Step three, complete.

She didn't even see Brody move. One moment Manuel was looming over her, the next he was face first in the dirt with the ranger's arm around his neck.

"Gun."

Olivia jumped at Brody's terse hiss and reached for the pistol tucked into Manuel's waistband. Before she could even straighten up, the tables had turned and suddenly Brody was on the bottom, being choked.

She didn't think, she simply pointed the gun at Manuel and pulled the trigger.

CHAPTER ELEVEN

Brody pushed the big man off with effort, the body rolling into the dirt. He took a moment to catch his breath before he got to his feet. Someone had probably heard the gunshot. Perhaps they'd thought it had happened out in the street. The earthen walls would muffle it somewhat, but they had to move fast.

Olivia stood with the gun in her hand, staring down at Manuel's body. She'd committed more acts of violence in the time they'd been together than she had in her entire life. Now she had killed a man again for him. He would owe her his life a few times over.

He took the gun from her without a blink. She looked at him with pain in her eyes. He wanted to take that away from her but he didn't know how.

"We need to go. Now."

She nodded but didn't move. He took her by the hand and led her up the stairs, keeping the sound to a minimum. Before they got completely up, he peered around but didn't see anyone. The kitchen was quiet so he took a chance and they climbed out of the trapdoor.

He shut the door as carefully as he could, then realized they weren't alone in the kitchen.

Elena.

She didn't say a word but stared at them in her intense

way. Her hair was down, out of the perpetual braid she wore. The long black waves only accentuated how beautiful she was. Too bad she was all icing and little cake.

"We're leaving." He found Olivia's hand and pulled her close.

"Bueno." Her gaze flicked to Olivia's. "You will not find him here."

Olivia caught her breath. "What?"

"The boy you look for. You will not find him here."

"Can you—" Olivia never finished her question. A crash out in the main tavern stopped all of them.

Elena started walking toward the corner of the kitchen. "Come."

Brody would have made his own decision two weeks ago. Today he looked to the woman at his side and when she nodded, they both followed Elena.

It appeared as though she was taking them straight toward a solid wall, and then she disappeared from view.

"What the hell?" Brody caught up to Elena and realized there was a hidden door behind the wall. It was built to blend in perfectly with the wall.

They squeezed through the small opening into a dark space. He had to trust Elena was not leading them into a trap as he followed her blindly. Olivia kept close behind him, her hand firmly attached to his.

After what seemed like twenty minutes, although was probably three, light penetrated the gloom. Elena held another small door open, gesturing with her hand to hurry.

What choice did he have? They might only have minutes before they were discovered. He had no reason to trust Elena, but who else could he trust? No one in this place.

Olivia poked him in the back. "What are you waiting for? Go."

She was right, of course. They either escaped or they were killed or captured again. Standing in the cramped passageway was only going to give him cobwebs in his hair or a crick in his neck.

Brody started moving again and crowded through the small door. To his surprise, they were in a barn. He hadn't realized the buildings were connected. Either they had walked underground, which was unlikely because the passageway wasn't sloped, or the passage was camouflaged from the outside. Anyone walking past wouldn't notice anything out of the ordinary. Lucinda and Rodrigo were smart, he knew that, but they were smarter than he'd thought.

Elena led them to the stalls where their horses munched placidly on feed. She stood there staring as Olivia and Brody started to saddle their horses with as little noise as possible.

He had just smoothed the blanket on the gelding's back when Elena appeared beside him.

"You must leave Mexico."

"I figured that one out on my own." Brody reached for the saddle. "I appreciate your help getting us out of there."

She waved her hand as though dismissing his gratitude. "My mother and brother do not own me. I do as I want, not as they want." She leaned in close, her breasts pushing into his arm. "You must tell her not to come back. The boy is not here."

As Brody looked into Elena's dark eyes, he thought he might be hearing the truth for the first time. "Where is he?"

"I do not know. Three boys were sold to work haciendas in Texas. One was not." She blinked rapidly. "He was left near the arroyo east of here."

Brody's jaw tightened to the point he heard teeth crack. "Who killed him?"

"Rodrigo. I do not know which boy, but I do know the one you seek is not here." Her fingers bit into his arm. "You must never come back."

After he nodded, she moved away. Brody would sort out all she'd told him later. For now, he would heed her warning and hightail it out of town. He finished saddling the horse and checked on Olivia. To his surprise, she was finished as well. He kept forgetting she was a rancher's daughter and likely spent every day on a horse.

Another reason he felt at home with her at his side. They were a perfect match, even if he didn't say it out loud.

"Lead the way." He turned to Elena but she was gone. "Shit."

"We need to go east, back toward Forgata. Then we can turn toward home." Olivia held up a sack. "She even gave me food."

The mystery of Elena would likely never be solved. She did things no woman ought to, yet she had showed remarkable kindness to them as well.

"She told me there's a back door to the barn that we can use." Olivia tied a dark cloth around her head to disguise her hair. She took her mare's reins and led the way.

Brody wondered how many women would be so calm in the face of mortal danger, or the aftermath of killing a man, or if any woman would have followed him this far into hell. Likely not.

"Here it is." She walked into another stall and sure enough there was a door just large enough for a horse to fit through if it ducked its head. Another clever escape route unnoticeable to most.

She went through the door first with Mariposa and he brought up the rear. They were hidden from view from almost every building in town since there were few with windows facing east.

"She also told me to avoid the arroyo just east of here but wouldn't tell me why." Olivia mounted her horse and turned to him, a challenge in her eyes. "You know, don't you?"

He avoided her gaze as he got on his own horse. They had to keep the horses as quiet as possible until they were out of earshot of town. That meant they couldn't do much more than a canter for now.

"I don't know."

"You have never lied to me, Brody. Don't start now. If you don't tell me why, I will head for that arroyo and find out what you're hiding." She kneed her horse into motion beside his.

He debated what to tell her but in the end kept silent. She didn't say anything for the next ten minutes as they put distance between themselves and town. He hoped she'd forgotten it.

But she hadn't.

"You have about two more minutes." Olivia leaned down and patted her horse's neck. "Mariposa is going to fly soon."

Brody glanced behind her at the town. "No one is following yet. We can pick up the pace now."

He urged his horse into a gallop and heard Liv do the same. If he wasn't careful she would find that arroyo and the body left out there by Rodrigo. The question was, should he tell her about it or let her find out herself?

"Elena said your brother wasn't there anymore."

"I know that. She told me too."

Brody hesitated. "One boy did end up in the arroyo but there—"

Before he could finish telling her there was no way to know which boy it was, she had taken off in a dead run. Her horse was fast as hell too.

Shit.

Olivia saw the edge of the arroyo from far away. She leaned down low over the horse, not caring what happened to her. She had to get to that arroyo. God whispered in her ear that she would not like what she found, but she would not be dissuaded from riding hell for leather toward it.

It couldn't be Benjy. It wouldn't be Benjy.

She did not want to be the person who found his body. What would she tell her family? Her heart ached so hard, tears stung her eyes and her breath stuck in her throat.

Closer, yet closer still. She couldn't get there fast enough. Why couldn't she reach the arroyo? Olivia didn't realize she was crying until the wind cooled the tears on her cheeks.

She finally got close enough to recognize a lump at the edge of the dry creek. That shape was definitely a human body, a small human body. Her stomach clenched up enough to send bile into the back of her throat. She had to remember that whatever she found, her family would survive. She would survive.

Olivia pulled Mariposa up hard, a cloud of dust bursting from her hooves. She jumped off the horse, wrenching her ankle but not stopping to care.

"Olivia, wait!" Brody's voice came from far away, too far for her to worry.

The smell hit her first, the rancid, familiar stench of rotting flesh. Then the sound of buzzing flies filled her ears. A small moan crept up her throat. She could do this.

She dropped to her knees and forced herself to look at the body. It was a small boy, dressed in tattered pants and shirt. His left arm was thrown up over his face, as though warding off a blow, and dusty hair was the only thing she could see.

The size and age were right. It could be Benjy. Her stomach roiled, pushing burning bile up her throat. She swallowed with difficulty but the taste remained on the back of her tongue.

She wasn't sure if she could touch him, but did she have a choice? Her heart pounded so hard, her ears hurt, but she reached with a shaking hand for the small arm.

"I just need to see your face, little one. I just need to see who you are." Her tears fell in the dust and her hands trembled as she moved his arm from his face. She clenched her eyes closed for a moment, then another until she had the courage to look into the face of the dead child.

It wasn't Benjy.

Grief welled up inside her, traveling through her heart, into her throat and finally exploding out of her mouth. She screamed with all the pent-up agony flowing through her. Tears fell in rivers from her eyes. She cried for herself, for Benjy, for her family and for the nameless child tossed away like a piece of refuse.

The little body was barely larger than the rock beside it, coated with dried, rusty blood. The sound of the flies filled her ears, the stench of death filled her nose, her mouth. She couldn't stop sobbing, couldn't stop the overwhelming anguish, couldn't find a way to pull herself out of the deep, dark hole she'd fallen into.

She wanted to hurt someone, cause as much damage to them as had been done to her. Her hands turned into claws, her nails digging into skin. She didn't realize Brody had come near her until she felt his hand at the center of her back.

"Liv, it's not him. Even I can see there's no resemblance."

She threw off his touch, turning to snarl at him. "I know it's not him. Do you think I'm an idiot?"

"No, I never thought that."

"Liar." She scrambled to her feet, not caring that snot and tears mingled on her face. "You thought me stupid from the moment you met me. I forced you to take me with you. And now this." A sob burst from her throat. "This poor child is dead and no one will bury him. His parents will never know what happened to him."

She could easily picture Benjy here, in the dirt and covered with maggots, left to rot in the sun. It could be him. A fresh wave of grief scraped her battered heart.

Brody's expression was pained, but she had no time for his hurt. He seemed to understand she just needed to let it all fly. There was no room for anything but her primal rage and sorrow. "He's in Texas."

It took a few moments for Olivia's mind to recognize what he'd said. Her heart jammed into her throat so fast, she choked.

"What?" She grabbed his arm. "How do you know?"

"Elena."

Mention of the whore, no matter whether she was a willing participant in her trade or not, made Olivia's fury rise. She punched him once, then twice, then found herself beating his chest, sobbing. Her mind, heart and soul screamed for Benjy, cried for the unknown boy and wept for her own pain.

She dropped to the ground, not caring that she sat in dirt and muck. The world was a dark, dangerous place and she had had enough. Her heart slowly cracked into a thousand pieces, the pain radiating out to every ounce of her being.

As she slipped further toward the precipice of nothingness, she vaguely recognized that Brody had picked her up. His strong arms held her boneless form. She didn't care where he took her. She couldn't care anymore. She had nothing left inside her to care.

Olivia had given up.

Brody had never been frightened before now. Oh, he'd been in situations where he felt a pinch of fear, but he'd kept his head and got through it. Seeing Olivia collapse into a pile of despair scared him to his bones.

She had been hard as nails, with brass balls any man would be happy to have. The discovery of the dead boy, who was not her brother, had broken her. It was the last thing he'd expected and he damn sure didn't know what to do about it.

The woman had been through hell and back without batting an eyelash, and yet the body of a child destroyed her. It was right sad what had happened to the boy, but he was nobody to her, just a nameless child. Brody didn't understand what had happened to Liv. It upset and scared him.

He didn't like it one little bit.

Olivia was strong, smart, clever and, dammit, he had already admitted to himself that he loved her. He hadn't found the courage to tell her yet and now he could've lost the chance. His stomach quivered at the thought she might not come back from this. He didn't think he would ever be the same if she didn't.

Brody carried her to her horse, realizing she probably wouldn't sit on the mare. He couldn't throw her over the saddle belly down or she would fall off, which meant he had to carry her on his own horse.

They were only half an hour outside of the town they'd just escaped from. No chance they could sit there until she found her head again. They had to keep moving and fast.

"I need you to sit up here for a minute, honey." He spoke softly into her ear and she moaned, a pitiful, disturbing sound. With a little bit of effort he got her up on his saddle, then held her there while he threw himself up behind her. It wasn't comfortable but it would do. They needed to get out of the area before Rodrigo realized exactly what had happened.

Brody hadn't intended on crossing the Mexican warlord. Rodrigo was smart, angry and hungry for power— three things that spelled trouble for anyone who got in his way. If Brody and Liv were lucky, Rodrigo would think they'd died after leaving his mother's tavern. After all, the desert was an unforgiving place.

Perhaps it would be hours before Manuel's body was discovered. Lord knew no one would believe Olivia had been the one to shoot him. Remembering just how close he'd come to dying at the big man's hands made his stomach twist.

Now here she was in his arms, a shell of the woman who had faced down the world with nothing but gumption and a gun. He had to believe she was just exhausted and overwhelmed by everything that had happened.

He had to believe.

Mariposa stood placidly by, waiting. The mare was attached to her mistress in a deep way. He'd never seen the like before. He leaned down to catch the horse's reins and lead her back to Texas. It was time to go home. Without Benjy.

As a man of the law, it stuck in his craw that they hadn't been able to find the boy. Elena had told him three children had been sold to work at haciendas in Texas. He hadn't lied to Olivia—one of those children was probably Benjamin Graham. Elena remembered the boy's eyes because they were so much like Olivia's.

His gelding was strong enough to carry both of them for a while, but not all day. He pushed him for the next two hours as fast as he could go without hurting the horse. They took the long way around Forgata, across the driest land he could find. The less evidence they left the better. In the softer soil, they would be easily tracked.

The next arroyo they found had water in it, which was lucky for them. He pulled the horses to a stop and glanced down at Olivia. Her eyes were open, but she wasn't really there.

"I'm going to get off now. Can you sit by yourself for second?"

She didn't answer but she sat up straighter. He took that as a positive sign and dismounted slowly, keeping his hand on her hip. Once his feet touched the ground, he reached up and pulled her off the saddle.

"We need to water the horses, then get going again." He led her to the edge of the creek as though she was a child. "Let me check it to make sure it's okay to drink."

There was grass growing around the edge and what appeared to be animal tracks on the opposite bank. All good signs, but he learned down to test it himself before he let his horse drink. He knelt with Olivia standing beside him. They were in luck—the water was cool and clear, perhaps fed from a high stream somewhere.

"Drink, Olivia."

To his surprise, she did as he told her without arguing or griping about how he ordered her around. This was not good at all. He had to snap her out of the trance she seemed to be in.

While she drank, Brody brought the anxious horses to the creek. He took in their surroundings, and watched the horizon for any movement. The air was still and fortunately there was no sign of anyone on their trail.

Ten minutes passed while the horses rested and Olivia sat on her haunches at the creek. He wondered if she was remembering the last arroyo and if she was still there. Damned if he had any idea how to ask or how to talk her out of the place she was hiding in.

He wondered if he ever would.

"Are you ready to ride?"

Quiet as the air around her, Olivia rose and took hold of Mariposa's reins. Her silence was spooky. She kept her eyes somewhere behind him, never meeting his gaze.

"We're going to have to ride hard again. I want to try to ride through the day and into the night if we can."

She walked the mare out until she could get in the saddle, then waited for him. Before he'd met Olivia, Brody had thought he might have wanted a quiet woman who would be his mate. That was almost a joke now that he'd met and fallen in love with the storm named Olivia.

Now she'd been reduced to a whisper of a breeze.

The sun sank behind them as they made their way north and west toward Texas. Brody was surprised to see no one following them. He'd truly expected Rodrigo to come after them, if only for his pride. Yet there was nothing.

Brody didn't relax his guard a bit though. He wouldn't be surprised at any sort of retaliation or revenge from a man who was driven like Rodrigo was. He'd never met a man who was as smart, clever or downright conniving. If they'd been on the same side of the border, they might have been friends. He would grudgingly admit to himself that he respected Rodrigo. The man was a force to be reckoned with.

One who had threatened his woman.

Olivia was quiet for the journey, always looking ahead and never at him. Brody hadn't realized just how much she colored the world around him until she had no color to give. He'd complained about her chatter, her enthusiasm and her stubbornness, but he'd do just about anything to get it all back.

"We'll stop once we cross the Rio Grande. Maybe by then you'll find your tongue again." Brody could have been talking to a rock for as much response as he got.

He didn't know who he was angrier at, Olivia or himself. Since their journey began, they had spent every waking and sleeping moment with each other, had the most amazing sex of his life and now here they were, together yet completely apart.

His brothers had died on the battlefield, alone and without family around them. His parents had died when he was a small boy, without family around them. Now he was alone in the world except for the brash, beautiful woman beside him. Was he dumb enough to throw their future away? To let her stay in her cave? If he did, then odds were Brody would die alone without family too.

"That's it. I'm done with this foolishness." Brody

grabbed her reins and his and kicked his horse into a gallop. Mariposa had no choice but to follow at the same speed.

Olivia hung on, her hair flying behind her, shirt still open to her breasts, face darkened by the clay and from the sun beating down on her today. Those blue-green eyes stood out like jewels in a beautiful statue. His heart clenched at the sight of her. She was incredible and, dammit, he wasn't going to let her go without a fight.

They raced across the last few miles to the river, full dark closing in around them. He jumped off his gelding and then yanked her down off Mariposa.

"We're crossing the river." He took her hand and the horses' reins, then led them across the shallow water.

When they reached the other side, he let the horses drink from the river while he found a place to stop for the night. In a cluster of bushes ten feet from the bank he set Olivia down on a rock.

"Stay here."

She again did as she was told.

"You know you're driving me completely loco." He gritted his teeth in frustration as he walked back to retrieve the horses.

After securing them to a mesquite tree near the campsite, he unsaddled both of them and rubbed them down. They had been sturdy mounts, loyal to their masters, even when pushed to the limits of endurance. The sweet grass nearby would be enough for the animals to fill their bellies.

Now it was time to deal with Olivia.

Olivia let the white noise surround her, cocoon her, feeling safe in a bubble of nothing. She couldn't let herself step out of the bubble or something bad would happen. There was pain out there and she wanted no part of it.

She knew Brody was taking care of her, guiding her horse, making her drink and talking to her. Through the bubble, she couldn't hear him and she couldn't respond to him. It was safe in there, so safe. Nothing could hurt her.

Brody picked her up and walked back toward the river. In the dark, the water looked almost menacing. She hung onto his neck, content in her bubble.

When he threw her in the water, the river grabbed her, pulling her under, filling her mouth, her nose, her ears. Olivia could have simply floated away on her bubble, free from pain and the ugliness in the world. She could have escaped for good.

"Dammit, Olivia, don't you dare give up on me."

Brody's shout popped the bubble as though he'd slapped her. She scrambled for purchase, even as the weight of her wet clothes and the water's current dragged her down. She sucked in a lungful of water and stars exploded behind her eyes. She was drowning.

As blackness crept in around her vision, she finally got her feet under her and tried to rise, only to fall down again. Brody's hand found hers and she hung on, pulling herself up using the tether he offered. When her head broke the surface, she tried to pull in air, only to be blocked by the water already in her lungs.

She gasped and stared into his scowling face. He appeared to understand what was happening because he started slapping her back. Water gushed out of her mouth as she coughed up the river from within her. After she got a breath in, she retched up more water from her stomach. Brody held her hand as she stood there shaking in the dark.

"You tried to drown me."

"Nope, if I had wanted that I would have let you float away. Hell, I could've shot you in the head and left you twenty miles back." He snorted. "I saved you from a hell of your own making."

She walked toward the bank. "I didn't make a hell. I was just, um, healing."

"You were hiding."

Olivia shivered as the night air hit her full force. She walked toward the horses, determined not to talk to him any longer. He had done something dangerous and she had almost paid the price with her life.

"You almost killed me."

He grabbed her shoulders and turned her so she faced him. Moonlight lit his blue eyes, making them glow. "I had to do something to wake you up. Truth is, you scared me."

She stared, momentarily silenced by his confession. If anyone had asked her whether the tough ranger was ever scared, she would've said no, never. He was unbendable, unbreakable steel, never blinking in the face of danger or mortal peril. The man was a rock, one she had clung to several times.

Now he told her she'd scared him. Scared him. *Him!* Her mind tried to take in that bit of information but found it was difficult to do. She'd hoped he had feelings for her since she was stupidly in love with him. Did this mean he did feel something? Being scared for her meant he cared about her. Didn't it?

"Why?" she blurted out.

"Why what?" He snagged a blanket from the saddle sitting on a rock and wrapped it around her.

The wool provided welcome warmth. She snuggled into it as she tried to decide whether she should ask him what she really wanted to know.

Do you love me? Because I love you.

"Why did I scare you?" She wasn't as brave as she wanted to be, that was for certain. This was the moment to open up her heart again, but she didn't.

He picked up kindling around the base of the trees and bushes, ignoring her question. She waited before she repeated it, not willing to move too far out onto that limb she was perched on. Brody knelt by the rocks and set the kindling down.

While he built a fire, the moments passed by slower than molasses. She stood there dripping and wondering if she should tell him how she felt. What was the worst that could happen? He could laugh, in which case she'd punch him. But he could also tell her he loved her back.

The prospect made her heart clench.

She opened her mouth to speak. "Brody, I—"

"I saw lots of men acting like you were during the war. Staring at nothing, not talking, not there. Most of those men ate a bullet while no one was looking." He snapped the sticks into smaller ones, the sound making her start. "I knew your brother would tan my hide if I brought you home like that."

Her mouth stayed open from shock while her heart screeched in pain. He'd been worried about what her brother would do? That was his big area of concern. Her brother?

"You're an ass." She walked away, deliberately not stomping her feet as he probably thought she would, and found a nice tree to sit under. Her wet clothes reminded her of the last time she'd been in the Rio Grande, and the chafing that followed. She would be better off removing her clothes now and letting them dry before morning. It would give her the chance to keep away from Brody for a while so she didn't punch him.

She set the blanket on the ground and started wrestling with her buttons to get them undone. Her temper rose and before she realized what she was about to do, she'd yanked hard enough to pop three of the buttons.

"Shit!"

"Did you need some help?" Damn the man for sounding amused.

"No, I don't need help. Especially your help. After all, we wouldn't want Matt to think you'd touched me, now would we?"

"What the hell are you talking about?" He reached for her, but she moved out of his way.

"You are not allowed to touch me right now. I'm liable to kick you in the balls." Her chest heaved with the deep breaths she sucked in. Perhaps if she'd been a woman more in control of her emotions, she could be a lady. Well, she wasn't and likely never would be.

He held his hands up and stepped back. "I almost want you quiet again so you won't cut me to pieces with that tongue of yours."

"Oh, you are one to talk." She took off her blouse and threw it at him. The wet splat gave her a measure of satisfaction. "You just told me you saved me so my brother wouldn't be angry. As though I was an order of wood left out in the rain."

Hurt crept into her tone, much as she didn't want it to. She turned her back on the man who had tied her in knots, then thrown her to the side. His retreating footsteps told her that her message had been received.

With clumsy fingers, she managed to get her riding skirt and boots off. She stood there, wet and naked, warming herself with the tears running down her cheeks.

Damn the man, he had reduced her to the one thing she hated: a crying woman.

She took another fifteen minutes to dry her face and let the night hide her swollen eyes. By the time she returned to Brody, he had built the fire and started a pot of coffee.

"You done yelling at me?" Brody didn't even glance up from the flames.

"You done being a jackass?" Her back went up as quickly as the words left his mouth.

Neither one answered the question, which didn't surprise her. The rest of the night passed in near silence. Brody stood guard, watching the horizon and feeding the tiny fire. He didn't take off his wet things but chose to wear them as they dried. She didn't care one way or the other. If he wanted chafed manly parts, that was his problem, not hers.

She sipped at the coffee in her hands, glad of the warmth, although she wasn't going to tell him thank you. After hanging her clothing on a bush nearby, she had donned the other clothes in her saddlebags. They were wrinkly and not even remotely clean, but they were dry.

The next several days would be difficult beyond measure. Riding with Brody, knowing how he felt, would be like a small knife pressing into her heart, mile after mile. There would be no touching, holding or pleasuring.

It would be a journey of shame, of heartache and sorrow. Not only hadn't she found Benjy, but she'd lost her heart and her hope.

The sight of the Graham ranch should have brought Brody relief. However, it had the opposite effect. His stomach curled into a ball, right next to the blackened remnants of his heart.

His adventure with Olivia was over.

The last few days had been downright torture. She

barely spoke to him, rarely looked at him and sure as hell didn't touch him. When she made up her mind about something, she did not change it.

Like a piece of granite, unable to do anything but be one shade.

The sun had darkened her skin after the mud staining had faded. Now freckles and a light tan made her look so healthy, so alive. If only her eyes were as alive as the rest of her. In the blue-green depths he saw dark emotions, pain and anger, disappointment and confusion. He recognized them as the same stupid emotions swimming around in his own heart. They had made a royal mess of everything and had no one to blame but themselves.

They were out of time and neither one of them was likely to fix anything now. His chest tightened as he watched her expression change from bleak to relieved at the sight of the ranch house.

"Home." It was the first word she'd spoken in eight hours. Perhaps the last he would hear from her.

Movement near the barn told him that someone had already spotted them. He braced himself for the onslaught of Grahams and the possibility of Matt coming after him with a gun. The last thing he wanted was to get into a fight with Olivia's big brother.

Dirt coated his hair, skin and clothes, creases of dust in every nook and cranny. Hell, he even had grit in his teeth. By the end of the day though, he knew he'd be on his way, grime and all. The Grahams wouldn't be welcoming him.

She kneed Mariposa into a gallop, leaving him to bring up the rear. He was in no hurry to do so considering the reception he expected. All he could see was a cloud of dust; all he could hear was a round of squeals and shouts.

What would it feel like to come home to that kind of reception? To know that your family would be happy to see you no matter what? It was a foreign notion, one he couldn't quite understand. A twinge of wistful need sliced through him. Somewhere deep inside he wanted to make that kind of family with Olivia, but his head smashed the notion. They had no future, no matter how much he might wish it.

By the time he arrived at the house, Olivia was in the midst of her three sisters, the girls squealing and hugging her like a pack of baby pigs. Caleb and Matt stood to the side, their gazes locked on Brody. The youngest brother, Nicholas, was on the porch with Eva and Hannah, Matt's wife, watching the general foolishness.

"Armstrong." Matt's tight voice caught everyone's attention. "Glad to see you brought her back alive."

What could he say to that? Any response would get him an ass-whooping with at least two of them on him. He decided to play the diplomat instead and dismounted in front of the porch.

He tipped his hat to Eva and Hannah. "Evening, ladies. I'm glad to see you both again. If it's all right with you, I'd like to get some water and be on my way."

Eva's brows went up and Hannah covered her mouth with one hand. Brody didn't know if they were amused or shocked.

"Ranger, you ain't leaving here that easy." Matt appeared by his side, fury blazing from every pore. "You took my sister to God knows where and you bring her back looking like a cat drug through the mud by a pack of dogs. Not to mention—"

"Shut up, Matt," Olivia snapped. "I'm tired and hungry and in no mood for a pissing match. *I* left and went with the ranger because I had to. The decision was *mine*, not his."

She walked to the house, her shoulders back and head high. Damn, he really did love that woman so much. His foolish eyes even burned at the sight of her.

"Eva, would you mind asking the boys to get water for a bath while I eat?"

"Por supuesto, hija." Eva put her arm around Olivia's waist. "Come inside and eat. You are so skinny!"

The ladies all disappeared inside the house, followed by a sullen Nicholas and Caleb. Both of them shot daggers at Brody with their gazes. Those boys had too much vinegar in them yet.

"You have a lot of explaining to do." Matt hadn't given up. Although his anger was evident, he hadn't shot Brody. Yet. "Where have you been?"

"I had some information I was following up on. Investigating the kidnappings and tracking the source." Brody led his gelding over to the trough, fully expecting Matt to follow.

He didn't disappoint.

"What in tarnation were you thinking when you took my sister with you?"

"Have you met your sister? I wasn't thinking anything. She took over like she was an army general and made me dance to her tune." Brody's laugh lacked any humor. "I couldn't say no."

"Jesus, I know she's like that. But it's been almost a week, Armstrong. A week without a word." Matt took off his hat and ran his hands through his brown hair. With at least a day or two worth of whiskers and a wrinkled shirt, he had obviously been on tenterhooks, waiting for Olivia's return.

The idea that Brody had been the cause of such worry, no matter what he told the Grahams, made him sick to his stomach. He knew what the family had gone through in the last year. Adding onto that pile of tragedy was the last thing he wanted to do.

"I didn't mean to cause any harm, Matt. Things got out of hand." Brody tied off his horse and turned to the other man. "I'm sorry."

Matt's anger deflated at the apology. He pinched the bridge of his nose with two fingers. "Did you find him?"

Brody contemplated how to tell Graham what they'd found. "Do you have any whiskey? I could use a drink to tell this story."

"No, but I've got some of that homemade firewater from Eva's cousin. It will take the paint off wood, but it's a stiff drink when you need one." Matt led him to the tack room in the barn where he pulled out a mason jar filled with clear liquid and two battered tin cups.

Brody sat down on one of the stools. He couldn't remember the last time he'd been so damn tired. When Matt handed him a cup, he started.

"You falling asleep sitting up?"

"I haven't slept in three days." Brody tried to blink away the grit in his eyes. "I was keeping watch when we stopped for the night."

Matt's gaze narrowed. "I'm ready for the story now. Get to explaining, Ranger."

Brody took a sip of the liquid, and it burned like a son of a bitch. Definitely firewater of the raunchiest caliber. Just what he needed. He took another sip and then a deep breath. There was so much to say, he started at the beginning, where his life took a hard right turn without his even knowing it.

He told Matt the story, from the moment Olivia latched onto him for information until their escape from Lucinda's and the harrowing journey back. He excluded the more intimate moments out of self-preservation. At times, he thought Matt might just decide to wallop him anyway. Yet he kept on urging Brody to continue, intent on the tale.

By the time he finished, Matt had swallowed what was left in his cup and stood there by the door, hands on his hips.

"You sure she said he's in Texas?" His question was full of hope and pain.

"No, she said three boys had been sold to haciendas in Texas and he could be one of them. She recognized Olivia because of the eye color." Brody threw back the last of his cup of firewater. "It's unique to your family." When he got to his feet, the world tilted left and then right. He grabbed hold of the bench and tried to stand up straight.

"Whoa there, Ranger. Let's get you in a bed before you fall on your head and break something." Matt led him to a room in the back with two cots. They belonged to the Vasquez brothers, who were obviously not currently using them. "Sleep here. I'll tell the boys to sleep under the stars tonight. They won't mind."

As Brody's head hit the pillow, sleep claimed him almost immediately. It would've been perfect if Olivia had been at his side.

Chapter Twelve

As she climbed into the bath, Eva and Hannah looked at Olivia with pity in their gazes. She knew she'd lost weight, but she didn't think she was that awful.

"Why are you two looking at me like that?"

Hannah looked guilty, her brown eyes wide. "You've been gone for a week alone with a man and you come back dirtier than any human being ought to be. You're thin, angry and about to bust from holding something in you need to let out."

Her sister-in-law was uncanny in her ability to read people. And dammit, she was right again.

Olivia tilted her head back and closed her eyes lest any tears decide to leak out. "It was a hard trip."

Eva cursed in Spanish under her breath. "That man is a *diablo* to keep you away from home so long."

"Not his fault, Eva. I made him do it. He would have left me behind the first day if he had a choice." Olivia took a deep breath. "I never gave him the chance."

The silence in the bedroom was broken only by breathing and by the low sound of murmuring from outside and in the kitchen.

"Did you find him?" Eva's soft question popped Olivia's self-control like an ax to an apple. There was no need to ask who "him" was—Benjy was always on everyone's mind.

"No." This time she let the emotions come, then accepted the comfort of Eva's embrace and Hannah's hands clasping her own. Safe in the fold of her family, Olivia told them her story, stopping only to take a breath.

The women were a rapt audience, caught up in the adventure of a lifetime. One that ended in sorrow and disappointment. And no Benjy.

She didn't tell them she'd fallen in love with the ranger, or that he'd rejected her, that she was just his obligation. There were things she couldn't share yet. Neither one of them pushed for more information, but she could see in their faces they knew it wasn't the whole story.

The bathwater grew cold and Olivia asked Hannah and Eva for privacy. They excused themselves and went to the kitchen to check on supper. Olivia took her time drying off, relishing these moments alone for the first time in a week.

She stood in her room and looked around. It was the place where she'd been a child, but now she was a woman. She was not the same person who had left the ranch, full of righteousness and brimming with energy. Now she was exhausted beyond measure and her view of the world jaded by what she'd seen, what she'd done and what she'd experienced.

The world was an ugly place outside the walls of this house and now she knew that firsthand. There were dangers waiting to surprise unsuspecting girls. There were men who would take advantage of them.

If she was fair to Brody, she had to admit he hadn't taken advantage of her. She'd bullied him into taking her with him and making her his partner. The first joining had also been her idea. She had been so certain she was in the know about it all. Now she recognized she had known nothing.

Brody had taught her a great deal in his own gruff way. Her own stupidity had taught her as well. There were images burned into her memory she could never scrub away. She had done things she could never undo.

Olivia would never be the same person again. It wasn't a bad thing, but it wasn't a good thing either. She couldn't go back to being the same naïve girl she'd been. Brody's touch would never be erased from her skin or her heart.

No matter what, she loved him and it would take an exceptionally long time for that to change. He had taken her heart and she didn't know how to get it back.

She pulled on a clean chemise, another one the talented Hannah had made for her, and crawled into her bed. The familiar scent and feel surrounded her and her breath caught. Home. She had finally come home. As sleep swept over her, she had the thought it was the first time in days she'd slept without Brody by her side.

And she missed him.

Olivia sat up straight in bed, startled to find herself back at the ranch and in her room. Her heart pounded as though it would jump out of her chest. She'd been dreaming of running from danger, but she'd kept tripping and falling, never getting any distance between herself and whatever chased her.

She had shouted his name. That's what woke her up. In her bad dream, Olivia had reached for Brody and he wasn't there. The dream didn't just scare her. It disturbed her at an elemental level that even her sleeping mind needed him.

She had to see him.

Olivia slipped on a clean dress, amazed by the feel of clean clothes and clean skin. Astonishing what she had gotten used to out on the trail, where a bath was splashing in a creek with a sliver of soap or just sand to get clean.

It never occurred to her he might have left already. He wouldn't go without saying good-bye, not even he was that low. That meant he was sleeping somewhere on the ranch and she had to find him.

Barefoot, she crept out of her room and into the kitchen. A shadow moved near the table and she stifled a scream.

"Relax, Liv, it's me." Matt's soft voice came from the head of the table.

She squinted into the darkness, making out his form in the meager moonlight. "What are you doing?"

"Couldn't sleep. I was drinking some milk. Hannah's idea, even though I don't think it will work." He yawned so hard, his jaw cracked. "But she could have been right."

Olivia put her hands on the back of the other chair. "I need to talk to him."

She didn't have to specify whom. Matt wasn't stupid. He had probably already talked to Brody, and hopefully hadn't shot him or punched him.

"Do you love him?"

Olivia expected the question and answered without even a second's hesitation. "Yes. But I'm not so sure he feels the same."

"Oh, I think you'd be surprised." Matt sipped the milk. "He told me what happened. Most of it anyway. I expect there were parts he didn't share."

Good thing it was dark enough he couldn't see her

heated cheeks. No doubt they were flushed and guilty looking.

"We didn't find him." The sorrow couldn't be contained.

"No, but you found out where he'd been. That's one piece of the puzzle." His chair scraped the floor as he stood and rounded the table. "You have got to be the most amazing woman I know, aside from my wife that is."

Her brother's unexpected praise made her eyes prick with tears. She was a lucky woman to have such love from her family. It was a blessing she sometimes took for granted.

"I did what you would have done if you'd been here."

He pulled her into a hug. "Nope, I would have stayed here with Hannah and let Armstrong do the work he's paid badly by Texas to do. You, dear sister, are a helluva fighter."

Olivia smiled into his shoulder. "Thank you." She had missed the noisy Grahams so much, even Catherine's constant chatter and Rebecca's posturing to be more grown up than she was. What she missed most was the way they were a family, despite all their faults and mistakes. They were the circle eight and she would spend the rest of her life trying to make it complete again by finding Benjy.

"Where is he?"

"In the bunkroom. Lorenzo and Javier are sleeping under the stars tonight." He kissed her forehead. "Be careful, little sister."

Olivia couldn't answer him. The last thing she'd been was careful around the ranger. She'd thrown her arms wide open and embraced the danger that filled his life.

Now she would throw caution to the wind once more and try to convince him that he couldn't live without her.

She would get her man, come hell or high water.

Brody dreamt of Olivia: the softness of her skin, the smell of her hair, the sweetness of her taste. She surrounded him, drew him into her world with that mischievous smile and incredible body. He hardened instantly, aching for her.

Her nimble fingers danced up and down his shaft, making his balls tighten. He grew an inch when she squeezed the head with her other hand. Then her mouth closed around the head of his cock and he gripped the bed. Pure fire leapt from the hot, wet recesses of her mouth. Her tongue lapped at him, even as her mouth sucked.

Her hand cupped his balls, her thumb pressing against the base of his dick. As she bobbed up and down on his length, he groaned aloud, coming fully awake.

It wasn't a dream.

Olivia was here, giving him the pleasure of a lifetime. He reached out and found her soft, clean hair and ran his fingers through it.

"You're really here."

He felt her chuckle against his taut skin. She nibbled at the sensitive head and he sucked in a breath.

"God, that feels good."

"Goddess."

It was his turn to chuckle. Olivia might be a loud-mouthed, stubborn, tenacious woman but she was *his* woman. There wasn't another one in the world like her, not that the world could have handled another one.

When his cock touched the back of her throat, he almost came right then and there. His fingers dug into the wooden frame of the cot, embedding a few splinters in the skin.

"Whoa, you need to stop."

"Nuh-uh." She did it again, going deep, pulling and sucking at him.

His eyes rolled back in his head. "If you don't, ah, don't stop, ah, I'm gonna . . . come right in your mouth."

Brody couldn't stop it. He'd warned her, told her to stop, but she kept going, sucking, licking and nibbling him. The orgasm rolled through him and he tried to pull her head away but she remained firm. He was blind for a moment, lost in the sweet rush of ecstasy as she continued to pleasure him even as he twitched.

Guilt filled him. "I'm sorry, honey."

She finally let him loose. "Don't be. I wanted to pleasure you, to feel your life, to conquer you." She chuckled. "Are you conquered?"

He smiled. "More than you know."

Before she could protest, he jumped off the bed and pulled her to her feet. A waft of soap and clean woman made him pause. He realized she smelled wonderful and he smelled like the wrong end of a cow.

"I stink."

"You could use a bath." She offered. "But you don't stink."

He pulled off her dress, followed quickly by her chemise, and then she was wonderfully naked. She shivered and her nipples hardened in the cool night air.

"God, I mean, Goddess, you are perfect." With something akin to reverence, he reached out and cupped the perfect orbs waiting for him. Her skin was softer than anything he'd ever touched, the nipples begging him to taste.

Now it was his turn to get on his knees. He laid her down on the narrow cot as though she was more precious than anything. Then he took off the rest of his clothes and he knelt down.

His mouth closed around her right nipple, so tight and hard. He sucked, nibbled and licked the pink peak. She shifted beneath him, a tiny moan coming from deep in her throat. He switched breasts, finding the left one just as tasty as the right. His hand closed around the now damp nipple, tweaking and tugging in rhythm with his mouth.

She tasted of sunshine, of woman, of Olivia. It was enough to make his cock roar to life, pulsing between his legs within minutes. He had to ignore it though. This was about Olivia and her pleasure.

He moved down her belly, kissing the angel-soft skin, biting and licking sensitive spots. She wiggled and shifted the lower he got. He gently pushed her legs open.

"Brody, what—"

"Shut up, Liv." It was said with as much love as he could put in his voice, but it worked.

Without any further protests, he positioned himself between her legs, sliding up the cot to reach the bounty that awaited. He kissed his way up her legs, delighting in the spot behind her knee that made her gasp each time he licked it. Moving past her knee, he found her inner thighs were as soft as down.

As he drew closer to her core, the scent of her arousal filled his nose. It sent a pulse through him that made his cock, now buried in the blanket, twitch.

He spread her nether lips, the moist folds glistening in the meager light. She was perfect. He ran his fingers down the edges, delighting in the way she shivered at his touch. Brody leaned in and ran his tongue from top to bottom in one long swipe.

Her groan made one of the horses whinny.

He should have told her to be quiet but was enjoying her noises too much. With her musky flavor on his tongue, he dove in for more. He found her nubbin of pleasure swollen, ready for him. As he licked at it, he slowly pushed two fingers into her. She closed around him, pulling him in farther. His cock protested, wanting to bury itself inside her folds, but he ignored it.

"Brody, I can't, it feels . . ."

He continued to lick and nibble at her, his own body reacting with each gasp, moan and shiver she made. Her thighs closed in around his head and he knew she was close. He pushed a third finger into the perfect rosette beneath her pussy.

"Now, now, now," she chanted.

He fucked her with his fingers and sucked her clit, feeling the flutter of her orgasm on his tongue as it began. She let loose a low keening cry and flooded his mouth with the sweet flavor of her pleasure. He kept sucking, licking and fucking her until she begged him to stop.

"Please, stop. I can't even see anymore."

Brody chuckled and kissed her one more time. She twitched and he smiled. He crawled up her body and lay on top of her. They had been in many positions over the week, but never in this one. She was a warm, soft body, but more than that, lying atop her felt like home, as though he had found where he belonged.

As he slid into her wet, tight folds, he shuddered at the emotions, the sensations overwhelming him. This wasn't the first time they'd been together of course, but it was the first time he'd accepted the fact he made love to Olivia.

"Brody." The sound of his name in her breathy tone made his eyes prick with tears even as his body hardened to the point of pain, wanting to move.

When he managed to get himself under control, he began to slide in and out. The delicious friction sent zings of pleasure through him. He clutched the blanket beneath them as he thrust into her welcoming core again, then again.

Her nails scratched at his back each time he pushed in. It was another tingle in the mass of pleasure flying through him. He leaned up on his elbows to look at her, to see the expression of ecstasy on her beautiful face.

Those unique green-blue eyes were half closed, her pupils wide, her expression full. She was exquisite, the most incredible sight he'd ever seen.

Brody loved Olivia. Completely, utterly.

"So close," she whispered. "Close."

He reached between them to find her clit, the swollen nubbin of pleasure slick with her juices. He flicked her once, twice, three times, then her eyes opened wide.

"I love you." Her body clenched around him as she reached her climax.

Moments later, Brody's orgasm roared through him. It was a powerful, knee-buckling force, slamming into him so that stars exploded behind his eyes. Pure joy flooded him as he found the ultimate ecstasy with the woman who owned his heart.

As he came back down to earth, reality hit him in the gut. A Texas Ranger couldn't have a wife, couldn't be tied down. He had to be ready to do his job at a moment's notice.

Brody would have to choose between his job and his woman. He'd never been so unsure of anything in his life.

Olivia knew he was gone the moment she woke. The sounds and smells of the morning went on around her— the hay, the horses, the gentle murmur of voices from the barn. Yet the warmth she had slept with was missing.

And so was Brody.

With a certain amount of pain, she opened her eyes and glanced around. She had been right. His saddlebags, his boots and that blasted black flat-brimmed hat were no longer lying on or beneath Javier's cot.

Still naked, she pulled on her chemise and dressed quickly, before anyone noted she was sleeping in Lorenzo's bed alone. It was embarrassing enough to seduce a man, tell him she loved him, then have him disappear like a thief in the night.

She wouldn't hold out hope that he was in the house having coffee and *huevos* with Eva. No, that wasn't Brody's way. He just did what he thought was necessary. In this case, leaving without saying good-bye.

Although she told herself not to look, Olivia opened the door a crack and peered out into the murky barn. His gelding was no longer in the first stall where he'd been the night before when she'd crept in.

Her heart squeezed so hard she couldn't get a breath in. When her former fiancée had left her following her parents' murder, she'd been sad and angry. She'd thought she had been nursing a broken heart. Now she knew better.

A broken heart was the most excruciating pain she'd

ever endured. She had put herself into his hands, her heart into his keeping, her life into his control. And he had left her behind like a piece of trash he didn't need to keep.

She sank to her knees and pressed her forehead into the wood. Finally, she was able to suck in short choppy breaths, enough to make the rushing sound in her head subside. She wouldn't cry; she had already shed enough tears to last a lifetime.

Her entire body shook as she rode the waves of pain racing through her. If only he had simply told her he was too devoted to being a ranger. Or even that he didn't want a wife to complicate things. Anything but disappearing as though he didn't care enough to even say good-bye.

Oh, God, it hurt. So damn much.

She didn't know how many minutes had passed before she was able to get to her feet. It was pitiful enough she had to use the door to do it; she was absurdly grateful no one could see her. Eva and Hannah didn't know the depth of her relationship with Brody. Thank God she hadn't confessed how intimate they'd become, although Matt knew. The worst possible thing she could imagine would be pity from any of them.

With still trembling hands, she opened the door to return to her own bed. She hoped no one would speak to her because she wasn't in any mood to converse.

Rodrigo stood there, the pistol in his hand pointed straight at her heart. "*Querida,* I've missed you. Why did you leave without saying good-bye?"

Brody rode back from town a changed man. He'd had every intention of riding away, back to Austin for good. Instead, he stopped five miles away and yelled at the sky until he recognized he couldn't live without Olivia by his side.

He'd acted a coward running off like that. She would have confronted the situation head on, ready to fuss and argue about it. Yet he had been the weak one, the man too afraid to tell her he loved her.

Her soft "I love you" the night before had knocked him sideways. She loved him. For all his hard, unyielding and hardass ways, she loved him.

His brothers had loved him in their own way, loyal and steadfast. Yet neither of them had ever shown him what affection was, or that his life would change because of one loudmouthed woman with a gun and an attitude.

There was no other choice but to return to the Graham farm and ask her to marry him, although the prospect made him break out in hives. She was tough enough to live on the trail if need be. He hadn't told her about the family farm he now owned but neglected. It was half a day's ride from her family's ranch, which was not too far from the Graham clan.

He couldn't even consider the prospect of her saying no. That couldn't happen. She'd said she loved him.

Then he'd snuck out and left her.

Granted, it was only for an hour but he had left. He winced at the thought she would be angry enough to say no, just because she was stubborn and hurt. If he was lucky, she hadn't woken up yet. He had left before the sun rose.

The closer he got to the Graham ranch, the tighter his stomach got and the drier his mouth. He was no good with words, no good with women. He had his badge, his gun and his smarts. What else did he need?

Olivia.

He knew it was the truth. Somehow or other he'd

found the woman who matched him in every way, who fought him like a soldier and loved him like a goddess. He'd be two times a fool if he let her get away.

His mind made up, Brody rode toward the ranch house with confidence mixed up with a whole lot of fear. She could still say no, after all.

The front door flew open and banged against the side of the house. Matt Graham stormed out, sparks shooting from his eyes.

"Where the hell is my sister?"

Brody's excitement vanished to be replaced by a very different kind of fear. "I left her here sleeping an hour ago."

"She isn't in the barn or the house or anywhere. Mariposa is in her stall, which means Olivia is missing." Matt pulled a shotgun out from behind him, keeping it pointed toward the ground. "I'm gonna ask you one more time, where is she?"

The air crackled with tension as Brody weighed what to do. He could shoot the rancher before the shotgun trigger was even touched. Not something he wanted to do. No, he had to do this the hard way and hope the other man could see reason.

Brody dismounted slowly, the creak of the saddle leather the only sound in the still morning air. As soon as his boot hit the ground, he raised his hands.

"I swear I don't know where she is." He figured this was the time for the truth. "We were in the bunkroom in the barn. That's where she was when I left. Why don't we go look there?"

"I already did." Matt moved a little closer, although he didn't yet point the muzzle of the shotgun at Brody. "She's not there."

Hannah appeared on the porch, her brown gaze frightened. "Matt, don't shoot the man. He's a ranger, for God's sake. Besides, you sent her out there."

Brody couldn't contain his surprise. Her brother had sent her to the barn, where he knew Brody was sleeping? Their relationship must be more obvious than he'd thought. Either that or this would be a shotgun wedding.

"Can I go look for her? I know I'm not your favorite person right now, but I can track." Brody moved toward the barn, wondering with each step if he was going to make it there without feeling the deadly heat of a shotgun blast.

"She's not there."

Brody ignored Matt and stepped back into the barn. There were fresh footprints in the dirt on the floor and what appeared to be a couple drag marks from bare feet. He squatted and stared at the markings. No rancher boot had made those prints. The heel was squared off and cut deeper than the toe.

"Any of your men wear *vaquero* boots?"

Matt stood in the door of the barn, watching, scowling so hard his eyebrows touched. "No. Lorenzo and Javier don't much like them. Why?"

Brody got to his feet and glanced in, glad to see none of her clothes were left behind. That meant she was dressed when she left. Thank God. She could've been dragged out of there buck naked. "Did she have any shoes on last night?"

Matt threw up his hands. "No, she was barefoot. What the hell is going on, Armstrong?"

The realization of what had happened hit him square between the eyes. Holy hell.

They hadn't lost Rodrigo after all. He had followed them all the way into Texas. To the Graham ranch, the very place where too much tragedy and bloodshed had already happened.

Brody's stomach lurched straight up his throat and he had to swallow down the bile that filled his mouth. Cold, raw fear slid through him.

Sweet Jesus.

"Your sister's been kidnapped."

"What?" Matt's eyes widened. "By who?"

"Who took Olivia?" Caleb's face was flushed.

Nicholas made a grunting sound and charged at the barn like a teenage bull. Matt threw his arm out and stopped his younger brother before he hurt himself.

"Who?" Matt repeated.

"An outlaw named Rodrigo who fancies the title of *caudillo*. We had dealings with him when we were in Mexico. I can tell you more later, but know this, he is ruthless and isn't afraid to kill to get what he wants." Brody would wait until Matt was calmer before he told him the outlaw had sold Benjy six months earlier. "For now let's get moving. They've already got a headstart."

Matt's blue-green eyes, so much like Olivia's, bored into him. "I'll agree to this for now. But later, you will tell me more about Rodrigo and how you got my sister wrapped up in this mess."

"Fair enough." Brody would tell him as much as he could, but there were things that would stay between Olivia and himself. There would be no discussion of who killed whom, or just how close the two of them had gotten. Or that she'd told him "I love you" and he had run off like a coward into the night. No, those would be his moments to hold onto.

"Everyone *move*. Now," Matt barked and everyone jumped.

The Grahams were like an army, commanded by Matt,

with Eva providing instructions when he wasn't in earshot. The horses were saddled, food and water gathered, and guns loaded. Matt, Caleb and Nicholas had the fiercest expressions on their faces that Brody had ever seen. That was real love. Olivia had brought him a forever kind of love and the family he'd never truly had.

"I'm going to blame you if anything happens to her, Ranger." Matt's horse grew restless beneath him, but he kept it under control with his knees.

"So will I." Brody would control his rage and fear for now. When he had Olivia back safely, he would let it all loose on Rodrigo. This time, the outlaw wouldn't live to hurt anyone again.

Olivia was furious—with Rodrigo, with Brody, but most of all with herself. She was tied up like a turkey thrown over the rear end of Rodrigo's horse. Rodrigo's hand pressed down on her back, keeping her in place as he navigated his way through the dense woods. He had obviously chosen this place well since it was the thickest forest within twenty miles of her home.

"*Querida,* you shouldn't have run from me." He pushed down on her back so hard, she couldn't get a breath in.

She considered kicking the horse to start it panicking, but knew she would get herself killed in the fall or trampled. However, she was running out of choices. Spots danced in front of her eyes as she maneuvered her bound feet to kick the horse right in its vulnerable leg. Just as she got in position, Rodrigo released the pressure and air rushed back into her lungs.

"I do not want to hurt you."

"You have a strange way of showing that, *maricon.*" She had learned a few curse words from Javier and

Lorenzo. That one tasted especially good since it shut him up for a few minutes.

He dug his fingers into her back but she closed her eyes and thought of Brody. The ranger wouldn't whine or complain if he were in the same situation. Neither would she.

"You have a filthy mouth. I will take pleasure in making sure it's too busy to talk." His laugh sent a chill up her spine. "I will enjoy it too. Your *hombre* is too protective of you. He should have let us have our pleasure. Now I must kill him."

"You'll never get the chance. He will kill you for taking me." Big words for a woman who had no idea where her man was. He'd already left, either scared or disgusted by her confession of love. He didn't even know she'd been kidnapped.

"Ah, you lie to me, *querida*. He rode away an hour before I took back what he stole. I listened and watched you both and the others at the house." He made a *tsking* sound with his mouth. "You lied to me, Olivia. Another sin to be punished for. Perhaps I will take the little blond girl for payment."

Olivia knew her first pinch of fear. He had been watching her family, her home. The man had hunted her, and now knew where her family lived. He threatened to take Catherine, for God's sake. Sweet, innocent Catherine.

She closed her eyes and took a deep breath, trying to stave off the panic that threatened. If she didn't focus, she couldn't get herself free or help her family. What she needed to do was assess the man, his weapons and the situation, then find his weak spot and strike. She needed a battle plan.

If she reacted to his threat, he would know he had her

beaten. No, she needed to do the unexpected and throw him off balance.

"Of course I lied to you, foolish man. Those people don't know what my life is or how I live it. Do you think I'm stupid? I chose to leave them, to live on the back of a horse, under the sky. Not cooped up in one place for all time." She managed to lift her hips enough to relieve the pressure on her stomach. "We were planning on taking what we needed and leaving by tomorrow."

Rodrigo was quiet for a few moments, perhaps gauging whether she was lying again or being truthful.

"Those people all look like you, the same eyes I think. I have seen eyes that color before."

Her mouth tasted of cold fear, but she managed to form the words she needed to speak. "The youngest. We needed money for guns so I convinced Jeb to take him. There are too many mouths to feed anyway. One less left more for me."

She told her stomach not to react, not to vomit for fear she would choke to death on it with her head hanging down. It was a difficult fight but, in the end, she managed not to throw up.

"You are a cold-hearted bitch, *querida*. I knew there was something about you I liked. You are like me. You want more than life gives you and you aren't afraid to take it." His hand moved to her rump, where he squeezed. "And you are round and soft in all the right places. We will be good together."

The very idea of being with Rodrigo, knowing what he did, what he'd done, and what he intended to do, made fury rise inside her. That was good. Anger would keep fear and panic at bay while she figured out how to get away from him.

"I'm not a cheap whore you can just take." She gritted her teeth.

"Ah, I did not think so." He chuckled, the sound grating on her nerves. "You will be a challenge. This I like."

Was there no putting this man off? He liked her docile. He liked her feisty. He liked her at his mercy. The man just wanted to own her, no matter how she behaved. He made her skin crawl. Fear fluttered back into her heart. Olivia dug deeply, way down to found another cup of courage.

"Well, I don't like being belly down on this goddamn horse. If you want me to be accommodating, you're going to have to be nicer to me." She managed to bang her head into his back. Her ears rang from the contact, but she had the satisfaction of hearing him grunt from the blow.

"I could tie you to the back and drag you instead." His playful tone had been replaced by one as sharp as the knife he'd held to her throat.

"I could bite off your dick too." What possessed her to threaten him, she'd never know. Her heart thumped so hard, her ears hurt, but she hung on and kept working on the knots. She could only reach the knots with her fingertips, but picking at them made her feel better.

She didn't know how much time had passed before they emerged from the woods. Being upside down, she could only see the ground and the horse's hindquarters. She had no idea where they were, or what direction he had chosen to take. The sad fact was she hadn't spent much time in the woods, or even beyond the boundaries of the Graham ranch, until she'd met Brody.

He had taken her on an adventure, shown her what was out there for her to discover. Now she regretted not taking the same opportunity at home. If she had, the ground, the rocks, something might have given her a clue as to where they were.

The sound of another horse's whinny sounded in the morning air. He pulled the horse to a stop and she was thankful for the reprieve from the constant jarring. She lifted her head, but her hair covered her face, obscuring her view. Maybe Brody had followed Rodrigo after all. She couldn't help the burst of hope in her belly.

The rapid-fire commands in Spanish told her it wasn't Brody's horse she'd heard, but someone with Rodrigo. Oh, God, he had brought one or possibly more of his followers. She had a chance against one, but not a group of men.

When she heard Elena's voice, Olivia wondered if Rodrigo had kidnapped her as well, or if she had come willingly. Her brother was a dangerous man, commanding everything and everyone around him. His sister was no exception, regardless of the fact she'd helped Brody and Olivia escape.

"Vamanos." Rodrigo kneed his horse into motion again and Olivia's eyes pricked with tears.

She hadn't cried and didn't intend on crying but, dammit, this entire situation was wearing her down. Discomfort, pain and heartbreak overwhelmed her.

You are too strong to buckle under now, Liv. You killed three men to save my life. You are a survivor, not a quitter.

Brody's voice was so clear in her head, she thought he was hanging right next to her. He was right. She'd be damned if she would give in now.

Olivia was ready to fight for her life.

Brody struggled with self-control. He wanted to howl at the heavens and beat his chest, screaming his fear and self-recrimination. Hiccups of bitter emotion bubbled up his throat and escaped as small grunts. He sounded like a wild boar and damned if he didn't feel like one. He was angry, reckless and ready to kill anything that got in his way.

The Grahams, on the other hand, were cool and collected. The three of them rode with their backs straight and their eyes focused on the horizon. He'd never met Stuart Graham before he died, but the man obviously knew how to raise boys to be men.

Being a soldier, then a ranger, Brody had thought he knew everything about how to be a man. But Olivia and her brothers had taught him the true meaning of loyalty, honor and courage. It was as humbling as it was frustrating.

He wanted a pack of snarling beasts at his side, ready to tear open the enemy. Instead, he got the Graham boys, who might freeze their enemy to death before they shot him. They were shooting frozen daggers at him from their blue-green eyes right now.

He couldn't look at them, to see the similarity between her brothers and Olivia. It reminded him of his failure to be the man she needed. He had to find her, to tell her he was sorry and that he loved her.

He loved her.

Why hadn't he just accepted that hours ago? Days ago? Stupid idiot that he was, he had ridden away from what was as plain as day, and now he risked losing the most precious gift he'd ever received.

While his mind spun in circles, his eyes were trained on the ground, looking for signs. He found the hoof prints straight off, the deep impressions telling him the horse was carrying two people. They had headed west, off the Graham ranch and into wooded areas. That might have been to throw him off the trail but it had the opposite effect.

A horse tromping through trees and brush left more signs to track. He dismounted as soon as they reached the edge of the forest.

"What are you doing, Armstrong?" Matt snapped. "Get the hell back on your horse and get to tracking."

"I am tracking, Graham. And if you think I'm going to let you order me around like you're my captain, you are mistaken." He turned a cool expression on the eldest Graham. "I am still a Texas Ranger. Right now I'm investigating a kidnapping."

"My sister's kidnapping," Caleb growled, looking much older than his eighteen years.

"It helps me focus if I don't think about her." Brody faltered, his voice breaking as his heart stuttered. "I need to focus on the task, not the person."

He pleaded silently for them to understand. Olivia was the most important thing in the world to him, and he couldn't risk her by going loco. Her brothers were angry with him, rightfully so, but they had to give him a chance to do what he did best. Track and hunt criminals.

Matt's expression relaxed a smidge. "You told me some of the story last night, but the boys don't know yet. You tell us who he is and what happened in Mexico and we'll help you catch him."

It was likely the best offer he would get from them. "Fine. I'll tell you what I know, but we need to keep moving."

Matt dismounted. "Lead the way, Ranger. We'll stay close so you can talk low."

Brody nodded tightly. "Let's go."

They all led their horses into the woods, keeping their

noise to a minimum. The soft bed of leaves and pine muffled the horses' hooves and their boots.

"He has a tavern about two hours into Mexico. Small town, barely a dot on the map. But he owns it. He talks and they jump. Including his sister, who he whores out." The memory of Elena's attempted seduction made him frown. "Tried it with us, but it didn't work. We convinced him we wanted to buy some merchandise, so he took us to his mother."

"What? His mother?" Nicholas's eyes widened and he stumbled on a tree root.

Brody caught his arm to steady him. "She's the coldest bitch I've ever met and I don't wonder where Rodrigo gets it from. We rode to her whorehouse in a bigger town. We tried to get her to buy the merchandise—"

"Wait, what merchandise?" Caleb frowned. "I thought you were looking for Benjy?"

Brody met Matt's sad gaze and realized the younger Graham boys were not quite men yet. "He was the merchandise."

Nicholas and Caleb's faces were ashen at that bit of information, but they kept on walking.

"We tried to make a deal with her, but she got suspicious, put us in a root cellar tied up." Brody had flashes of the root cellar and what had happened in the darkness—holding Olivia, kissing her, pleasuring her. He had to physically shake his head to stop the memories from overwhelming him.

"Then what happened?" Nicholas urged.

"We lured one of his men downstairs and killed him." Brody couldn't snatch the words back, but he sure as hell wanted to.

"Who killed him?"

"Olivia."

"You turned my sister into a murderer?"

Brody held up his hand to stop the questions. "He was going to kill us. We survived."

The Grahams all nodded, thank God.

"How did you get away?" Matt's gaze probed his. "You must have been watched."

"Rodrigo's sister, Elena, helped us. She did everything he said, but then she helped us. After we managed to get away, I thought Rodrigo wouldn't bother to chase us down." His words trailed off as he noted the horsehair stuck in the bark of a nearby tree and the broken leaves. The trail was easy to follow, almost too easy. Rodrigo wasn't that stupid.

"He's leading us somewhere. Setting a trap more than likely." Brody stopped and listened. The only sounds around them were the normal birds, squirrels and drone of insects. Wherever he was, the outlaw wasn't in the woods any longer.

A terrible realization hit him and he stopped in his tracks. Elena hadn't bucked her brother's authority when she'd led them out of Lucinda's house. *He had told her to.*

"She let us go on purpose so they could follow us. Probably didn't want his mama to know. Son of a bitch. It was a trap. A goddamn trap." He wanted to punch himself for being dumb enough to fall for it. They had led Rodrigo and his army right to the Grahams' doorstep.

After the terrible tragedy they had already suffered, now there was more to be had. Now that Rodrigo knew where the Grahams lived, he could pick them off one by one.

"Fucking bastard." Brody punched the tree hard enough to draw blood.

"What do we do?" Matt was finally looking to Brody

for his lead, an expression of confusion and fear on his face.

Brody stared at each Graham brother in turn. "We kill him and save Olivia."

It was a moment when they could have all backed away, but none of them did. He saw young Nicholas swallow hard, but the boy held firm, his sixteen-year-old shoulders straight as an arrow. Brody gave them a lot of respect for their decision—they were ranchers, not men of the law. He knew Matt and Caleb had fought in the war, but this was much more personal.

It was family.

"The trail heads northwest, and I'm guessing it leads somewhere on the other side of these woods. He's probably positioned himself and a few men there to pick us off like ducks in a pond." Brody pulled out his pistol and checked to be sure it was loaded.

"What kind of pistol is that?" Nicholas stared at the weapon.

"It's a Colt pistol. Friend of mine just patented it and gave me one." He pointed to the cylinder. "This is a revolving cylinder that spins to the next bullet after you fire."

Nicholas whistled. "That's a nice gun, Mr. Armstrong."

Brody told himself he would gift the gun to the boy if they all survived. "I'm hoping one of you knows your way around here so we can circle the other way and surprise them."

"I do," Caleb volunteered. "I was sneaking off to see a girl last year and her house isn't far from here."

Matt's brows went up, but he didn't say anything. It wasn't the time.

"Good. We're going to have to leave the horses at least half a mile from wherever he's waiting to ambush us. Otherwise, he'll hear us coming. How far do these woods go?" Brody pulled his rifle from its scabbard and checked it too. It wouldn't be as handy as the pistol, but he would get at least one more shot with it.

"About five miles, then there is a creek, about fifty yards wide, then there's more woods on the other side of it." Caleb glanced around at them. "Are we going to die?"

It was a question all of them were probably asking themselves but only Caleb had the balls to ask it.

"I don't know, but if we do nothing, Olivia will die." It was a bald but true statement. "You three can go back home if you want. I won't force you to put yourselves in harm's way. I'm going after her."

"Me too."

"I'm not going home."

"I'm staying too."

Brody nodded at each of them. "I don't know how many men he'll have, but I'm sure he already knows how many you had at the house. He's probably expecting all of you, including your ranch hands and me. If he thinks we have six men, then he'll have seven, or give himself enough of an advantage to kill us all so he can take what he wants from your ranch."

"Like the girls?" Nicholas's frown looked so much like Matt's, Brody had to bite back a snort.

"Yes, the girls, the horses, the cattle, the furniture, everything. He will take what he wants and leave the rest to rot or burn. I know what he is. He's a locust, a man driven to conquer everything and everyone." Brody hadn't realized, however, to what lengths Rodrigo would go to win. Although he should have, considering the outlaw used his own sister as a whore.

"Then we kill him." Matt had always struck him as a

good man, but right about then he appeared more like an avenging angel of death. His grimace bared a few teeth and his eyes were burning with retribution.

It was time.

"We head back out of the woods and circle around. Have your hand on your weapon at all times and be ready to use it." Brody turned his gelding around and the Grahams followed suit.

As they walked back out of the woods single file, Brody had the feeling they were heading into the most important battle of their lives. Someone was going to die that day. If it was him, he would accept it as long as he knew Olivia survived.

Nothing mattered but her. Nothing.

CHAPTER THIRTEEN

Olivia's head throbbed from hanging upside down for too long. She decided against mentioning it to Rodrigo since his fingers were digging into her back again. She could hear several horses and knew Elena had not been alone.

She had been more angry than anything when Rodrigo had taken her. Then when Elena had appeared, along with the others, fear crept up her spine. Why were there so many of them? What did they want with her?

Logic told her Rodrigo had decided to take over Jeb's business for himself and eliminate the middleman. That meant he had followed them back to Texas, and possibly arranged for them to escape from Lucinda's root cellar. If that was true, then she and Brody were still playing the outlaw's game.

She didn't want to be a pawn for Rodrigo, or for anyone. Her frustration grew at the thought that she had no control over what would happen to her. The idea of being tied up and at a man's mercy made her ire rise.

The horse walked through water, splashing cold water on her face. She twisted her head to avoid it, but it got in her eyes and nose and she started to cough. By the time they reached the other side, she was having trouble pulling in a breath.

In a split second, she was torn from the horse and thrown to the ground. She hit the dirt hard and stars exploded in her head. Olivia rolled over, pressing her face into the cool grass, desperate for air. Her throat was tight, so tight no air could pass.

Someone slapped her back and she was finally able to suck in a breath. The next slap was to the side of her head. Dirt and pebbles filled her mouth. As she spat them out, a third slap landed right on her ear.

"Puta." Elena sounded different, wild and harsh. "Stop being so stupid and pretending to choke."

"I wasn't pretending." Olivia's ear rang from the blow while the pain in her pounding head grew.

"Una mentira."

"I don't lie, you bitch." Olivia had no idea what possessed her to snarl, but it felt damn good to do it. "Don't you dare fucking hit me again." The curses tasted like hot candy in her mouth, a perfect side dish to her fury over how she was being treated.

Rodrigo chuckled. "She does not like to be hit, *hermana.*"

"Puta." Elena spat on the ground beside Olivia.

Looking up through her hair at the other woman, Olivia was not entirely surprised to see the snarling visage of a mad woman. Rodrigo was dangerous but his was a cool, calculating manner. His sister was a different story.

"Why do you keep calling me whore?" Olivia decided to keep pushing and poking at Elena. Perhaps she could get the woman to lose control, and change the odds in Olivia's favor. "You're the one who whored yourself to me and to my man. Didn't I see you on your knees because your brother told you to?"

Elena lunged at Olivia with her fingers curved into claws, but her brother snatched her by the waist.

"No, you will not kill her. We need her." Rodrigo's voice was hard as granite and it had the desired effect on Elena. She seemed to shake off the fury that had driven her to slap Olivia. However, she wasn't done yet.

She kicked Olivia in the stomach, driving out the breath she'd just been able to suck in.

"*Matarlo, puta.*" Elena's threat was deadlier than Rodrigo's. There was true venom in her voice. She intended to kill Olivia.

If she were smart, Olivia would be afraid of the enraged woman. However, her brain told her to be strong, and her heart told her to not give in. A Graham *never* gave in.

"Try it and I promise you I won't be the one dead, *puta.*" Olivia bared her teeth and was pleased to see Elena blink hard.

"Enough playing, *chicas*. We need to move behind these trees." Rodrigo pulled Olivia to her feet. He grinned at her, a darkly amused expression on his face. "I may decide to keep you after all, *querida*. You have fire."

Olivia drew on every bit of her fury and spit in his face. The amused look vanished, replaced by cold hatred. He backhanded her across the cheek with a snap of his wrist. Blood filled her mouth and she felt a loose tooth, along with pain. She spat again; this time blood coated his face too.

Despite the throbbing in her face, she stood tall with her back straight and her pride intact. He grabbed her by the hair and dragged her into the woods. Olivia tried to bite his hand or arm but couldn't reach.

The small rocks littering the bank of the creek scraped

her legs and knees raw. The leaves and pine needles offered some relief but stung the already open wounds. In another moment, her hair would rip out by its roots. She'd been beaten, slapped and kicked, but the pain from her hair brought tears to her eyes.

Rodrigo let her go as soon as they reached deeper cover behind the trees. She lay there for a few moments, trying to block the pain but only succeeding in breathing. It was enough to give her the strength to sit up.

She glanced around and couldn't help the gasp of surprise that flew from her mouth. Rodrigo didn't just have Elena with him. A group of men stood by, heavily armed, all of them hidden from view from anyone in the creek or on the opposite bank.

It would be a slaughter.

"Who do you think is coming after me? Brody is, ah, gone. He left hours ago. I wasn't enough for him." Real emotion filled her voice and her throat tightened. "No one else will follow. I was just staying the night in the barn at that ranch."

Rodrigo shook his head. "Now that is *una mentira.* You lie, *querida.*" He squatted down and cupped the same cheek he had backhanded. "I knew who you were the second I saw you. Your eyes told the story I needed to know. That boy with your eyes was a *diablo* too. He had a big mouth and he kicked anyone who got near him. I sold him to a rancher who would teach him manners."

True horror blossomed inside her at the realization that he'd known she was Benjy's sister all along. "I don't know what you mean."

"That is your family at that ranch. I see things, I hear things, I know things. No more lies, eh? You are a brave woman, Olivia, but it is time to stop playing games." Rodrigo's accent disappeared again and she saw the real man reflected in his eyes. He was emotionless, conniving and calculating.

She realized it was the second time he'd called her Olivia. He knew her name. He knew where Benjy was. He knew her family. He was going to kill her and them.

Hopelessness shredded through her and she struggled to keep that brave face so he wouldn't know how badly he'd wounded her.

"What do you want from me?" she whispered.

Rodrigo smiled. "That's better. I want you to be a pretty target for the men following us. They crashed through the woods like cattle after you. I heard them a mile away. When they get here, you will lure them over so I can kill them." He tapped the barrel of the pistol against her nose. "If you don't, I kill you first and then them."

"Why?" Her voice was raw and shaking. "My family never did anything to hurt you."

He cocked his head. "Business, *querida*. I want the merchandise at your ranch, and a place to do business in Texas. I need to get rid of those who would stop me. This will be an easy way."

Oh, God. Oh, God. She had to stop him. Rodrigo would murder half her family, and decimate the rest, scattering them to the winds like dandelion puffs. Her stomach roiled and for a moment, she thought she would vomit on his *vaquero* boots. He must have sensed what she was close to doing because he stood up and backed away.

"I will kill you if you make a sound. Don't doubt that, *querida*." He put his finger to his lips in a shushing gesture.

The sound of cracking branches and shuffling carried on the wind from the opposite bank of the creek. Olivia clenched her hands into fists, knowing she was about to witness the massacre of her family.

She couldn't let that happen.

Brody kept his face calm and his hands steady, but his guts churned like a twister. He was the ex-soldier and Texas Ranger; he shouldn't be such a mess. Olivia had turned him inside out and he didn't know how to change himself back. Deep down, he didn't want to.

Caleb led them back through the woods and around in a large half-circle. It took a lot longer than Brody wanted but he couldn't fault the boy. Caleb was sure in his steps and kept a brisk pace they could all follow.

When they reached a creek, Caleb stopped and dismounted. The other three did the same, securing their horses to the trees and out of sight. Brody waited by the edge of the water, a knot in his stomach. Caleb appeared beside him.

Brody glanced down the creek. "How far upstream are we?"

"About two miles. It's marshy most of the way, so they won't hear us coming." Caleb turned to look at Brody, his eyes too much like Olivia's. For a young man, his lashes were ridiculously long. "Do you think we'll find her?"

Brody grimaced. "We'll find her, but I don't plan on leaving anything of him to find." He would kill Rodrigo and bury the son of a bitch in a hole deep enough to reach hell.

"How deep are the woods we're walking through? Is the creek straight or does it twist and turn?" He noted the water was two feet deep where they stood. "And does the water depth change?"

"The woods are thicker in places, but it's mostly like

this. The creek is shallow, never more than three feet."
Caleb pointed at the water. "It's straight for another mile
and a half, then it winds west like a snake. That's a good
spot for an ambush."

Brody grimaced. "Then that's where they'll be." He
turned back to Matt and young Nicholas. "Last chance
to turn back. It's going to be vicious and bloody." He
didn't want Olivia's brothers to die because he'd let her
down.

"We're in this together, Ranger. Not a one of us is
backing out now." Matt put his hands on his hips. "A
Graham stands with his family, no matter what."

"Just wanted to give you the chance to change your
mind. I wouldn't think any less of you for it. Hell, I've
been in battles that made me shit my drawers, but I've
never been more scared of not beating the enemy than
now." The words tumbled out of his mouth before he
could stop them. The last thing he needed was them
thinking he was a coward.

Sweat crept down his back as Matt stared at him for a
full minute before he spoke. "It's different when you're
fighting for someone you love."

Brody took a deep breath. "I do plan on asking her to
marry me."

Matt nodded. "Good thing. I wouldn't want to have
to shoot you. Hannah would be mad at me if I did."

Brody felt the urge to grin, but it passed quickly. After he had Olivia back in his arms, he would celebrate
with her and her family. Now he had to kill the man
who'd taken her.

"Same rules. Hand on your gun, keep low and keep
quiet. Walk the same steps as the man in front of you."
He looked at each of them in turn. "I'm glad to be fighting alongside brothers again."

He could see Matt wanted to ask questions, but now wasn't the time. They waded across the creek single file, then walked into the marshy area. There was no conversation and very little noise. The tall grass and saturated ground masked their steps.

Brody focused on the woods around him and on the other side of the creek. The two miles should have taken thirty minutes at most, but it felt more like twenty hours. The drone of insects, the song of birds and the chatter of squirrels went on around them as though they didn't exist. That was fine by him; they needed to be as invisible as possible.

Once they arrived at the bend in the creek, he changed the pace to a slow walk. Within moments, the sound of a horse's bridle made him freeze in his tracks. He held up his hand and everyone else stopped. Brody drew his pistol and crouched down. His heart thumped, pushing the blood through his body in a steady tattoo. He strained to listen while he peered through the trees.

There, in the distance, was the flash of a horse's tail in a patch of sunlight.

Yes.

The battle wasn't won yet, but the fact they'd tracked Rodrigo down tasted sweet. He crept forward slower than a turtle, keeping his gaze locked on the spot he'd seen the horse. When they were fifty yards away, he could distinguish more than one horse between the trees.

It didn't surprise him Rodrigo had men with him. He'd expected it, but he didn't like it, especially with a sixteen-year-old along. He didn't want anyone he fought with killed, especially since they were all Olivia's brothers.

He crawled through the grass, the mud squishing through his fingers and soaking his trousers. Before he could use his gun, he'd need to dry off his hands. He couldn't risk losing his grip because his hands were slippery.

The low murmur of voices carried in the air. Brody stopped again, unsure if the Grahams were behind him until he turned around. They were all on their knees, even quieter than he was. He nodded and turned his attention back to the horses ahead.

From what he could see, there were seven of them. Jesus Christmas. Seven? That meant he and the Grahams were definitely outnumbered, but if they had the element of surprise, they could overpower Rodrigo. The most important thing was to protect Olivia from harm.

Conchos winked in the sunlight, so Rodrigo's men were likely Mexican *vaqueros* or *banditos*. The saddles themselves looked well cared for, with the exception of two of them that were practically falling apart. A man appeared in his line of vision and Brody hoped like hell the tall grass hid him from view. It was the first time in his life he wished he hadn't worn black.

He'd never told Olivia why he always wore black and only black. Another confession he'd need to make to her when he had her by his side again.

The Graham boys were in browns and blues, disguising them much better than Brody. Too late to change his clothes, or his habits, now. He just remained as still as possible, ignoring the mosquito whining near his ear and the ants crawling on his boot.

The man moved away without raising an alarm or even looking in their direction. Brody let out his breath slowly while his pulse pounded in his head. He turned to look back at the Grahams, gesturing them to move closer.

The four of them huddled together, nearly nose to

nose. It wasn't awkward being so close. The thirst for revenge and the common goal of rescuing Olivia created an instant camaraderie. It was always that way in battle, and he was pleased to see it was the case with this little band of soldiers.

Brody spoke so softly, he could barely hear himself but he dared not make too much noise.

"We've got to flank them. Nicholas, you stay with Matt on the left, come in from the woods. Caleb, stay near the edge of the creek and come from the right."

"What about you?" Matt scowled.

"I'm going straight toward them to scatter the horses and cause confusion." Brody picked a handful of grass. "And dry your hands before you handle your weapon."

Each of them used the tall grass to get rid of as much mud as possible. Brody wiped his hands on his shirt to make sure he was ready. Dropping his gun would be suicide.

"Wait for my signal and then start shooting every *vaquero* you can see except Rodrigo. He's about my size and he'll be the one holding Olivia. Everyone else is fair game." Brody gazed at his new family, his new battalion. They were ready. "Good luck."

They formed a line side by side, each facing the direction assigned. Brody checked the rifle slung on his back, the knife in the scabbard tucked into his trousers, then the pistol. He took a deep breath and nodded to the others that it was time.

As they silently moved away, Brody focused on getting to the horses without being seen. If Rodrigo's men spotted him, he would lose the element of surprise. Rodrigo might decide to kill all of them, starting with Olivia. No, he had to be stealthy and smart to outwit the outlaw.

He snatched up a handful of sweet grass and stuck it in his teeth, baring them as though he was an animal on the hunt. Inch by inch he made his way to the first horse he found, a paint with an intelligent gaze. The mare watched him as he crept up to her. She had obviously been trained to stay put no matter what.

Brody held out some of the sweet grass to her and she sniffed delicately before taking it off his palm. The gelding to her right was either nosy or hungry because he pushed her aside and went straight for the sweet grass in Brody's mouth.

He didn't want to hurt the animals so he had to do this right. After feeding the gelding, another horse bumped his back, sending him toward the ground. He stopped himself before he had a nasty accident with a rather large rock. When he turned around to look at the anxious horse, a large black stallion eyed him. This had to be Rodrigo's horse.

With a triumphant grin, Brody untied the reins of the three horses, then held out the sweet grass to the stallion as he backed away slowly. The horse now bared his teeth, but he followed, as did the mare and the gelding, anxious for the delicious treat that wasn't growing close enough for them to reach.

He led them to the patch of sweet grass, then left them happily gorging and returned to the other four horses. They were much closer to the voices and he couldn't lure them away without being noticed.

Brody needed to see the men to know what he was up against. He crept up behind two horses that stood close together. The murmuring was in Spanish and he wished he had Olivia's fluency with the language so he could understand everything. He understood enough to know they were talking about women.

He had to act fast or they would notice the horses missing. First, he made quick work of loosening the other horses' reins from the tree branches. Then Brody peered through the scrubby brush until he could count five men and two women.

Shit. He sure as hell didn't expect to see Elena there, but that liquid black hair was unmistakable.

Olivia's hands were tied to a tree branch over her head, while she kneeled on the ground. Her face was a mass of welts, bruises and dried blood, her hair a matted snarl. The pretty dress she'd been wearing was torn and covered in dirt and blood, as though she'd been dragged.

Red fury slammed into him and he clenched his teeth. In the short time they'd had her, she'd already been beaten and treated worse than a mongrel dog.

He would kill every fucking one of them and leave Rodrigo for last. Only a coward beat a woman and he was one who deserved a bullet in his head.

This time Brody would not fail. He would not be responsible for his new brothers' deaths as he had been for his actual brothers. This battle was personal and he intended to be the victor come hell or high water.

Brody got to his feet and positioned himself behind a tree. His heart pounded in a steady rhythm and he got his breath under control before he counted to three. Pistol in one hand and knife in the other, Brody stepped into view and let loose a Texas roar of rage they probably heard in Austin.

Then he started firing.

Olivia's arms ached so badly she kept trying to stand up to relieve the pressure on them. Elena would kick her each time, forcing her back to her knees. It was a slow and insidious way to torture someone. The beautiful woman had obviously had practice at hurting people.

Olivia was about to ask for a drink of water when the most god-awful roar split the air, then gunshots rang out. Two *vaqueros* jumped to their feet only to be cut down, blood and brains splattering on the ground behind them.

Through the trees, she spotted Brody coming toward them, his face a mask of rage. He looked like an animal, snarling and gnashing his teeth as he fought with another *vaquero*. To her surprise, Matt appeared from another direction with Nicholas to take on two more of Rodrigo's men.

That left Rodrigo and Elena. Caleb popped up behind Elena and when he grabbed her arm, she slashed him with the knife that appeared in her hand.

Death and gore was all around Olivia. She watched in horror as Elena stabbed Caleb in the shoulder, but he managed to knock the knife from her hand and it fell to the ground only a foot from Olivia. With a feral grin, he aimed his gun at Elena, but she kicked him in the balls, sending him into a crouch.

Olivia couldn't stand by and let her family, and her man, die. Using her foot, she pulled the knife close enough that she could grab it with her knees. With every bit of strength she had, she got to her feet, the agony of pins and needles cutting into her useless arms and shoulders. The knife was still between her knees.

Shaking with effort, she grabbed the branch above her and slowly brought her knees up, the bloody knife getting closer and closer. Olivia caught a glimpse of Rodrigo and Brody rolling on the ground fighting and it gave her a final burst of strength. She reached the hilt with her fingers and pulled it from her knees.

Although she cut herself half a dozen times, it was nothing compared to Caleb's knife wound. She cut the ropes and freed one hand. The second was free moments later.

Olivia shook her arms to try to stop the pain as the blood flowed back into them. She couldn't keep standing there while her family continued fighting.

She couldn't see Brody and Rodrigo, but she saw Elena on top of Caleb, a rock in her hand. Olivia ran toward her, letting out her own battle cry. She slammed into the other woman with a bone-jarring grunt.

They rolled onto the ground with Olivia on top, but Elena didn't stop. She started kicking and punching, snapping her teeth as she tried to get close enough to bite Olivia. It was like fighting a wildcat, but Olivia managed to get to her knees, out of Elena's grasp. She staggered out of reach.

"*Puta*. Come back here and let me show you how to fight." Elena's mouth was coated in blood as though she'd been feasting on raw flesh. Olivia didn't want to know whose blood it was—she just wanted to stop her. The beautiful girl had turned into a hideous caricature of herself, completely mad and lost in a world of darkness.

Olivia held up the knife. "You come near me or my brother and I will kill you."

Caleb interjected from behind her. "Don't fight with her, Liv. Let me handle this."

She didn't reply, but in her heart she knew there was no way she would let her brave brother die for her.

"Stay out of this, Caleb. Find your own battle. This bitch is mine." Now it was Olivia's turn to bare her teeth in a snarl. "We have something to settle between us."

Elena's screeching laugh made Olivia's ears hurt. "The

only thing to settle is who will die first. You bleed, *puta*. Your hands shake and are slippery. The knife will slide from your hands quick."

Olivia didn't need a reminder of just how bad her hands were. The multiple cuts stung and her palms were wet with her own blood. Before she could change her mind, she yanked off her sleeve and wrapped it around her hand.

"Now I've got you." Olivia circled around, waiting for Elena to strike. It was only a matter of seconds before she did, leaping at her with her fingers shaped like talons and her mouth open in a scream.

As battles raged around him, Brody had to focus on Rodrigo or he might lose him. The bastard had already broken his nose and knocked his knife into the woods. After a tussle on the ground, Rodrigo had retreated into the brush, hiding.

If he didn't kill the outlaw now, Rodrigo would be a ghost haunting Brody for the rest of his life. He couldn't lose sight of him, even though he ached to check on Olivia. But she was strong and had three brothers to help her. He had to believe the Grahams would survive.

A movement in the bushes to his left revealed Rodrigo's whereabouts. Brody lunged around to flank him, surprising the outlaw as he crouched down. He resembled a dark demon released from hell to wreak havoc on earth.

"Come on then, Ranger, shoot me." Rodrigo got to his feet, his hand on the pistol strapped to his hip.

Brody was startled to realize the outlaw had called him "ranger." Rodrigo knew exactly who he was and what his mission was.

"Ah, you are surprised, no? I know many things,

Ranger. I know you are a coward who ran from battle and your brothers died."

Brody reeled back as though Rodrigo had punched him. His breath was trapped in his throat, leaving him unable to speak or breathe. How could Rodrigo know?

"The second I saw you, I sent a man to Texas and he returned with much to say." Rodrigo chuckled, a nerve-scraping sound. "I know you, Armstrong, and your cowardice."

It had been his first battle, but not the last. Brody had made a horrible mistake. He'd been making up for it ever since. He wouldn't let a piece of dog shit like Rodrigo make him feel guilty.

"And I know you, Robert Hansen."

It was time for Rodrigo to be surprised. His mouth dropped open and he cocked his head as though listening to something only he could hear. Brody wanted to crow in triumph. He'd had a list of Texans who had worked for Mexico in the war. Based on the man's stories, he'd hazarded a guess at the "real" Rodrigo. And Brody had been dead right.

"You're not the only one who can find information. I'll be sure to bring your dead body to your daddy so you can get a proper burial." Brody's colt cleared leather before Rodrigo's gun did.

It was a test of speed, accuracy and courage. Gunshots echoed around them as Brody fired once, twice, three times. He felt a sting on his left side but ignored it.

When the smoke cleared, he stood and Rodrigo lay still on the ground. Blood leaked from three wounds in his chest, staining the leaves and pine needles beneath him with a crimson river. Brody took a deep breath to slow his heart.

An unholy scream came from his left. He turned to

find Elena bearing down on him, blood dripping from the knife stuck in her chest. She wailed and threw herself on her brother's body, then lay still.

He saw Nicholas, bleeding but alive, standing beside Caleb and Matt, also looking as though they'd been in a battle. The Graham boys had survived, but what about Olivia? He couldn't see her anywhere and panic clawed at his heart.

Just as he stepped toward where he'd last seen her, a hand landed on his shoulder and he spun around, gun cocked. Olivia stood there, looking even worse than when he'd seen her ten minutes earlier. Her left hand was cut up and bloody, most of the top half of her dress was wrapped around her right hand, which was as bloody as the rest of her.

"I thought you'd left me."

Brody dropped the gun and snatched her up in his arms, holding her tightly against him until he didn't know where she ended and he began. Their blood mixed together, as did their tears.

He wept for what he'd almost lost and for the amazing gift he'd found. Words couldn't even begin to express just how overwhelmed he was with gratitude. He'd almost lost her, the woman who owned his heart, his soul, his life.

Against impossible odds, they had triumphed, using heart and love to guide them. The Grahams had taught Brody so many things, but the most important was this: Nothing mattered at the end of the day except the woman in his arms and the men at his back. Family.

They had survived together.

They left the bodies where they lay, taking the horses back with them to the ranch. Olivia rode one of the *va-*

quero's horses, unwilling to go near Elena's or Rodrigo's. As soon as they could, the Grahams would sell the animals to put money in their hands for winter.

Olivia wanted to ask all of them what had happened and how they had found her, and most of all, why Brody had left. She let him bandage her up as best he could; then he let her do the same to him. By the time they mounted up, everyone had some sort of clothing used as a bandage.

She was sore, exhausted and in pain, but she kept her back straight and rode home with her family. Brody rode beside her, shirtless, the gunshot wound in his side seeping blood through the makeshift bandage. She was worried about him, but he didn't even wobble a bit in the saddle. Eva would be able to doctor him when they got home.

Home.

It was Olivia's home but not Brody's. Would he leave again? She wouldn't know the answer to that until she found out why he had left the first time. After she'd told him she loved him, he hadn't done the same. He had shown her the depth of his feelings by tracking the outlaws down and killing them, but the man hadn't said a word to her since the fight was over.

He'd just held her so tightly she could hardly breathe, then examined all her wounds before bandaging the worst ones with his own shirt. As much as she enjoyed looking at him bare chested, in the bright sunlight, she saw the scars that littered his body. The one on his jaw stood out the most. It looked like a saber slice, possibly from the war since it was pinker than the other scars.

He was a mystery to her still, even after all the time they'd spent together. There were so many questions she wanted to ask, they crowded up her throat and she couldn't get even one out.

Olivia stopped the horse, earning surprised glances from everyone.

"Liv, what are you doing?" The entire left side of Matt's face was swollen and starting to purple. Someone must have hit him with a big branch.

"I need to talk to Brody."

"Now?" Caleb had his arm in a sling, the knife wound from Elena's mad attack making his left arm useless.

"Yes, now. You three take the rest of the horses. We'll be along in a few minutes."

"Jesus, Liv, I—" Matt began.

"Now."

Although she knew they wanted to argue the point with her, they did as she asked, leaving her alone with her man. Was he her man though? He had never made a declaration of love or even commitment of any kind. Their deal had been to find Benjy, which they hadn't, and return to Texas, which they had. Nothing else was said or promised.

"What's wrong?" Brody's voice was scratchy and exhausted sounding. He looked like he could sleep for a week.

"Why did you leave this morning?" She had to ask. She had to *know*.

He sighed, the sound making her heart pinch. "I'm a coward."

Of all the things he could have said, that was the last she expected. In fact, she laughed at the notion.

"You? I might believe that of any other man, but you? No." She shook her head.

He looked at the retreating group of horses and

brothers. "There are a lot of things you don't know about me."

"Understatement."

He clucked his tongue with a frustrated sound. "I know I don't talk much and I'm a pain in the ass, but you talk a lot and are a bigger pain in the ass."

"Flattering too."

He threw up his hands. "I am a coward, a yellow-bellied coward who left his comrades to die at the hands of the Mexicans. I hid up a tree until they left, until the bodies of eighteen men were all that was left." He rubbed his hands down his face, the rasp of whiskers loud in the quiet air. She tried to imagine Brody hiding from battle but couldn't do it. "I was scared, Liv, shitting my pants scared. After I was sliced in the face, I ran. First battle off the farm and I wet myself. Because of my cowardice, my brothers died while I watched."

She sucked in a breath. "Oh, Brody, I'm so sorry."

His eyes glistened with unshed tears. "I told everyone I had been hit in the head and was unconscious during the battle. Said the Mexicans thought I was dead so they didn't shoot me. The wound on my jaw lent truth to my story. Lies, all lies."

Olivia moved her horse closer and took his hand. "You survived and that's what your brothers would have wanted."

"You don't know that. I could only think about me and how small a man I was." His chuckle sounded more like a painful sob. "After that I was a machine, fighting and killing, trying to win a shred of my pride back. Then the war was over and I still hadn't found what I was looking for. Whatever it was I needed to be a man again."

She kissed the back of his shaking hand, willing him

to go on. This was what she needed to hear, what he needed to say.

He turned to look at her. "When I met you, you drove me loco, pushy and bossy as you were. Somewhere along the way my heart got involved and I got scared. When I left your ranch this morning, I was running again. Coward that I was. That's when I realized, all that time I was fighting and killing, being a ranger and chasing people, I was searching for you."

Olivia's heart pounded hard against her ribs at the love in his eyes. She didn't need to hear the words. He would say them in time.

"You found me." She managed a smile although her entire face hurt at the effort.

"I almost lost you. Jesus, Liv, I almost lost you." He squeezed her hand. "I ain't a poet or even any good with words, but I'd be right pleased if you'd marry me."

Shirtless, bloody and filthy, Brody Armstrong proposed to Olivia Graham, equally bloody and filthy. She didn't even feel any pain when she launched herself onto his horse and kissed him. The saddle horn dug into her hip, but she didn't care.

Like Brody, she had finally found what she was looking for. Love.

Chapter Fourteen

Eva and Hannah fussed over everyone like mother hens, stitching, washing, bandaging and even removing the bullet lodged just under Brody's skin. Supper was canceled and everyone ate whatever they could find. No one minded, of course, because the Grahams had all returned home safely, if not in tip-top shape.

Brody sat on a rocking chair on the front porch, smoking a pipe, with Matt beside him on the other chair. It was a beautiful night with a velvet sky full of stars, and the symphony of insects singing around them.

"All this bloodshed and we still haven't found Benjy." Matt's voice was tinged with a sadness that ran deep.

"No, but we know Rodrigo had him at one point, and that he sold him to a hacienda in Texas." Brody tasted the bittersweet knowledge that the boy had been in Texas all the while they were in Mexico searching for him.

"Do you know which one?"

"No, but I will." Whether or not he remained as a Texas Ranger, Brody would find Benjamin Graham.

"I appreciate that. Liv wanted so badly to find him. She was closest to him, a second mother. The day it happened—" Matt swallowed audibly. "He had a sore throat and stayed home. I can't help wondering if she had stayed with him what might have happened. I made her come with us to watch over the other little ones."

"Life changes course on a whim. A few seconds here, a minute there, and things would be different." Brody had suffered from that kind of thinking too many times to fall into it again. "You can't play that 'if' game, Matt. It will eat you alive."

"I know, but I'm going to sleep better knowing he survived. He's a tough little boy, so much like my dad."

Brody thought every Graham boy must be just like Stuart Graham had been. The man had given them courage, honor, dignity and an unerring sense of what was right. Brody envied them for that.

"Olivia must take after him too."

Matt snorted. "She is stubborn as a mule and twice as ornery, isn't she?"

Brody didn't need to answer such an obvious question.

"You ask her to marry you?" Matt took a sip of whatever was in his tin cup; it didn't smell like coffee. Brody was tempted to ask for a cup of his own since he was now facing the head of the family and discussing Olivia.

"Yep, but she didn't answer me." His gut had been churning since they'd returned. She had kissed him and hugged him, giving him the peace he needed after his confession. Yet she hadn't answered the question. It was slowly driving him mad.

"Really? Hmm." Matt took another sip. "She usually isn't afraid to tell everyone how she feels or what she thinks."

"I've noticed that about her." Brody couldn't see the other man smile, but he could feel it.

"Do you love her?"

"Yes." No hesitation, no question. He loved her with every bit of whoever he was. Soldier, killer, ranger, man.

"Have you told her?"

This time Brody hesitated. He didn't know what to say because he was embarrassed to admit he hadn't told her. After a minute of silence, Matt spoke again.

"Took me a while to tell Hannah too. She was patient, to a point, but what she needed from me was to tell her I loved her." Matt offered his cup to Brody. "You may as well drink the rest of this. You're going to need it if you plan on telling Olivia you love her."

Brody took the cup gratefully. He knocked back some of the strongest homemade liquor he'd ever tasted. His throat burned as it slid down his gullet, but he didn't dare cough or even gasp, although his eyes watered.

"Until you two get hitched, I can't let you sleep in the same room with her. And I sure as hell ain't going to let her follow you to the barn again." Matt had every right to protect his sister, although he obviously already knew Brody and Olivia had been together in the biblical sense.

Brody finally found his voice, although it was damn raspy. "I respect that, Matt. I want to do this right. I'll stay in town until we can get married or until she tells me no."

"She won't say no." Matt turned to look at him in the semi-darkness. His eyes were the only thing visible. "She had a beau once who left her high and dry after my parents died. I never saw her look at him the way she looks at you."

Brody's heart thumped at the knowledge others could see the love between them. It was as obvious as the sun in the sky. He'd be a fool a million times over if he didn't grab her for his own.

He got to his feet and handed the empty cup back to Matt. "Much obliged, brother."

Matt's smile gleamed in the moonlight. "Go get her."

Brody walked back into the house to find Eva and Mrs. Dolan at the table drinking coffee. They both looked up at him and waited, brows raised.

"Where is Olivia?"

"Taking a bath, so you best not disturb her, young man. You don't need to be spying on her naked." Martha Dolan, Hannah's grandmother, was a wisecracking woman who never let a thought stay in her head when she could speak it out loud.

Eva shook her head. "I think that horse has already left the barn, *amiga*."

Brody's cheeks heated at the bawdy talk between the two older women. "Is she in her room?"

Eva stared at him, without blinking, until he felt the crazy urge to shuffle his feet like a naughty schoolboy. She was a hell of a guard dog.

"If you break her heart, I break you, *comprendes?*"

Brody understood all too well how intense the love was between the Grahams, and that went for Eva and her boys too as extended members of the family. He hadn't met anyone like them before.

"*Comprendo, Eva. Yo amo Olivia.*" He loved her and now he'd said it out loud, albeit in Spanish. Surely he could tell Olivia too?

"*Bueno.* You marry her then and make babies so she can get out of my hair, *sí?*" Eva laughed and Mrs. Dolan joined in.

He left them cackling at the table and walked down to Olivia's room in the corner. The littlest Graham, Catherine, popped up in the doorway to his right.

"That's my sister's room." She folded her arms and glared up at him.

Brody squatted down, his experience with children limited. He didn't want to scare her, or worse yet, make her think he was a bad man coming to hurt Olivia.

"I know. Olivia is my sweetheart. Do you know what that means?"

Catherine frowned, then slowly shook her head.

"It means that I love her." There, he'd said it again. It was almost rolling off his tongue now. "I'm going to marry her and be part of your family."

"Oh, another brother. That's no fun."

Brody smothered the laugh that bubbled up. "I promise I won't be like your other brothers. I'll do fun things like go fishing with you."

"Really?" Her face lit up with a smile that reminded him of Olivia. "Then I don't mind another brother." She reached over and hugged his neck before kissing his cheek, then skipped back into her room.

Brody knew he'd have a family with the Grahams, but he wasn't prepared for the way his heart stuttered at the little girl's affection. He was just getting used to Olivia's love, and now he had even more to get used to. The lonely boy he'd been wanted to hug Catherine back, but the man he'd become wasn't quite ready. He would be one day and for now, would secretly treasure his new little sister.

He got to his feet and shook off the swell of emotion that had overcome him, then raised his hand to knock on her door. A splash sounded from behind the barrier. His entire body tensed, including his cock. She was in the bath, naked, a few feet away.

Oh, hell, his erection grew another two inches and pressed against his trouser buttons.

"Who is it?" Her voice floated through the door.

He pressed his head against the wood, focusing on keeping his breathing steady. "Brody."

"I'm bathing."

He gritted his teeth against the onslaught of images. "I know that, honey. I need to talk to you and it can't wait."

A pause. "Does Eva know you're here? At my door, I mean."

"Yes, she does. So does your brother and Mrs. Dolan."

Please let me come in, Olivia. I need you.

The words went unsaid and he could have kicked himself for being unable or unwilling to get the knot out of his tongue.

"Come in." She sounded hesitant and that was unlike his Olivia.

He pushed the door open and stepped in, closing it behind him. Brody didn't dare look at her until he got his words out. He was having a hard enough time dealing with the marvelous smells in the air, including soap, woman and her unique scent. He was nearly overpowered with the urge to take her. After a stern but short conversation with his wayward cock, he now leaned his head against the other side of the door.

"What are you doing?"

"I can't look at you, Liv, or I won't be able to control myself." His hands pressed against the wood, his palms itching to weigh her perfect breasts in his hands again.

She giggled. "I like the sound of that. You out of control is an unusual sight."

"Don't laugh, please. This is uh, hard for me." As soon as he said it, he wanted to swallow the words back into his stupid mouth. He was hard all right, but that wasn't the biggest issue.

There was a long pause before she spoke. Her voice this time was small and unsure. "You're leaving."

"No, hell no. I'm not going anywhere. Well, wait, I am going to sleep in town, but only because your brother ordered me to." His thoughts whirled around until he could hardly find one to pluck out. "I need to talk to you."

"You are talking to me."

He whirled around, annoyed that she'd gotten him riled in under thirty seconds. She sat in a small hip bath, her body glistening with water, knees not hiding the magnificent pink-tipped breasts behind them.

"Holy God."

"Remember, Goddess is fine if you have to call me that." She smirked and the knot in his tongue loosened just a bit.

Brody took off his hat, partly to hide the erection in his trousers, but it was the polite thing to do as well. "You never answered me," he blurted.

She frowned. "What was the question?"

Tell her. Tell her. Tell her. NOW.

"I, um, asked you to marry me but you didn't answer."

"Yes, I most certainly did. I distinctly remember answering you before I joined you on your horse." She nodded as though her recollection was the only important one.

"No, you squealed, jumped onto my saddle and kissed the bejesus outta me, but you didn't say yes." He pulled at his shirt collar, hot and bothered in so many ways. "I remember every second of it."

She stared at him, her eyes wide. "Ask me again."

This was the moment, the time for him to be the man she wanted him to be, the man he wanted to be. The moonshine burned a hole in his stomach, sitting there bubbling up, pushing him.

Tell her. Tell her. Tell her. NOW.

"I ain't good at talking, especially to women, and I sure as hell ain't no catch. I'm mean, stubborn and talk hardly at all."

"You paint quite a picture for me, Brody." The little minx raised one brow.

Tell her NOW.

He almost felt the cork pop within him and words started pouring out of his mouth. "I can't imagine spending one more minute of my life without you by my side. I want to marry you, Olivia Graham, and spend the rest of my life making love to you, waking up beside you and growing old with you. I want to make beautiful babies who have their mama's eyes. I want to go to sleep each night with your face the last thing I see before I shut my eyes."

Brody approached the tub and dropped to his knees. His voice cracked like a young boy's when he finally said the words they both needed to hear.

"I love you."

She was out of the tub in a flash, pressing her wet, naked body to his and her lips against his waiting mouth. He could hardly get ahold of her she was so dang slippery. His cock hammered against her belly, wanting to join in the party.

Brody managed to grab her shoulders and break the kiss. They were both breathing heavily and damned if her hard nipples didn't make his mouth water.

"You didn't answer the question."

She grinned. "Yes, you silly ranger. Of course, I'll marry you." She placed his hands on her nipples. "Now show me how much you love me."

"Your brother will kick my ass." Brody had just made his peace with Matt five minutes earlier, but the feel of Olivia in his arms, naked, was overpowering.

"Then lock the door."

He didn't need to be told twice. Without letting go of her perfectly delectable body, he reached over and turned the key in the lock. The soft *snick* echoed in the room.

"Make love to me, Brody."

"My pleasure."

They didn't have much time before someone came knocking. Brody shucked his trousers and shirt quick as lightning. His cock bobbed toward her, eager to touch, plunge, rub.

She stood there waiting, still wet, incredibly beautiful. He stopped in mid-motion, dumbstruck by the extraordinary gift of a woman like Olivia. She frowned.

"What's the matter?"

"Nothing. I'm just counting my blessings is all." He scooped her up and she giggled. "You, Olivia Graham, are the beginning, middle and end of the list."

She smiled, her eyes filled with the love he now cherished. "You're not so bad yourself, Ranger Armstrong. I'm still waiting for that lovemaking to start, though."

Brody kissed her hard, then set her on the bed. He intended to see to her pleasure, but she opened her arms and gestured for him to lie on her now. His cock didn't mind that at all.

As he crawled on top of his woman, flesh met flesh, heat met heat. Goose bumps raced up and down his skin at the sensation. Before he could gather his thoughts, her legs fell open. He inched forward, his staff nudging her entrance.

He levered himself up on his elbows so he could see her face. Her amazingly expressive face. There wasn't an emotion she didn't feel that wasn't on that face. This time he saw love, pleasure and joy.

It was the joy that made his throat tighten up. That was the strange emotion knocking around inside his heart. *Joy.*

Brody didn't remember feeling joy before he met Olivia. There were quite a few emotions he'd not experienced before her, but joy was unexpected.

As he slid into her, he watched her face and she watched him. Her eyes opened wide when he was fully sheathed within her. His cock pulsed with the need to move but he stopped.

It was the most perfect moment of his life and time slowed. He felt his heart thump against hers, and her warm breath against his chin. She surrounded him, physically and emotionally, just as he did her.

Brody had never understood the fuss about loving someone, but this exquisite moment gave him all the understanding in the world. This was what life was all about. The perfect moments were the treasures to be tucked away in his heart, to build into the life they would share together.

"God, I love you." The words were out, his voice thick with unshed tears.

One brow went up and her smile grew wider.

Brody smiled back. "Goddess, I love you."

"I love you too, Ranger."

He began to move within her, slow measured thrusts to build the pleasure together. She raised her knees, drawing him in deeper, then deeper still.

Brody leaned down and captured one dark pink nipple, sucking and nibbling at it. She made kittenish moans each time his teeth closed around it. He could time the squeeze of her inner walls with the moan and the bite. It was a rhythm he moved to, heightening his and her pleasure.

When he switched to the other nipple, she scratched at his back in protest. The rhythm began again, and this time Olivia pushed up as he pushed in. It was like diving into a pool of pure bliss.

His balls tightened without warning and his orgasm hovered. He reached over and tweaked her other nipple, pinching and tugging. She contracted tighter and tighter around him. He knew she was close and he hung on, squeezing his eyes shut to hold back the floodgates of his own release.

"Brody, now, now, now." She arched her back as her hands dug into the bed frame.

She tightened around him so fast and hard, his orgasm slammed into him instantly. He whispered her name, unable to form any coherent thought except Olivia.

Ecstasy roared through him, wave after wave crashing over him. It was the beginning of a new life for him, for her, for them, perhaps even a new life within her.

Brody shook with the force of his orgasm, completely overcome. He managed to roll off her and lie on his back, breathing heavily as his entire body tingled and pulsed.

"Holy shit," she whispered.

Joy bubbled up inside him and he pulled her closer, kissing her until neither one of them could see straight. Then they made love again.

Brody had finally found where he belonged.

Hot coffee in hand, Olivia walked out to the front porch to watch the sunrise. She sat on her favorite rocker and pulled her legs up beneath her. Eva would have admonished her for not sitting like a lady, but Olivia didn't worry about that. Life as she knew it had changed so much, she needed to feel comfortable. She needed to remember sitting in that same chair with her mother, watching the horizon for her father, Matt and Caleb to return home.

The chair she sat in grounded her, gave her a solid place to be, physically and mentally. Olivia didn't get much of a chance to be alone. None of them did. She'd heard Matt and Hannah leave for their early morning ride and snuck out to the porch to think.

As she sipped the coffee, she watched the sun paint the sky in vivid tones of pink, orange and red. Peace. That's what she was feeling, a measure of peace, although it was tempered by other thoughts and emotions. So much had happened in the last two weeks, she'd barely had time to catch her breath. And things were going to change again.

She was getting married in a few hours. A week after her return from Mexico and she was about to become a missus. Life hadn't turned out the way she'd dreamed it, that was for sure. Mama would have been pleased with her man, gruff and bossy as he was. Brody was the right choice, there was no question of that.

What weighed heavily on her mind was the loss of Benjy, the idea that he was somewhere in Texas, in her own country, yet she didn't know where. There was a hole in her heart that could only be filled by finding him.

He'd been the baby, the youngest Graham, with a big smile and an inquisitive nature. From the time he could walk, he'd followed Olivia around, her shadow with chubby knees and a penchant for finding things he shouldn't be getting into. He kept them all busy, that was for sure. She'd be content with chasing after him twenty-four hours a day if he were back here with his family.

"Good morning, Liv." Brody's soft voice didn't surprise her. He'd been arriving early in the morning all week long and having breakfast with them. Although he told her it was because he missed her so much, she secretly suspected it was Eva's cooking that drew him so early. He sat down in the chair next to her and tried to take her coffee. She held it away from him.

"Go get your own and come back out here."

He stood up and saluted. "Yes, general."

She smothered a laugh and waited for him to return. Benjy was the unspoken conversation between them, and they needed to have it before they went in front of the preacher.

"You're thinking about him, aren't you?" He sat back down with a steaming cup of black coffee, then sipped it noisily. She loved her ranger just the way he was.

"Yes. I need to know what we can do to find him. What you can do to find him." She shook her head. "It's hard to just do nothing when I know he's somewhere in Texas."

"I have been sending letters to other rangers, and back up to Austin. Nothing yet, but I did get a list of the largest hacienda owners in Texas." He slurped the coffee again. "They're spread out so it will take some time to visit all of them."

Olivia turned to him. "We haven't talked about what happens after the wedding."

His lascivious grin made her laugh.

"Not that part, foolish man. I mean, what will you do? What will I do? Where will we live? I want so badly to find Benjy, but I don't want to miss my chance to have a happy life with you." Her heart pinched at the mixed emotions she felt. She didn't want to give up her future with Brody. At the same time, she didn't want to simply abandon the littlest Graham.

"I've been thinking a lot about that."

"Me too."

He nodded. "I figured that. After you pushed, shoved, bullied and plowed your way through our, ah, adventure together, I knew you wouldn't forget about him when we got back."

"Bullied?" She frowned at him.

He ignored her question, for which she would punish him later somehow. "If I keep on as a ranger, I can't search for Benjy. If I quit being a ranger, I can search for him, but I can't feed us without the meager pay I get for being a ranger."

Olivia wasn't about to tell him how pleased she was to hear his thoughts. He was thinking about her, about Benjy and about the future. She silently hugged herself, infinitely happy with the man she'd fallen in love with.

"We could live here. During the week we could work on the ranch and spend weekends looking for Benjy." To her it was a practical choice.

He grimaced. "No, I can't do that, Liv. There's barely enough room in that house as it is. To add another man would make things downright uncomfortable."

"Then where will we live?" She'd never considered moving away from her family, or worse, living full time on the trail. Not that she couldn't do it, but it would be hard.

"My family had a cotton farm not too far from here and—"

"Wait, you were a cotton farmer?" Olivia couldn't help grinning at him. The big, strong ranger had picked cotton?

He made a face at her. "My pa taught my brothers what to do and they taught me." He shrugged. "We scraped by. It's an honest living."

She held up her hand. "I know, it's just, well funny to picture you farming. In farmer's clothes."

"Shut up, Liv."

That made her laugh. "I'm sorry, go on about the farm. Where is it?"

"Half a day's ride east. It's not much, but it's mine now that my brothers are gone. Pa owned it free and clear. It's dusty and needs work, but it's a home."

He sounded unsure of himself and she smothered the smile that threatened. Brody was bossy and decisive; this side of him was unexpected and completely endearing.

"I'm sure I'll love it. I'm not afraid of getting my hands dirty either." She rocked, the only sound the gentle squeak of the porch beneath the rockers.

"Or muddy." He smirked.

A laugh burst from her throat. "It was clay! Not mud." She shook her finger at him. "Behave yourself, Ranger Armstrong."

He looked away, his gaze somewhere she couldn't reach. "I'm going to quit being a ranger."

She gasped. "Brody. I don't want you to give up what you love for me. We can still look for Benjy in between your assignments."

It broke her heart not to get on Mariposa and start searching for her brother as soon as she could. Yet Brody had taken his place in her heart and he was even more important than her burning need to find Benjy.

He shook his head. "I joined the army because my brothers did. After they died, I kept on fighting and killing because I had to. After the war, being a ranger made sense. All I knew was how to carry a gun and put my life at risk. But I wasn't living. I didn't have a home." He turned to look at her, his blue eyes full of old pain. "I didn't belong anywhere until I met you."

Her heart thumped at the love and honesty in his voice. She leaned over and kissed him, blinking back the sudden tears in her eyes.

"That doesn't mean you need to quit being a ranger."

He looked away again. "Yep, it does. I was a ranger because I had to do something. I can do more good looking for Benjy with you. If we can find him, maybe we can find others."

Olivia was humbled by his idea. She had been so focused on finding Benjy, she'd never thought of other children. So many had disappeared, not just the smallest Graham.

"I think that's a good idea. I would love to be a rescuer of stolen children. It feels like the right thing to do." The more she thought about it, the more she wanted to do it. Brody and she made a good team; together they could do anything.

"We can start looking for Benjy as soon as you want."

Brody took another noisy slurp of his coffee. Her love for Brody grew deeper by the second. He was such a good man, a man of honor and integrity. She was so lucky to have found him.

"Maybe we should go to your home and—"

"Our home."

She smiled. "To our home and get things squared away so we have a place to come back to."

"I will go anywhere with you, honey. Even better, now I can make a home with you, plant cotton, raise horses, find lost brothers." He grinned. "Make babies."

The thought of holding Brody's child made her knees

weak. She managed to swallow the lump in her throat. "I can't wait to do all those things with you."

It was his turn to kiss her, a soft flutter of lips. "We can start now."

A burst of excitement raced through her, sending tingles over her body. She leaned forward to invite him to a secret spot behind the barn but a heavy footfall behind her made her jump.

Matt stood there, arms crossed, scowling. "Don't let me interrupt."

Olivia jumped to her feet. "We were just watching the sunrise."

"Uh-huh, sure." He rocked back on his heels, directing his scowl at Brody. "Isn't the groom not supposed to see the bride on the wedding day?"

"I didn't know she'd be out here so early." Brody plastered an innocent look on his face. "I came for the coffee and *huevos*."

"Uh-huh, sure." Matt jerked his head toward the house. "You go to your room and get ready for your wedding, Liv. I'll keep your groom occupied."

Olivia kissed Brody. Matt growled and she laughed, darting into the house. Eva stood at the stove, shaking her head but with a smile playing at the corners of her mouth.

"You love your man very much, *hija*. You risk your brother's anger for him."

Olivia thought about all they'd been through together. There wasn't anything she wouldn't risk for Brody, even her life.

"I love him."

Eva smiled broadly. "*Sí, hija,* and I am so happy for you." She pulled Olivia into a hug. "Your mama, she is smiling at you from heaven."

Olivia hadn't intended on crying once on her wedding day and now for the second time that morning, she felt tears threaten. "*Gracias,* Eva. I think she would have liked him."

Eva held her at arm's length, her brown eyes suspiciously wet. "Both your parents would have liked him."

Olivia nodded, emotions crowding her throat. She missed her parents so much in that moment, it took her breath away.

"Come, *hija,* let's get you ready for your wedding. I will be your mama's hands." Eva took her elbow and led her to her room.

Today Olivia would marry the man she loved.

Caleb stared at the ranger, or rather the man who was marrying his sister Olivia. He was big and dark, always wore black except for today. Someone must have made him a blue shirt, likely Hannah, who was a genius with a sewing needle.

Aside from the fact that he was an intimidating man, Brody Armstrong was a Texas Ranger. As soon as Caleb had heard that bit of news, he'd taken every opportunity to study the other man. Being a ranger in the Republic of Texas was an honor, but to Caleb's disgust, Brody was throwing it away for a woman.

A woman!

After the war, all Caleb had wanted to do was go home, be with his family. The blood, the smells, the killing, had all shaken him to his eighteen-year-old core. He wasn't hiding at the ranch, but finding a place he could be safe and think.

Over the last six months, he'd been thinking about volunteering to be a Texas Ranger. Armstrong had been the one to take Jeb Stinson down, and the speed with which he'd killed the outlaw Rodrigo was astonishing. Caleb had never seen anyone draw that fast.

Now the man was giving up the life of a ranger. Granted, it wasn't a glamorous life with lots of money and women, but it was a good life. Rangers were the law Texas needed to survive as a country. Without them, Mexico might try to sneak back in or Texans might get the idea it was okay to do what they pleased with no consequences.

Being a man of the law, being a Texas Ranger, had been on Caleb's mind since he'd met Armstrong. In fact, he'd been fixing to ask the ranger how to sign up when Caleb found out about the wedding.

It left a sour taste in his mouth that the man he wanted to be like had fallen under the charms of a female. Caleb liked the opposite sex, but not that much.

Unable to keep his peace any longer, Caleb approached the ranger.

"You sure about this, Armstrong?"

Brody nodded. "Yep, I'm sure, Caleb. It's the right thing."

Caleb glanced around at the flowers the girls had arranged for the wedding. "Seems like an awful lot to give up, if you don't mind me saying so."

"It might look that way, but I'm getting a helluva lot more than I'm giving up." Armstrong met Caleb's gaze, his blue eyes as intense as a summer sky. "I love your sister. I know you don't understand what a man would do for the woman he loves, but one day you will."

"Oh, I don't think so." Caleb did not intend on being a fool and letting a woman lead him around by his dick.

A smile spread across Armstrong's face, the first Caleb had ever seen from the man. The transformation was a bit spooky.

"I do and when it happens, don't fight it."

Caleb nodded, unwilling to argue the point. He wasn't going to ever be in that situation so there was no need to plan for it.

"I was thinking of joining the rangers."

Armstrong's brows went up. "Does Matt know about that?"

"No, not yet. I don't need his permission. I'm nineteen, a man old enough to make his own choices." Caleb hadn't told his older brother because he knew Matt would fight his decision. It would be better if Caleb simply left one night and didn't come back. He'd leave a note, of course, but it would save some arguing.

"I can appreciate that. Rangering is hard work, Caleb. Lonely too. You don't get much in the way of home cooking or soft beds." He gestured to the house. "This is a good place to be, an honest place. You don't want to leave it behind just to scratch an itch."

Caleb appreciated the fact that he had a good family and a place to call home. But he wanted, no, he *needed* more.

"I know. I'll do what's right."

After Caleb walked away, Brody looked around at the guests, noting a few neighbors he'd met while investigating, and of course the Graham clan and the Vasquez brothers. Rebecca, Elizabeth and Catherine had picked wildflowers, decorating everything they could reach. Caleb, Matt and Nicholas had strung up the flower chains behind the house, creating a wonderland for the event.

Reverend Beechum drove up to the ranch accompanied by Frederick Stinson, who appeared twenty years older than he had six months ago. Beechum's round belly told stories about just how often he liked to visit ranches and sample the rich foods folks would make for him. This was no exception. Eva had been cooking for two days and the house was fairly bursting with delicious scents and sights.

Brody stood beneath the huge tree, his stomach in a knot that had nothing to do with marrying Olivia. He couldn't wait to call her his wife.

The knot was there because of who wasn't at his wedding. No parents, no brothers, nobody. He had been alone in the world for a long time, even when his family was alive.

He stood apart, watching the smiles, the handshakes and the conversation. Caleb had talked to him for a bit, but only to ask about rangering. He sure hoped the boy didn't go down that path. It was a hard road to follow, especially for someone used to a big family, lots of love and a regular place to hang his hat. Brody didn't think Caleb was ranger material, but he had a feeling the boy would do it anyway. It was hard being the younger brother of such a strong, capable man as Matt. Brody knew that feeling all too well.

"What are you doing over here by yourself?" Catherine appeared beside him, her smocked yellow dress already smudged with dirt and leaves. She put her small hand inside his and tugged. "You can't hide by the tree anymore, silly."

Brody couldn't remember the last time anyone had called him "silly." The youngest Graham present was a force to be reckoned with already. She pulled him toward the cluster of men standing around and chatting. At the center of the circle stood Matt. He nodded to Brody.

"I told him he couldn't hide anymore." Catherine squeezed his hand. "He's too big anyway."

"Thought you were changing your mind over there." Matt's gaze was questioning.

Brody's smile was an easy one. "No, just trying to be patient."

The man laughed and slapped him on the back. Matt shook his hand, genuine affection in his expression.

"Welcome to the family, Brody."

For the first time in a very long time, Brody Armstrong felt like he was truly part of a family. He couldn't imagine a more precious gift, until he spotted Olivia standing by the corner of the house, waiting.

She took his breath away.

Olivia's stomach hopped and skipped like Catherine after she had some peppermints. She'd never been so nervous in all her life and all for what? The man she loved wanted to marry her, have babies with her and spend their time looking for Benjy. It was perfect, she couldn't want for anything more.

Yet she was jittery and fidgety. She stood at the corner of the house, noting the menfolk standing around jawing, like they always did. Eva stood beside her, fussing with her hair. Catherine had presented her with a crown of wildflowers to wear. It was a little crooked and a good third of the petals were missing, but Olivia wore it anyway.

The men separated and she saw Brody. Her heart skipped a beat at the sight. He was spiffed up, shaved, with his hair combed too. The black hat was missing, thank God. He smiled at her and she felt it touch her from twenty feet away.

Matt stepped toward her, smiling. When he reached her, he held out his arm. "Ready, Liv?"

"More than you know."

He chuckled. "Your man there is a little nervous, I think."

"Me too."

"That's normal." Hannah appeared on the other side of Olivia. "I thought I would lose my breakfast the day we got married."

Matt made a face. "Glad I didn't know about that."

She swatted at his arm. "Stop it, Matthew. Now, are you ready to give your sister away?"

"More than you know."

This time it was Olivia who swatted him.

"I'm fooling with you, Liv." Matt took her hand in his. "I am very proud of you. You're courageous, smart and have more honor than most men I know. Love you, sis." When he kissed her cheek, Olivia couldn't stop the tears that spilled from her eyes.

The Grahams loved each other, but to hear the words from Matt meant the world to her. Hannah squeaked and whipped out a handkerchief to dab at Olivia's eyes.

After getting herself back under control, Olivia took her brother's arm again.

"I'm ready."

She looked ahead at the preacher standing under the tree with his Bible, at her family and her neighbors. Each one held a place in her heart. Then she moved her gaze to Brody, who waited for her beneath the flowers.

The nervousness blew away on the breeze like dandelion fluff, and Olivia felt nothing but joy and love. As she walked toward the man who held her heart, Olivia smiled.

Today was the first day of the rest of her life.

Have you read MATTHEW, the first in the Circle Eight series?

It is a vast spread in the eastern wilds of the newly independent Republic of Texas, the ranch their parents fought for . . . and died for. To the eight Graham siblings, no matter how much hard work or hard love it takes, life is unthinkable without it. . . .

In the wake of his parents' murder, Matthew Graham must take the reins at the Circle Eight. He also needs to find a wife in just thirty days, or risk losing it all. Plain but practical, Hannah Foley seems the perfect bride for him . . . until after the wedding night. Their marriage may make all the sense in the world, but neither one anticipates the jealousies that will result, the treacherous danger they're walking into, or the wildfire of attraction that will sweep over them, changing their lives forever. . . .

Praise for Emma Lang and her novels

"A sweet and sensual western in which the heroine discovers her inner strength with the help of a delightfully sexy hero."
—Angela Knight, *New York Times* bestselling author

"With a fresh voice and engaging characters, Emma Lang's *Restless Heart* kept me reading late into the night."
—Tina Leonard, bestselling author